"Look at this rose. Did you ever see anything so fragile, so beautiful?" Lainey asked.

He wasn't looking at the flower.

"Come touch it. Did you ever feel anything so soft?"

Zac moved his hand from the rose to her cheek, then trailed his fingers to cup her chin. "Yes, I have. Something softer, more beautiful than any rose."

A flash of pain moved into her eyes, and she shook off his hand. "No, I'm not. Not beautiful and not delicate, either. Maybe I was once, but no more. It's over, all over. And you can't get it back."

It was the vodka talking, but Zac was certain there was more here. "What can't you get back?"

"Myself. What was inside me. He took it, he robbed me, and there's nothing left." Her face was full of anguish; then a wrenching sound escaped from deep inside her.

Zac quickly cradled her against his chest. "It's all right," he whispered gently. "I'll take care of you."

Dear Reader,

In a world of constant dizzying change, some things, fortunately, remain the same. One of those things is the Silhouette **Special Edition** commitment to our readers—a commitment, renewed each month, to bring you six stimulating, sensitive, substantial novels of living and loving in today's world, novels blending deep, vivid emotions with high romance.

This month, six fabulous authors step up to fulfill that commitment: Terese Ramin brings you the uproarious, unforgettable and decidedly adult *Accompanying Alice;* Jo Ann Algermissen lends her unique voice—and heart—to fond family feuding in *Would You Marry Me Anyway?;* Judi Edwards stirs our deepest hunger for love and healing in *Step from a Dream;* Christine Flynn enchants the senses with a tale of legendary love in *Out of the Mist;* Pat Warren deftly balances both the fears and the courage intimacy generates in *Till I Loved You;* and Dee Holmes delivers a mature, perceptive novel of the true nature of loving and heroism in *The Return of Slade Garner*. All six novels are sterling examples of the Silhouette **Special Edition** experience: romance you can believe in.

Next month also features a sensational array of talent, including two tantalizing volumes many of you have been clamoring for, by bestselling authors Ginna Gray and Debbie Macomber.

So don't miss a moment of the Silhouette **Special Edition** experience!

From all the authors and editors of Silhouette **Special Edition**—warmest wishes.

PAT WARREN
Till I Loved You

Silhouette Special Edition

Published by Silhouette Books New York

America's Publisher of Contemporary Romance

For Rose and for Helen, sisters *extraordinaire*—
for putting up with me all these years

SILHOUETTE BOOKS
300 East 42nd St., New York, N.Y. 10017

Books by Pat Warren

Silhouette Special Edition

With This Ring #375
Final Verdict #410
Look Homeward, Love #442
Summer Shadows #458
The Evolution of Adam #480
Build Me a Dream #514
The Long Road Home #548
The Lyon and the Lamb #582
My First Love, My Last #610
Winter Wishes #632
Till I Loved You #659

Silhouette Romance

Season of the Heart #553

Silhouette Intimate Moments

Perfect Strangers #288

PAT WARREN,

the mother of four, lives in Arizona with her travel agent husband and a lazy white cat. She's a former newspaper columnist whose lifetime dream was to become a novelist. A strong romantic streak, a sense of humor and a keen interest in developing relationships led her to try romance novels, with which she feels very much at home.

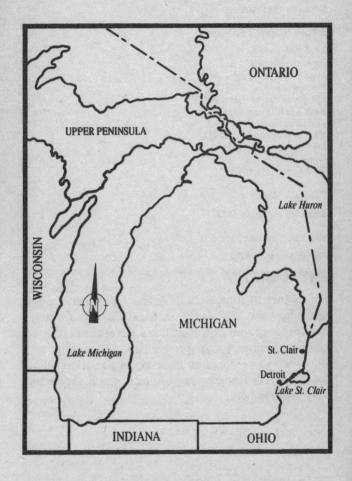

Chapter One

She was definitely not accustomed to manual labor.

Zac Sinclair leaned against the weathered boards of the barn door and watched the woman with the pitchfork. She was as lovely as she was inexperienced at pitching hay, he thought as she wielded the long-handled tool somewhat awkwardly. Absorbed in her work, she hadn't heard him approach.

She was tall, easily five-nine in leather boots that looked new and barely worn. Her hair was long, jet black, tied back at her nape with a red kerchief. Beneath her oversize cotton shirt and stone-washed jeans, she looked to be almost too slender, yet the curve of her hips and the length of her shapely legs were clearly feminine. As a builder, he appreciated clean, classic lines and unmistakable style. As a man, he appreciated an attractive woman despite her efforts to underplay her looks.

He'd come to her ranch on impulse, and perhaps out of boredom coupled with a healthy dose of curiosity. Sam, the salesman behind the counter of St. Clair's only lumber and hardware store, had told Zac that Zac's new neighbor was looking for a handyman. While that wasn't exactly a job description he would list among his areas of expertise, he supposed he could qualify. He'd been working with his hands since he was twelve years old and now, some twenty years later, there was precious little in construction that he couldn't do.

Truth of the matter was, he'd done everything that needed doing to renovate his own ranch house during the past month. He was too restless to be idle long. And he loved challenges. Looking about at the neglected condition of his neighbor's barn—to say nothing of the house he'd glanced at on the way in—this job would definitely be a challenge.

Zac stepped out of the sunshine of the open doorway and moved closer, but she was still too preoccupied to notice him. The lone occupant of the barn, a big-eyed gray mare, bobbed her large head in her owner's direction, obviously wanting attention. With unhurried movements, the woman tossed a mound of new hay into the mare's clean stall.

"I know you're lonely, Trixie, but be patient with me," she told the animal, whose brown eyes watched her. "As soon as I find someone to repair these other stalls and fix this roof, I'll get you some companions." She stopped to nuzzle the horse's long nose. "Don't worry, it won't be long."

Turning back to the pile of hay, she plunged the pitchfork in and hefted another batch. Suddenly a squeaky sound distracted her and she jumped back as a tiny mouse scurried past her. "Oh!" she cried out, and dropped the pitchfork.

Zac laughed out loud.

She swung about to face him, blindly grabbing the stall door to steady herself. Not just lovely, he thought. Beautiful, with elegant cheekbones, a complexion that needed no makeup, and a soft, inviting mouth. Her wide-set eyes were a fascinating combination of blue and violet, their expression changing from startled to wary.

"Who are you?" she asked as she stepped back and quickly retrieved the pitchfork, holding it in front of her with a defensive grip.

Awfully skittish, Zac thought. "Sam at the lumber store told me you were looking for a handyman." He gave her his best friendly smile. "I'm fairly familiar with a saw and hammer."

Lainey Roberts shifted the pitchfork into her other hand. She closed Trixie's stall door, buying a little time as she studied the man whose unexpected presence had unnerved her far more than the mouse's. She was unused to being alone in close quarters with men, feeling vulnerable when she was. Though she knew that Ben Porter, her semi-retired, part-time caretaker and ranch hand, was around back somewhere, the man before her still made her uneasy.

Not your ordinary handyman, she thought, though he wore the standard denim work shirt, faded jeans and dusty boots. His lean face was weathered, the taut skin quite tan though it was early June. He was well over six feet, with a rangy build; yet he looked hard, with muscles that rippled along his arms where his sleeves were rolled up.

Still, his boots were hand-tooled and expensive, his brown hair was stylishly cut despite its present wind-blown disarray, and his calm gray eyes had a look of quiet confidence that she suspected had been hard won. And he was a long way from Ben's sixty-five. She'd been hoping to hire another older man—not one who exuded that unmistakable masculinity she wanted to avoid.

But, after three weeks of placing ads and asking around, she'd had no applicants for the job. And frankly, she'd come to realize the work was far too much for her to tackle alone. Raising her eyes, she supposed she had little choice but to check out the man's credentials.

"How long have you been doing this kind of work?" Lainey asked.

Giving her the breathing room that she obviously needed, Zac strolled over toward the hayloft. "About twenty years." He checked the sturdiness of the wooden ladder leading up, then tested the first two rungs. Rickety and downright dangerous. He turned back to face her. "Just what is it you want done?"

The list was incredibly long. Perhaps she should start slowly, so as not to overwhelm him. "The barn has been neglected, as you can see. An elderly widow owned this place and simply couldn't keep it up. I want the structure reinforced, the stalls repaired, the floor of the hayloft replaced where necessary and the roof checked. It leaks in several places."

"I see." Zac walked over to inspect one of the horse stalls.

Maybe she should find out what he was capable of doing before she outlined the rest, Lainey thought. "And then there's the house." Still holding the pitchfork, she moved alongside him. "Just how experienced are you?"

Lainey saw the amusement in his eyes as he looked over at her. She felt heat move into her face and wished she'd phrased her question differently. Odd how in a few short months she'd lost her ability to verbally fence with an attractive man. But then she'd never been really good at it, anyway.

She cleared her throat. "What I mean is—"

"I know what you mean," Zac interrupted, wondering when he'd last seen a grown woman blush. He caught her scent over the barn smells—something light and delicate, like the lilacs his mother used to grow along the back fence. She had an innocent air about her that delighted him.

Lainey fought a quick urge to bolt for the door, to stand outside in the warm sunshine of midday. There was something too intimate about sharing the dimness of the quiet barn, about the probing look in his gray eyes. "Perhaps this is all too much for you."

Zac stuck his hands into his back pockets and wandered over to Trixie's stall, gazing up at the rafters as he spoke. "I can build from the ground up, do finished carpentry, plumbing, roofing, electrical, most furnace work." Stopping, he patted the horse's sleek hide, then turned back to her. "Will that do?"

Like a teenager in high school, he'd listed his abilities to her, Zac thought with a flash of irritation. Just why he'd wanted to impress her, he wasn't certain. Perhaps it was to prove to her that he wasn't some unqualified drifter wanting to work only long enough to pay for the next bottle. Or perhaps it was that hesitant vulnerability he saw in her dark eyes. Or was it because he wasn't ready to return to the rat race of the paper shuffle in his executive offices?

More amused than annoyed at her reluctance, he tossed her a smile. "I have references."

It wasn't the man's ability that worried her, but rather her own ability to ignore his rugged presence, day in and day out, until the work was completed. Still, no other applicants had been beating a path to her door. He was probably the most qualified she was likely to run across, if he was telling the truth. She'd soon find out if he was.

"That won't be necessary."

A sound from outside the barn interrupted, then—a low howl that sent a shiver up Lainey's spine. "What on earth!" Carrying the pitchfork, she hurried out.

In three long strides, Zac was beside her. "Don't let Willie scare you," he told her, heading for his blue pickup truck parked several yards from the door. "He hates to be kept waiting."

Lainey broke into a reluctant smile as she heard the cocoa-brown hound dog give a final deep-throated howl before putting his front paws up on the windowsill of the truck's cab, his wagging tail shaking his whole body. Zac rubbed the dog's droopy ears as she raised her hand to touch his smooth head.

"Behave yourself, Willie," Zac scolded. "We'll be going home soon."

"You must be a hunter," Lainey guessed, squinting as she looked up at him.

"No. I inherited Willie from one of my ranch hands when he moved out of state."

So she'd been right. He wasn't just a simple handyman. "You have a ranch nearby?"

Zac pointed into the trees beyond her house. "Right through those woods. I'm your neighbor." He held out his hand. "Zac Sinclair."

It would be unneighborly to refuse the gesture. His hand was large, callused and waiting. She touched hers to his skin and immediately felt the heat, the jolt. Quickly she pulled back. "Lainey Roberts." The dog was safer, she thought as she returned her attention to petting him. "Willie's an odd name for a dog."

She was coiled tighter than a spring, touchy as a newborn kitten, and he wondered why. "His former owner had a thing for western music. Even now, when Willie Nelson comes on the radio, he howls along. But he can't carry a tune half as well."

Lainey leaned on the tailgate, forcing herself to relax. Standing in bright sunshine, she found no reason to be frightened of a neighbor with a hound dog who liked to sing. There was subtle appreciation in the way he looked at her, but it wasn't overt. "Why do you want to work for me if you own the ranch next door? I've been by that spread, and it's much larger than my measly five acres." She'd seen it when she'd been searching for this property. Neat, well kept. A breeding ranch, she'd heard.

Zac was scarcely aware his eyes had taken on a sadness he struggled to control. "I've owned the ranch for quite a while. I used to spend a lot of time there. But now I've got a foreman running it. I'm more comfortable with construction work. My company's based in Detroit, and lately the paperwork's really got to me. So I came up here because I like the people and the peace and quiet. And because I needed a change." He examined his hands, running a thumb along a recent cut. "I enjoy working with my hands more than anything."

Lainey knew all about needing a change, and about searching for a quiet, peaceful place. For the first time since she'd turned to see Zac watching her, she gave him a genuine smile. "Let me show you what I'd like done in the house. That is, if you're interested in taking on all this."

"Yes, I am." He fell in step with her as she led the way. They skirted a sporty little Mustang parked in a graveled area alongside the barn. "I'm curious. What are your plans once the barn is renovated? More horses, I take it."

"Yes, and as soon as possible. I'm planning on opening a riding stable, mostly for children."

"I thought there were several riding academies around here."

She hadn't spoken aloud of her dreams to anyone except Dionne and now found herself excited to verbalize her ideas. "Not for these children. My students will be referred by Dr. Dionne Keller, a clinical psychologist specializing in traumatized kids. Some are handicapped, physically or emotionally, and some are temporarily disabled. It's Dionne's theory that horseback riding gives children confidence and learned skills that help them along the road to recovery. She's a marvelous therapist."

"How did you get to know her?"

"She's my...a good friend." Lainey climbed the two wooden steps onto the porch of her house. "Obviously, this needs a lot of work," she said, her hand on the wobbly railing. "I'd like the porch extended so it wraps around the south side of the house. The view of the woods and the stream is best from there." She stopped, realizing that angle faced his ranch. "I guess you already know that."

"Yes. I think there's even an overgrown path that leads from your place to mine. Probably hasn't been used in years."

That thought made her slightly uncomfortable. She much preferred being able to hear him approach along her wide driveway than having him arrive quietly and unexpectedly through the woods. But then, she hadn't heard his truck today. Perhaps she was being paranoid again.

Zac bent to pry loose a rotted board. "I think you're lucky not to have fallen through this porch."

"I'm a careful person," Lainey said, opening the door.

He would put money on that, Zac thought as he followed her in. Not a big house, but good-sized rooms. Originally well-constructed, but neglected for a long while now. The living room was large, with a big Michigan-fieldstone fireplace at one end and a parquet floor that badly needed refinishing.

"I'm sick about this floor," Lainey told him as she stooped to run her fingers over the chipped inlaid wood pieces.

Zac hunched down and rubbed at several spots. "Don't be. These can be replaced. And feel this." When she didn't move, he picked up her hand and stroked her fingers across a lumpy accumulation. "Wax buildup, mostly around the edges. Someone used a cheap solution, but it'll come off." He stood and drew her up with him, still holding her hand. "I like wood in a house. It lends warmth and richness."

Looking into her eyes, he noticed that they were filled with confusion and a sudden unease. He could see the pulse in her throat hammering, but it wasn't with desire. She seemed suddenly afraid, though he couldn't imagine why. He dropped her hand. "What is it?"

"Nothing." Lainey turned away, rubbing her hands along her upper arms to still their trembling. She walked toward the fireplace and stared at the empty grate. "It's chilly in here, don't you think?"

It had to be eighty outside, slightly cooler inside, but he didn't comment. Something was bothering her, but it was none of his business. "Would you like me to lay a fire for you, for later?" Even in summer, the evenings were often cool this far north.

"No, but thank you. I have a man who helps me out. Ben—Ben Porter." Slowly she turned back to him and raised her chin just a fraction. "He's back of the barn now, clearing an area for a garden. He's a grandfather, but he's very strong. Ben's here every day, so I'm rarely alone." She had to let him know that, just in case he was getting any ideas. He seemed all right, with that hint of sadness on his face as they'd talked out by his truck earlier. But you could never tell about a man, especially one she'd known less than an hour.

A warning, was that what she was giving him? Zac didn't think he'd acted out of line. She certainly was one jumpy female. He wished he could tell her to relax, that the last thing in this world he wanted was to get involved, especially with a jittery woman.

He crossed his arms over his chest. "I like gardening, too. You want to show me the rest of the house and what needs doing?"

She hurried him quickly past her bedroom, assuring him it was fine, then showed him the spare room where she wanted shelves and a bookcase built. The bathroom needed a lot of attention, but it was in the large, comfortable kitchen that he saw she was most enthused.

"I'm refinishing these cupboards myself," Lainey told him with a trace of pride. "I've never attempted anything like this before, but I'm discovering beautiful wood beneath all these layers of paint. Why do you suppose people do that?"

"I've never understood it, either." He ran his hand along the solid pine panels. "You're doing a good job."

"Thanks." She indicated the worn linoleum. "And I'm going to have a brick floor laid, then get a big oval rug for under the table."

Zac leaned against the counter thoughtfully. The only room that had much of anything in it was her room, where he'd caught a glimpse of an expensive brass bed and a lovely old chest of drawers before she'd closed the door. The second bedroom was piled high with unopened boxes and a massive oak rolltop desk. An antique rocker was the only piece of furniture in the living room, and the kitchen contained old appliances. A card table and two chairs sat by the window. A few of her things were classic and in good taste, making him wonder about her income.

Of course, she could come from a wealthy family, from perhaps Grosse Pointe or Bloomfield Hills. If so, why would she bury herself in this small town and plan to spend her days with horses and children? And if she had lots of money, why didn't she just hire a contractor and get all the renovations done in one fell swoop, never having to dirty her hands?

Puzzling. He'd always been intrigued with puzzles.

"Are you from around here?" he began.

"No." Lainey closed the cupboard door. "Shall we talk about money and see if we can agree on a price?"

"In a minute. Tell me, why didn't you hire all this done by a subcontractor or a remodeling company? Why advertise for a lone handyman?"

She took a deep breath, wondering if he'd understand, wondering why she felt she should explain. "Because I want to be in on everything. I want to plan it, to watch it get finished, to be in charge of the purchasing of each and every single thing that goes into this house. I've never had a place of my own, one that I felt truly at home in. I want this to be mine and only mine."

Her plans, her reasons, didn't disturb him. The woman herself he found disturbing, though he couldn't put into words why. He nodded toward her relic of a stove and the old refrigerator. "You going to replace those?"

"Of course, eventually."

"Do they work?"

"Yes. Why?"

He glanced at his watch. "Because it's lunchtime."

"I'm not much of a cook." Probably because she hadn't had much of an appetite for some time now.

"You should eat more. You're too thin."

She'd heard it before and she didn't need to hear it again. Wouldn't he drop over if he knew she'd actually gained ten pounds in the last few weeks? She reached into a paper bag on the counter and pulled out a red licorice stick. "This is what I usually have for lunch."

She saw him make a face and opened the refrigerator door, offering him a look inside. She hoped he didn't think that meals came with the job. "You see? I'm not much for meal planning."

An understatement if he'd ever heard one. Frozen pizza, ice-cream bars, peanut butter and a soggy sack of doughnuts. He shook his head as he closed the door.

"If you don't mind, when I go for supplies I'll stop at the grocery store and stash a few things in your fridge so I won't have to run home for lunch every day. Maybe you can live on licorice sticks, but I can't."

A little nervy, she thought. "I think I should tell you I value my privacy."

He held his ground. "I won't get in your way."

Lainey took a deep, steadying breath. If she had one other applicant, just one, she'd tell him to go fly a kite. But she didn't. And she needed to get the barn done quickly. She'd put up with his quirks, but she didn't have to like it. "I suppose it'll be all right, then."

Zac opened the back door. "I'm going to measure the barn for lumber and make a list of other supplies. I'll check with you before I go get the stuff." He walked outside.

Lainey stepped out onto the porch and felt the warmth of the noonday sun. She pulled the scarf off and shook back her heavy hair. "But we haven't discussed your fee," she called after him.

Zac glanced over his shoulder, then stopped in midstride and turned around. His breathing slowed and his heartbeat lurched as he took in the black cloud framing her oval face and falling down past her shoulders. Even across a distance of some twenty feet, he felt the pull and tug of sexual reaction. It hadn't happened to him in a long while, and he wasn't pleased to have it happen now.

He frowned in her direction. "Don't worry. We'll get to it."

Lainey watched his long-legged stride as he headed toward the barn, and wondered what she'd gotten herself into.

* * *

"She comes across as a tough lady with a mind of her own, no mistaking that," Ben said as he hefted his end of a stack of lumber and followed Zac into the coolness of the barn.

"That she does," Zac agreed, slowing his pace so the older man wouldn't strain. He hadn't really needed help unloading the supplies from his truck, but he'd accepted Ben's offer, thinking it would be a good chance to get acquainted. At the far wall, he lowered the last of the boards to the ground as Ben set down his end.

Taking a snowy white handkerchief from the pocket of his bib overalls, Ben wiped his damp face. "My Clara's like that. She sounds real strong, but she's got a lot of soft spots. Children and animals and any living thing that needs help. Any stray, human or beast." He stuffed the kerchief back and regarded the tall man before him. "Women like that can get hurt easily, maybe get taken advantage of by someone who discovers one of those soft spots."

Another warning? Zac almost smiled. Though Ben had just told him he'd worked for Lainey less than a month, he'd evidently taken on the role of her champion. Perhaps he could put the man's mind at ease, since they'd be spending a fair amount of time together.

"Only a heel would take advantage of a vulnerable woman, I agree. If anyone comes along like that and bothers Lainey, you and I will send them on their way, right?"

Ben scratched his balding head. "May not need to, you know. She don't trust too many, 'specially men." His pale blue eyes narrowed as he studied Zac's face. "I'm real surprised she hired you so quick."

So was he. Zac tried to look amiable. "I do good work and I have an honest face. What more could she ask for?"

Ben didn't comment, but rather took out a tin of chewing tobacco and stuck a wad into the corner of his mouth.

Walking back outside, Zac gestured toward Trixie's empty stall. "How long does she usually ride? I got two boxes full of groceries in the truck."

"I wouldn't put 'em in her kitchen till she gets back. Lainey wouldn't like that."

He'd had no such intention. Shielding his eyes, he gazed toward the back of her property. "She'll need that corral fencing rebuilt for those riding lessons. It looks pretty makeshift. Do you know this Dr. Keller who's sending over those kids?"

"Dionne? You bet. Spitfire of a woman—a redhead—but she's real good with kids. She's already brought one out a few times. Little tyke about six. He's on some kind of medicine to slow him down."

Zac leaned against his truck. "He's hyperactive?"

"Yeah, that's it. He sure loves to ride that horse. Come to think of it, I'm real surprised you didn't have to pass inspection by Dionne before being hired."

Zac's brows rose. "Does Dionne have an interest in this property?"

"Don't think so. It's just that Lainey don't make too many moves without checking with Dionne. Only natural, I suppose."

"Natural?"

"Yeah. Dionne being her doctor and all." Ben shifted his wad to the other side of his mouth.

"You're saying that Lainey is Dionne's patient? I thought she specialized in treating traumatized children?"

"Maybe so, but she treats Lainey, too. They've known each other since school days. Lainey even lived with Dionne for a while there, before she bought this place." Looking as if he'd probably said enough, Ben picked up his shovel from where it leaned against the barn. "Guess I'd best be getting back to my garden."

Zac thought he'd try to get in one last question. "Do you know where Lainey came from before she moved here?"

"Nope. She's closemouthed about her past. I wouldn't go upsetting her with a lot of questions." He looked at Zac straight on, his eyes steady. "That's why I told you this stuff, so you wouldn't be asking her. Like I said before, Lainey acts tough, but she ain't. She's soft like my Clara, maybe even delicate, you know. My guess is someone hurt her. I don't want to see that happen again."

"She has nothing to fear from me." Evidently Zac had struck the right note of sincerity, for the older man nodded before he strolled off toward the other side of the barn.

Absently, Zac watched him go, but his thoughts were on Lainey Roberts. So she was being treated by a doctor who specialized in trauma. Had someone hurt her, and she was accepting the help of a trained medical friend to get over the pain?

And, Zac wondered, even more important, why did he care? All he wanted was to do do some physical labor for a while before returning to his construction firm.

A month ago, he'd taken a long look at himself and realized he was on a treadmill to nowhere. He'd had his reasons for the long hours he'd put in—good reasons. But work and work alone, he'd discovered, wasn't enough. He'd become an automaton who enjoyed little, felt almost nothing.

He'd decided then and there that it was time to get back to basics, to once again do the work he loved instead of the work he'd somehow been trapped into doing. He'd turned over the operations of his company to his best friend and partner, Colby Winters, and driven from Detroit up to his place in the small town of St. Clair on Michigan's eastern shoreline. The simplicity and peace of his ranch had always soothed him.

The rustic house had needed work, and he'd gladly plunged in, the feel of wood and tools in his hands a welcome diversion. He was beginning to feel better, tasting his food again, noticing trees and blue sky and sunsets. The sadness and despair that he'd lived with the past several years still lingered, but it was easing. Yet, a month's self-imposed sabbatical wasn't enough. Which was why he'd impulsively answered Lainey's ad.

Perhaps she would relax more around him if she learned that he had no interest in a serious relationship, for he was still mourning a lost one, still healing himself. It he let himself get too close to another soft, vulnerable woman, he'd risk being hurt again. Loving had such a high price-tag.

But friendship was another thing. From what he'd heard just now from Ben, she could use a friend. And so could he. Working mostly with men, he missed the softer sex.

Zac heard the rumble of horse's hooves approaching and straightened, his eyes trained on the horizon. He moved to the fence and leaned on the top board. The wind had picked up and he could smell the heat of the day, the dust swirling in the humid air, the earthy animal odor of the barn. Then he saw her.

She was riding bareback, leaning forward, one with the animal. Her small hands were buried in the horse's mane, her slender legs gripping Trixie's thick sides, her black hair flying behind her like a silken flag unfurling. He watched her murmur to Trixie, though they were too far away for him to hear the words. The horse responded, slowing reluctantly as she approached the fenced area.

Now he could see her eyes, a deep violet, dark with the pleasure of her exertion. Then she spotted him, and the exhilaration on her face slowly faded as she straightened. Zac wished the sight of him hadn't caused that sudden guarded look. Expertly she guided the horse. Trixie obeyed, slowing to a walk as she passed through the fence's gate.

At the far end, Lainey dismounted with a fluid drop to the grass, then moved to the horse's head to whisper quietly to her. She walked Trixie along the fence line slowly, letting her cool down as she chatted softly to her. Her back to him, she gathered her hair at her nape and wound a rubber band around it, forming a ponytail. With a final pat on Trixie's neck, she left her there near an old maple shading the far corner and headed for the gate.

Zac watched her walk toward him, trying to remember what he'd planned to say to her.

She stopped several feet from him, and he finally found his tongue. "Where'd you learn to ride like that?"

"Here and there."

A careful answer. "You're very good. But shouldn't you use a saddle?"

Lainey had felt a rush of annoyance when she'd seen him leaning on the fence, watching her, waiting for her. She wanted him to get to work, to get the job done, and to get out of her life. He was too visible, too unnerving, too damn male. She'd only just hired him, and already she was beginning to question her decision. Squaring her shoulders, she looked up at him.

"I've been riding since I was fifteen. Shouldn't you be worrying about getting started on the barn instead of my safety?"

"I wouldn't want you to fall and hurt yourself."

"I never have."

Her fragrance was emphasized by the heat of her body. With some effort, he ignored its pull on his senses. "There's a first time for everything."

"Very original." She looked past him to his truck. "Did you find everything you need?"

"Yes."

"Fine. Then I'll leave you to your work." She stepped around him.

"Wait! We haven't had lunch."

Lainey stopped. She should have guessed he wouldn't have forgotten. Glancing at her watch, she turned back to him. "It's four o'clock. A bit late for lunch."

He gave her his most winning smile. "Then we'll call it dinner."

"Why don't we just call it off and start fresh tomorrow?"

For the life of him, Zac didn't know why he was persisting. He only knew that somehow it was important that he win this one. "Because I've got two boxes of food in my truck that will spoil if we don't do something with them.''

Lainey let out a ragged sigh. The man was as tenacious as a bulldog. "All right, come on.'' She swung about and headed for the house.

Fantasies. Every woman had them, Lainey thought. Right now, hers centered around picturing herself pouring a bowl of hot soup over Zac Sinclair's stubborn head.

Chapter Two

She couldn't remember the last time she'd had two helpings of anything. Lainey finished the final bite of spaghetti on her plate and leaned back in satisfaction. "I can't believe I ate all that," she told Zac.

Having consumed twice as much, Zac wasn't impressed. "You didn't touch the bread or your salad."

She gave him a mock frown. "I never eat salad, but I ate your main course, didn't I? Back off, Sinclair, and be happy with your small victory."

While he'd made the dinner, she'd washed up and changed into a floppy black shirt over white slacks. She looked freshly scrubbed and smelled better than his sauce. Zac raised his wineglass. "Here's to even bigger victories."

Lainey wasn't sure why, but his toast seemed to veil a threat. Or was she making too much out of a light comment? Probably, because she'd rather enjoyed the past hour, fussing around the kitchen storing the enormous array of food he'd brought while he'd opened bottles and cans and tossed spices into his special sauce. They'd stayed out of each other's way and chatted about nothing. It was a new experience for Lainey, and she found herself hesitant to trust the comfortable feelings.

She clinked her glass to his, but didn't drink. "Wine makes me fuzzy," she said by way of explanation.

Zac leaned back, stretching his long legs. "What do you like to drink?"

"Not much, except maybe peach brandy." She saw him make a face. "No, you'd like this. My Grandmother Nolan made it." As always, when she thought of her grandmother, she grew melancholy. "She used to make a batch every summer. She died five years ago, and I have only one bottle left."

"You two were close?"

"Yes, very. She was the kindest, the gentlest woman I've ever known." Lainey had often wondered how such a sweet person could have given birth to a cool, ambitious person like her mother.

"What about your grandfather?"

"He was sweet, too. He died a long time ago. I think the reason I hired Ben was that he reminded me of my grandfather." She stopped then, embarrassed at having revealed so much to a virtual stranger. "Enough about me." She stood to clear the table.

"Ben's quite a character," Zac said, wanting to keep her talking. "He warned me earlier not to upset you."

She smiled at that. "Did he really? Are you going to follow his advice?"

"Do I look like a man who enjoys upsetting women?"

Perhaps not, but she wasn't like most other women. "Maybe not intentionally, but..."

"But?"

"But you like your way, like most men. For instance, you're in here, aren't you? Having dinner in my kitchen, where no one..." She hesitated. He was making her uncomfortable, defensive. "I'm not a very social being."

He had trouble accepting that. "But you have friends, surely. Dionne Keller and...and..."

She sat down again. "And very few others. I've worked hard all my life, Zac. I've never had time to form friendships." Now she wished she had. But soon there'd be the children. And the horses. They would do. Many had less.

"What did you work hard doing, before you decided to open a riding stable, Lainey?" He was curious, he told himself. That was all.

She looked up to find his serious gray eyes on her. A relentless man. She would tell him only enough to satisfy him, then she would send him home. Questions always exhausted her. "I was a model, in New York, since I was seventeen."

He should have guessed—with her classic features. "That's why you don't eat much."

She shrugged. "Old habits die hard."

"Would I have seen your picture anywhere?"

"Only if you read fashion magazines."

"Were you successful?"

"Most would think so."

"Are you going back, then? Just doing this for the summer?"

"No. I like it here."

"Isn't it hard for you to give up that life?"

"Modeling can be arduous."

"Then why'd you do it?"

"It paid the bills." And rather well.

He watched her take a careful sip of her wine, and felt a rush of empathy. He, too, had been working at a job he'd grown weary of. "I understand."

She returned her gaze to his and shook her head. "I'm not sure anyone can, unless they've been there."

"I understand how empty a life is when you aren't enthusiastic about your work. And I understand loneliness."

With a frown, Lainey got to her feet. "I'm *not* lonely."

A smart man knew when to back off and when to take his leave. Zac stood. "Good for you, Lainey. People who never know loneliness are rare indeed." He moved to the kitchen door and opened it. "Thanks for sharing dinner with me. I cooked, so I guess you won't mind cleaning up."

Lainey followed him to the door and watched him inhale a deep breath of fresh air. No more wine, she thought. And no more cozy, chatty dinners. Both made her drop her guard.

He turned back and gave her a lazy smile. "See you in the morning."

Lainey closed the inner door a little too roughly. Quickly she ran the sink full of hot, soapy water while she listened to his truck rumble down the drive. The man had nerve, telling her what she did and did not feel. Impatiently she stuck her hand in the water and yelped when she found it scalding. She turned on the cold, then sucked on her throbbing fingers as she leaned against the counter.

The room seemed too quiet and suddenly very empty. She was *not* lonely, damn it. She was *not*.

Leaving the dishes to soak, she stomped outside. Trixie would be glad to see her, she knew. She much preferred the company of animals over people, anyway.

"No, I don't think it's premature to send over another student," Lainey said over the phone. "The barn's being renovated first, and the work is going along quite well. I hope to get a couple more horses soon. But until then, Trixie's more than capable of working with two children."

Holding the receiver on her end, Dionne Keller slipped out of her high-heeled pumps with a grateful sigh. It had been a long day for her, and it was far from over yet. "This new handyman's pretty good, then?"

"Yes, yes, he's fine."

Ever alert to nuances of the voice, Dionne frowned as she leaned back in her swivel chair and put a match to her cigarette. "Tell me about him."

"There isn't much to tell. He's a skilled carpenter, but he can also do electrical work and a number of other things. He owns some small construction company in Detroit."

"Then why is he up here hammering on your barn? Most owners wear three-piece suits and stay in their offices."

"He likes to work with his hands. He also owns the ranch next to mine. He breeds horses."

It was sounding "curiouser and curiouser." Dionne ran restless fingers through her short red hair as her busy mind considered possibilities. "Is his wife there with him?"

"His wife? I never asked if he had one." Lainey released an exasperated sigh. "Look, Dionne, I don't care if he's got a harem, as long as he does his job and stays out of my way."

"How old is he?" Dionne asked, hoping her friend would say the man was old enough to be her father. Lainey was too vulnerable right now to have to cope with a robust male looking for even a mild flirtation. She should have driven over and talked with this handyman before he'd been hired.

"I don't know. In his thirties, I'd guess. I didn't ask his political preferences or his favorite brand of toothpaste, either. Dionne, I know you mean well, but—"

"You're right, of course. I didn't mean to hover." Dionne tapped the ash from her cigarette thoughtfully. "But damn, Lainey, I just don't want some joker to make a move on you and set you back." Lainey needed a special kind of man—one with a great deal of intelligence and sensitivity—to help her learn to trust again. Both as a doctor and as a woman, Dionne knew that kind were scarcer than hen's teeth.

"I know. I'm fine, really. You're welcome to come meet him, to see for yourself that he's just doing his job."

"Sort of like a big brother, would you say?" Dionne asked hopefully.

Lainey hesitated, then said, "Yes, a big brother. Now, tell me about this new child."

The silence had dragged out too long. Something there, Dionne thought as she searched around for the right file on her cluttered desk. She'd have to make time to get over to Lainey's place soon. "Her name is Shelly Morgan, and she's seven. She was in an automobile accident and saw her mother die and her father badly hurt. He's still on the critical list. Oddly, Shelly wasn't even injured. But she hasn't said a word since.''

"Oh, God," Lainey whispered. "The poor kid."

She'd known that Shelly would get to Lainey. All creatures great and small got to Lainey, which was just one reason why she worried about her. "She's staying with her aunt and uncle who have four small children of their own. Physically she's fine, but she'd not communicating much. I hope that she'll relate to Trixie. And to you."

"I'm certainly willing to give her a try."

Dionne stared a moment longer at the file picture of Shelly with her long blond hair and serious blue eyes. So young to hurt so badly. With a snap, she closed the folder. "Great. I'll work out a time and give you a call soon."

"I'll be waiting."

"Take care, Lainey. And remember, I'm always here if you need to talk."

Lainey felt her eyes fill. Nearly six months of doctors and therapy, and her emotions were still so close to the surface. When would it end? Slowly she replaced the receiver, having finished her conversation with Dionne. She shuddered to think what she'd have done without Dionne these past several months.

Her heart went out to Shelly, her mind already wondering how best to help her. Yes, she could relate, all right. All too well.

Through the screen door, she heard a string of expletives shouted into the soft summer air. Peering out, she saw Zac favoring a thumb, he'd evidently whacked a good one. She'd have to warn him about that swearing when the children were around.

Dionne had wanted to know if he was married. If he was, where was his wife? Why was he up here alone for weeks at a time? None of her business, she reminded herself.

She watched Zac wipe the sweat from his damp face before stooping down and resuming his hammering. Perhaps she should make some lemonade and take a glass out to both Ben and Zac. After all, it was hot today, with the humidity still climbing. Lainey opened the refrigerator.

Rounding the corner of the barn on her way back from taking Ben a cold drink, Lainey felt an unfamiliar ripple of pleasure. The garden was coming along nicely; the soil was rich and fertile. Ben had nurtured some small tomato plants at his place throughout the spring and now was planting them for her. Soon she'd get some pepper plants, maybe corn. But no lettuce. She still had trouble enjoying a salad after having practically lived on them for years.

Stepping back from the ladder leaning against the barn, she shielded her eyes and looked up. Zac was squatting on the middle section of the lightly pitched roof, his back to her as he pounded a shingle into place. He would never hear her above the hammering. Gripping the large plastic tumbler, she grabbed hold of the ladder and started up.

The top of the ladder stretched a foot and a half above the edge of the roof. Lainey leaned against the rungs just as Zac gave a final slam to the nail and turned around. His teeth were very white against the tan of his face as he smiled at her.

"Good morning. Always nice to have a visitor." Yellow was certainly her color, he thought. The loose cotton blouse billowed in the breeze, and her hair hung down her back in a single long braid. He scooted closer, liking what he saw.

"Good morning. I thought you could use a cold drink." She stretched out her arm, holding the tumbler toward him.

Instead of taking the glass, he grabbed her wrist and tugged. "Come on up. I can't offer you a chair, but I've got the best view for miles around."

Caught off guard, Lainey climbed automatically so as not to lose her balance. "I wasn't planning on going all the way up."

"You'll love it." With a quick movement, he had her up and over the ladder's edge and seated alongside him. Taking the glass from her, he gestured at the panoramic view before them. "Isn't that worth the climb?"

It really was, Lainey decided. Except for the tallest poplars, they were above the treetops. Through a path in the thick vegetation separating their properties, she could see the stream in the distance and beyond that, Zac's house and barn painted a cheery red. The sky was clear and very blue, and she could hear the twittering of birds in the branches close by. The air was hot and tinged with the smell of hay and leather and the musky scent of the man beside her.

Lainey inched away from him, his nearness making her all too aware. Fighting the uncomfortable unease, she glanced behind her at the section he'd been working on. "I see you're making great headway. How many leaks have you found?"

Zac drained the last of the lemonade before answering. "Three. I've got one more to patch after this spot. But the wood underneath wasn't damaged, so it's not too bad." Why, he wondered, looking at her roomy tan cotton slacks, did she wear such baggy clothes?

"That's good. Think you'll finish it today?"

He glanced up at the cloudless sky. "Should. No rain in sight." His gaze swung to the north where, just beyond the next farm, Lake St. Clair could be seen. "My wife loved it here. We used to keep a boat at Gil's Marina and go fishing at night. And we'd stop at Ernie's Restaurant just off the coastal highway. Fish so fresh they would almost flop around on your plate."

Lainey focused on the word *wife* and felt a sigh of relief tremble through her. Thank goodness he was married. "Is your wife coming up to join you soon?"

Zac dangled his arms on his knees and stared into the ice cubes in his plastic tumbler. "Nancy died two years ago last month." The pain, a dull ache now, was still there every time he spoke of her. He was certain it always would be.

Even turned sideways, she could see the sadness in his face. "I'm so sorry. Were you married long?"

"From the time we were both nineteen." A long time, but not nearly long enough. He leaned back on his elbows, shifting his gaze to the sky. "I quit college after only a year and went to work full-time for this construction company I'd worked for for several summers. After a while, the owner got sick and I took out this huge loan and bought him out. Midwest Construction Corporation. Nancy worked in the office, and I was out in the field."

Lainey angled her body so she was facing him. "I've heard of Midwest Construction. I didn't realize that was you." She'd been wrong. Not some small outfit, but one of the largest and most successful construction firms in the state. And here the owner was, patching her roof.

"Yeah, that's me. We worked our buns off, expanded, then moved our offices to the suburbs. My manager bought in as a partner and finally, we could ease up. Only then, we learned that Nancy had cancer."

Without thinking, she reached out to touch his arm. "I shouldn't have pried."

His gray eyes were dark with remembrance, and he continued as if he hadn't heard her. "She lived for a year and a half. Nancy was very brave, even when the pain got so bad that I knew she felt like screaming. I never want to watch anyone go through something like that again as long as I live."

Lainey could add nothing to his words.

"You ever been in love, Lainey?"

She looked down at her hand on his arm. It had been a very long time since she'd voluntarily touched a man. Quickly she pulled back, lacing her fingers tightly together in her lap. "No."

"It's best to steer clear of it. Losing somebody you care about is far worse than never having found them at all."

"I intend to."

"Smart girl." He sat up and rubbed a hand across his eyes. "I didn't mean to bore you with the story of my life."

"I'm glad you told me." Very glad. He'd been hurt by his loss. He wasn't anxious to risk involvement. She could breathe easier, knowing that he wanted to go it alone as she did. She could regard him as the big brother Dionne had suggested he might be.

His gray eyes were clear once more. "I'm not usually so talkative. You're a good listener."

"Thanks." Lainey scrambled to her feet. "I guess I'd better go back down and let you get on with your work."

Zac rose and adjusted his wide carpenter's belt more comfortably. "I've run out of nails. I'll go down first." Stepping agilely over the ladder's top, he placed his feet solidly on the rungs. "Need any help?"

"No, I'm fine." She waited until he was halfway down before she stepped onto the ladder. It must have been horrid, watching the woman he'd married die such a painful death. He sounded as if he was still in love with her. The poor man.

Nearly to the bottom, she glanced over her shoulder and noticed he was waiting for her. She saw him hold up a hand to help her, and she frowned, not wanting assistance. "It's okay," she said, moving quickly to avoid his grasp. But she miscalculated and suddenly found herself sliding down the last couple of rungs and landing hard on the sparse grass.

Zac grabbed her shoulders and swiveled her about. "You all right?"

"Yes, of course." She took a moment to catch her breath, but her heart wouldn't stop racing. It wasn't the near fall, she realized, but the nearness of the man, who was much too close for comfort. The broad expanse of his bare chest was directly in front of her, tan and muscular and liberally coated with dark hair. Her hands were resting there from when she'd reached out to keep her balance. His skin was smooth and damp and hard beneath her fingertips. She could smell the heat of him, the maleness. Feelings somersaulted through her system as, with pulse pounding, she raised her eyes to his.

His eyes had darkened to pewter and filled with a sharp awareness. She could feel the trembling begin deep inside. *No!*

Lainey jerked back two steps, angling out of his loose hold. Turning, she started toward the house, then broke into a run until she reached the porch, taking the steps in a mad dash. Inside the kitchen, she quickly closed the door, then moved to the sink, breathing hard.

Her hands braced on the edge, she forced long breaths into her lungs, her eyes tightly closed, fighting the pull of her dark memories. She wouldn't allow them to take over. She couldn't.

It had been only Zac, the soft-spoken man who'd moments before told her of his wife's agonizing death. Zac, who wanted to steer clear of women as much as she wanted to steer clear of men. Zac, who could be the big brother she'd never had. Lord, he must think she'd suddenly lost her mind.

She'd overreacted, that was all. Dionne had told her it would happen, and it had.

Finally calming, Lainey splashed cold water on her face and grabbed the towel. Walking over to the mirror, she dried off, then stared at her shaky image.

It had been desire she'd seen in his eyes, not a hurtful lust. And crazy as it seemed, she'd felt it, too. For a long moment there, she hadn't felt in the least sisterly toward Zac. Then the fear had whipped through her. Now she was left with anger at herself for allowing her emotions to take over.

After months of therapy, she'd come to the conclusion that the only way she could insulate herself against further pain was to avoid close contact with men. With most of them, at least. Grandfatherly types like Ben didn't make her uneasy. But many others did.

So she'd decided to work with horses and children and their safe parents who brought them to her ranch. And she'd downplay her looks, never emphasizing her face or figure. While she didn't wish to look ugly, she also didn't want to unwittingly entice someone again.

And her plan had been working—until Zac Sinclair had touched her.

Perhaps it was time for another session with Dionne.

Lainey clamped the old red felt hat onto the straw scarecrow's head and stood back to admire her work. "What do you think, Ben? Will he keep the birds from eating our seeds?"

Ben walked over, carrying the sprinkling can he'd been using to water the tender plants and new seedlings. Angling his nearly bald head, he smiled at Lainey. "He sure will. Where'd you get that old plaid shirt?"

"It was hanging on a nail in the barn when I bought this place. Probably been there for a long time. I washed it and put it on old Henry, here." She straightened one stick arm. "Makes him look sporty, don't you think?"

Ben shifted his ever-present wad of tobacco and chuckled as he returned to his watering. "Yup. He's the best scarecrow for miles around."

He was humoring her, but Lainey didn't mind. She stepped over the carefully tended rows, realizing that she was in a better mood than usual this afternoon. Probably because she'd had a long conversation with Dionne this morning. Her doctor had helped put the incident by the ladder several days ago and her reactions to Zac in perspective.

She'd told Dionne everything she knew about Zac, and her friend had assured Lainey that her feelings were quite normal, but very much at war with each other. On the one hand, she felt the tug of attraction to a very virile man. On the other hand, his nearness triggered a remembrance of the fear she'd lived with since leaving New York. Dionne seemed to feel that Zac sounded nonthreatening. Since she was coming tomorrow to bring her new student to meet Lainey, however, she'd look him over.

Meantime, Dionne thought it best that she act normally but not seek out his company, which was what she'd been doing anyway. Zac, perhaps sensing something had upset her though not knowing the cause, had stayed out of her path, working long hours in the barn. He'd been polite; friendly, but distant. After stocking her refrigerator, he'd either skipped lunch or eaten it elsewhere. She was both relieved and surprised at his sensitivity. She hadn't known an abundance of sensitive men.

"See you later, Ben," Lainey called out as she strolled around the bend, catching his wave. A streak of brown fur and dust came whirling at her, and she just had time to brace herself before Willie came running over to her.

"Easy, Willie," she said, bending to scratch his long ears as he wound between her legs, looking for the attention he knew he could get from her. Zac had taken to bringing the friendly dog with him almost daily and letting him run loose, which suited Willie just fine. It suited Lainey, too; Willie's boundless energy and playful spirit were infectious.

"Come on, boy," she continued, straightening. "Let's go to the barn and check on Trixie. I'll bet she could use some fresh water on such a warm afternoon." Willie scampered on ahead of her, as if he understood.

Lainey blinked as she entered the barn, letting her eyes adjust to the dimness. Zac's truck was parked where he usually left it, but he was nowhere in sight. She would just complete this one last chore, then get back to her work on the kitchen cupboards. Avoiding him was easier than confronting him, though it made her feel a shade cowardly. She couldn't seem to make up her mind whether to apologize for her behavior that day, or to let the whole incident go.

Willie stayed back to roll around in a mound of hay near the door while she ran a bucket of water to fill Trixie's box. "Hey, girl, how you doing?" she murmured to the horse, causing the mare's ears to twitch in welcome. "Got a new young rider coming to meet you tomorrow."

Lainey turned off the water and walked to Trixie's stall, opening the gate. She filled the trough, then set down the bucket as the horse dipped her head to drink. Glancing around, she noticed that the progress Zac had made was remarkable for such a short time. The roof was all finished and three of the four stalls were like new, the fresh wood fragrant in the musty barn. All that was left was reinforcing the back wall and redoing the hayloft.

She hadn't dared hope one man working alone could get so much done so quickly. Then he would start on the house. Where would she hide while he was working there? she wondered. Sighing, Lainey hoped that by that time, she'd be more used to his presence and able to relax around him. She would be patient the few weeks it would take to complete the job, being friendly but standoffish. Then he'd return to his ranch, or back to his company in the city. Either way, Zac Sinclair and his uncanny ability to confuse her emotions would be history. She'd hang on to that thought.

Leaning down to pick up the bucket, she heard Willie yip, then howl loudly. Lainey hurried out of the stall and turned toward the door. Her hand rose to her throat along with a lump of fear as she saw the creature crouched in a standoff with Willie. Where on earth had a wolverine come from?

Willie growled low in his throat as Lainey frantically looked about for a weapon. The pitchfork was leaning alongside Trixie's stall, and she grabbed it quickly. "Hey!" she yelled, trying to distract the animal.

The weasel-like creature gave her a perfunctory glance, then ignored her as he inched closer to Willie. Lainey saw a small mouse burrow into the haystack and guessed that it was what the predator had been after. She should have had Ben check for a nest of mice after spotting that first one. She'd been told that wolverines stayed mostly north of this area and lived in the thick of the woods, but this stray looked hungry and mean. She knew that though they were small, wolverines were extremely strong. Moving nearer, she raised the handle of the pitchfork, hoping to get close enough to scare him away.

Willie bared his teeth and advanced, but the weasel was unafraid and determined. Lainey watched in horror as suddenly the wolverine lunged and attacked, grabbing one of Willie's ears in his small, sharp bite. The dog yelped loudly, and Lainey rushed to his defense, swiping at the wolverine. He spared her only a quick look as he whirled about and raced through the open door. Running after him, the handle of the pitchfork raised high, Lainey yelled her fury as she chased the black critter. She caught only the edge of his furry tail before he picked up speed.

From the corner of her eye, she saw movement and realized Zac had appeared from somewhere and joined the chase.

"Lainey!" he shouted, gaining on her. "Let him go!"

"No!" she shrieked back at him. "He's hurt Willie." She ran on.

Finally reaching her at the edge of the woods, he grabbed her by the arms and swung her around. "Stop!" He gave her a quick shake. "He's gone. Where's Willie?"

Catching her breath, Lainey shook off his hands. "In the barn. I think he's bleeding."

She saw Zac turn and run toward the barn, and she was close on his heels as she tossed aside the pitchfork. "There're mice in that haystack. It's got to be cleaned out or that wolverine will be back."

Slowing at the door, Zac saw Willie hunched on the ground by the hay mound. His ear was ripped and hanging, blood dripped onto his front paws, and his eyes were filled with pain as he whimpered at the sight of his master. Zac crouched down and touched his bony head. "It's going to be okay, boy."

Lainey grabbed a jacket she'd had hanging on a wall hook. "Let's wrap him in this. I'll hold him and you drive. The vet's only two miles from here."

Zac knew exactly where the nearest vet was. He took the jacket and wrapped the injured dog in it, then rose with him in his arms and made for his truck.

Stopping only to latch Trixie's stall door, Lainey ran after him and scrambled up into the passenger seat, then held out her arms for Willie. The dog gave out a low whine as Zac placed him in her lap. "I know, Willie. I know it hurts. We're going to get you fixed up just fine."

Zac closed the door and hurried behind the wheel. His hands were bloody, and he wiped them on his jeans before starting the truck. Any wounds about the head always bled so damn much. In a swirl of dust, he aimed the truck toward the path leading to the road, almost running over the pitchfork Lainey had thrown aside.

"What were you thinking, chasing after that vicious animal?" he asked her, his voice rough. Didn't she realize she could have gotten herself hurt, as well, and he'd now be driving two for medical treatment? "Wolverines are strong enough to kill a dog twice the size of Willie. They're often rabid, and this one could have turned on you."

"I was mad, so I chased him." She cradled the trembling dog close to her body, uncertain who was shaking more in the aftermath—she or Willie. The eerie feral eyes of the wolverine as they'd locked with hers for mere seconds were something she would not soon forget.

"You weren't even holding the pitchfork end toward him, just the handle," he went on. "What were you going to do? Rap him on the knuckles?" He struggled with his unreasonable anger, knowing it was directed mostly at himself for not having been there to protect her and his dog.

Lainey gritted her teeth. "I didn't have time to find a better weapon. Look, will you just drive? You can rant and rave at me some more while the doctor works on Willie."

With a jerk of the wheel, Zac zoomed onto the main road. Damn fool woman.

* * *

"I'm sorry I yelled at you. I shouldn't have." Zac stood looking out the window of the veterinarian's small reception area. Fortunately no one else had been waiting when they'd arrived, and Dr. Davis and his assistant were already working on Willie. Zac had calmed down outwardly, but inside he was still angry.

Lainey hadn't said a word since she'd sat down in the blue plastic chair. He turned to look at her. "Did you hear me?"

"Yes, and I agree. You shouldn't have yelled at me."

He walked closer to her, needing to make her see. "Still, you could have gotten badly hurt yourself. You didn't think. You were careless and—"

Lainey jumped to her feet, her eyes suddenly blazing. "But I *didn't* get hurt. And don't you *dare* call me careless. I knew exactly what I was doing—chasing away something harmful and ugly the best way I knew how. And where the hell were you while I was defending your dog?"

That hit home. His face reddening, Zac stepped back. She couldn't be angrier at him than he was at himself. He'd been on the ladder around back, checking the structural damage of the far wall. But that was no excuse.

Lainey marched to the window and stood staring out unseeingly, her mind focused on another time, on another voice berating her.

"How could you have been so careless, Lainey?" her mother had asked in that low, disapproving tone. "Why didn't you use your head, protect yourself?"

Lainey felt again the helpless defensiveness she'd felt then. "Things don't always happen because someone's careless or unthinking," she said, scarcely aware she'd spoken aloud. "Some things just . . . happen." She had to hang on to that thought. It hadn't been her fault.

Zac waited until she turned back to face him, and then he saw that the anger in her eyes had been replaced with a raw pain, and wondered what she was remembering. "I'm sorry. Tell me what I said to upset you, and I'll try to understand."

"I don't need you to understand me. I need you to finish your work and leave me alone." She walked quickly to the door, fighting her emotions. "I'll wait for you and Willie in the truck," she called over her shoulder.

Jamming his hands into his jeans pockets, Zac watched her go. Damned if he'd ever understand women.

The door to the doctor's office swung open, and Zac turned.

"Willie's going to be just fine," Dr. Davis told him, wiping his hands on a paper towel. "His one ear is going to be shorter and a bit ragged, that's all."

"That's great," Zac said with relief. "I was worried."

"Shouldn't be. He'll heal in no time."

Everyone said that time healed all wounds. But Zac wondered about that as he turned to look out the window at the woman sitting so erect in his truck. Lainey Roberts certainly seemed as though she was carrying around one hell of a wound. He couldn't help speculate what it was and how long it would be before hers would heal.

Chapter Three

The child was lovely, with curly blond hair and huge blue eyes in a heart-shaped face, Lainey thought as she walked toward Dionne's red Corvette pulling up near her back door. The car was capable of astounding speed, but Dionne kept well within the speed limits when one of her young patients was seated beside her. Lainey watched her new student climb carefully out of the car and immediately reach for Dionne's hand. She looked small, lost and fragile. So many fragile creatures in the world, Lainey reflected, and they came in all shapes and ages.

"There you are," Dionne called in greeting. "How are you?"

Smiling a welcome, Lainey stopped in front of the two. "Fine. Good to see you." And it was. Dionne's presence always gave her a boost.

She looked every inch the professional in a white linen suit worn with a green silk blouse, her short red hair lifting softly in the wind, her intelligent brown eyes missing nothing. Her glance at the little girl beside her was warm and reassuring.

"Shelly, this is Lainey Roberts, the lady I told you about who teaches children about horses. Lainey, meet Shelly Morgan."

Lainey held out her hand. "Nice meeting you, Shelly." The child looked up at her with solemn blue eyes and touched her small hand to hers briefly, then returned it to her jeans pocket.

"Shelly's anxious to meet Trixie," Dionne went on.

Before anyone could say another word, Willie scampered around the corner in a swirl of brown dust and came to a halt at Lainey's feet, his bandaged ear hanging at a tilted angle. Lainey stooped down to rub his head.

"Do you like dogs, Shelly? This is Willie, and he had a bad day yesterday. But he's brave and he'll be just fine." The little girl looked at Dionne hesitantly, then let go of her hand and took a step closer. "You can pet him if you like. He's very gentle."

Willie rolled over on his back and looked up at Shelly with mournful brown eyes. Overcoming her shyness, Shelly squatted down beside him and rubbed his soft chest hair. The dog rolled his head happily and licked her hand.

"You didn't tell me you had a dog," Dionne said, watching the two get acquainted.

Lainey rose to her feet. "He belongs to Zac. Poor thing went head-on with a wolverine yesterday and lost."

"A wolverine around here?"

"The first I've seen. He was after some mice that were nesting in the barn. Zac cleaned them all out last night."

Dionne looked around. "And where is your gentleman carpenter today?"

"Up measuring the hayloft, I think. We need to get that reinforced so I'll have a place to stack the hay and bags of feed, once I get a couple more horses."

Dionne studied Lainey from under her lowered lashes, noticing that Lainey was getting some sun, chasing away that pale look, and that her eyes didn't look quite as haunted. She had on a gray short-sleeved sweatshirt that was two sizes too large, and matching baggy sweatpants. If she still felt more comfortable in a shapeless outfit, Dionne wasn't about to criticize. Her clothes were the least of her concerns over her patient and friend.

She touched Lainey's arm. "Any more incidents?" she inquired quietly.

"Not really," Lainey hedged. "He's been busy working on the barn, and I'm refinishing the cupboards in the kitchen. That day, I overreacted."

"And you might again. Perfectly natural."

"No, I won't because I'm going to make sure the opportunity doesn't present itself again."

Dionne frowned. That wasn't the answer she'd been hoping for. "For the rest of your life?"

Lainey tried to find a smile and almost made it. "No. Just the next thirty or forty years."

"Lainey, I . . ." A sound from the direction of the barn drew Dionne's attention.

Dionne stared at him openly. Zac Sinclair was more than she'd been expecting. More rugged, more masculine, more sensual. Even from this distance, there was a confidence in his stance, a raw appeal, yet a gentleness in the way he was leading Trixie out of the barn. Then he smiled at Lainey, and it was unmistakably friendly and nonthreatening. Dionne let herself relax a notch.

"I thought you might want Trixie out in the corral," he called to Lainey. "There's a lot of sawdust floating around in the barn."

Considerate and sensitive coupled with sexy good looks, Dionne thought. A dangerous combination. She couldn't help wondering if Lainey was up to handling a man like this so soon.

"Thank you," Lainey answered, then bent to Shelly. "Would you like to meet Trixie?"

Reluctantly rising from the dog, who was obviously thrilled by her attention, Shelly nodded. Looking up expectantly at Dionne, she took hold of her hand.

Dionne was watching Zac murmur to the horse as he walked her into the corral. "Yes, let's go over and meet both of them."

Willie howled his displeasure at being abandoned, causing both Lainey and Dionne to laugh, breaking the tension. Strolling over, Dionne could sense Lainey's watchful eyes on her reaction to Zac's presence.

"Do you want me to get the small saddle?" Zac asked Lainey as she stopped at the gate.

"No, I don't think so, thanks. This first time, I think we'll just get acquainted." She looked down at Shelly and held out her hand. "Want to go closer with me?"

The child hesitated only a moment, then slipped her hand from Dionne's into Lainey's. Zac let the reins drop and walked over.

Lainey kept her eyes on Shelly as she introduced them.

Staying at a comfortable distance, Zac smiled warmly. "I know you'll like Trixie, Shelly. She's a great horse." He stepped over to Dionne and held out his hand. "I've heard a lot about you."

Dionne shook his hand firmly. "And I about you."

"Let's just walk over nice and slowly, Shelly, and talk to Trixie," Lainey said to the child, leading her to the middle of the corral where the mare stood patiently waiting. "We'll circle around so we can approach her from the front. Horses get frightened easily if they're surprised."

Zac swung the gate closed and leaned on the top rung, bracing one dusty boot on the bottom board, his eyes on Lainey. "Is she as good with children as she is with animals?" he asked Dionne.

"Even better." Dionne scrounged around in her leather shoulder bag, found a cigarette and stuck it into her mouth.

Zac turned toward her as he removed a book of matches from his pocket. "Allow me." He struck a match, sheltering the flame in his cupped hands.

And gentlemanly, Dionne thought as she leaned in to his light. "Thanks." She blew smoke into the hot summer air, glancing at him assessingly. "I understand you own the ranch next door. I've heard it's one of the best stud farms for miles around. I'm surprised you're over here doing repairs a first-year apprentice could do."

Zac gave her a measured look. "I like working with my hands more than running my ranch or business from behind a desk. It's as simple as that."

His gray eyes were sincere enough, yet Dionne had a feeling this deceptively quiet man was anything but simple. She glanced over at Shelly, who was listening intently to Lainey. But her thoughts were on the man who casually leaned on the fence railing, looking relaxed and at ease. "Your home is in Detroit?" she asked, wondering just how open he'd be with her.

"Yes. And you live in St. Clair, I imagine. Were you born here?"

So it was going to be question for question, was it? She inhaled on her cigarette before answering. "No, I'm originally from Detroit, too."

"And that's where you went to school with Lainey?"

"She told you that?" Odd, considering Lainey was not the chatty type.

"No, Ben mentioned it. Along with a warning not to ask too many questions or I might upset Lainey."

"Ben's very protective of Lainey."

"As I believe you are. Why does she need so much protection?"

She swung her gaze toward the woman they were discussing and saw her instructing Shelly how to hold the reins as they walked Trixie along the fence. "Lainey's one of the fragile ones. People tend to feel protective toward someone like her."

Zac dug the toe of his boot into the dirt, his jaw clamped together. After a moment he leveled his gaze on her. "I agree," he said, and she tried hard to hide her surprise at his unexpected response. "My wife was like that. Small, almost delicate, yet tougher than she seemed when she needed to be."

She'd been right. The sensitivity was there, the quick perception. "Yes, there is that core of strength in Lainey, too."

Zac braced his arms on the fence railing and watched Lainey demonstrate how best to stroke the horse's muzzle. "She'd have to be fairly strong to survive ten years' modeling in New York."

That information had to have come from Lainey, and again Dionne was surprised at how much her friend had revealed to this relative stranger. Perhaps it was because, along with obvious masculine appeal, Zac Sinclair exuded a resilient durability that attracted Lainey despite her wariness. "Modeling can be a tough life. Zac, perhaps I should tell you that Lainey's had a rough time lately. She's been hurt and—"

"And here comes the warning." Zac swung about and crossed his arms over his chest. "Perhaps I should tell you that I won't hurt her. I've had a relationship— a good one—and it hurt like hell when it had to end. I'm not masochistic enough to want to go through that again. But simple human friendship is another thing. For years I worked too hard to form many. I have the time now, and Lainey interests me."

Dionne drew deeply on her cigarette, buying some time. He seemed honest enough, and her instincts told her he was. She'd made a lot of judgment calls before, and her instincts had seldom let her down. Still, she had some reservations and she might as well lay them out for him. "Do you think it's possible for a man and a woman to have a simple friendship without the physical part getting in the way?"

Zac eyed her with a gleam of admiration. "Yes, I do." He stepped back, shoving both hands into his pockets. "I'm not saying I don't find Lainey attractive. But I'm not a person who pushes. I take it she's known a few who do."

Dionne adjusted the strap of her bag over her shoulder and braced her elbow on the fence. "Yes, she has. I just don't want anyone to hurt her."

"I don't blame you. Was it a husband?"

"I don't think it's necessary for you to have a run-down on everyone in Lainey's life in order to offer her simple friendship. And I think that if she wants you to know any more, she'll tell you herself."

"Fair enough. Then I have your permission to pursue this friendship?" he asked with a smile.

The smile changed his face, bringing even more warmth to his gray eyes. Yes, she would go with her instincts on this. "You never needed it. Lainey's her own person."

"But you're her doctor."

"I'm her friend."

"So am I. She just hasn't realized it yet." Zac removed his measuring tape from his belt. "Time to get back to work. I hope I've put your mind at ease."

Dionne gave in to a smile. The man didn't lack for charm. "You have, surprisingly. And I'm not an easy sell."

"No, I don't imagine you are. Any last words of advice?"

"Go slowly."

Zac raised his eyes and let them rest on Lainey a long moment. "Thanks," he said, then turned and walked toward the barn.

Dionne crushed her cigarette underfoot and turned back toward the corral. She knew she didn't trust easily or quickly, but she had a feeling Zac Sinclair was on the level. He might also be exactly what Lainey needed to help her face reality again. For her friend's sake, she hoped she was right.

Lainey lifted the cardboard container from where it rested atop several others and set it on the floor of her spare room. Sitting down cross-legged, she opened the box she hadn't looked inside in years, hoping she was ready for this self-imposed stroll down memory lane.

She'd worked hard all week, finished the kitchen cupboards yesterday and filled them this morning with the few things she had in the way of cooking paraphernalia. That done, she thought she'd go through some of the boxes she'd brought from her father's house when she'd moved to St. Clair a few months ago. They'd been stored in his basement since she'd left for New York. Her father had been glad to get rid of them. And of her.

Her father, Lainey thought with a sigh as she picked up the first item and removed the newspaper wrapping. A framed photo of Edward Adam Roberts, taken a long time ago, in happier times, though she could remember very few. Unsmiling, unshakable in his beliefs, he stared into the camera with his cool blue eyes, his back ramrod straight. Not a bad-looking man, she decided, trying to be objective. Possibly even attractive if he'd smiled more, enjoyed life a little. Perhaps he didn't know how. Then and now, he had very rigid standards, and little patience for those who didn't measure up. Unfortunately, both she and her mother were in that number.

Feeling the melancholia build, Lainey forced herself to go on. Dionne's words—that she had to face her past and come to grips with it before she could enjoy her future—rang in her ears as she unwrapped the next picture. Irene Roberts, in a somewhat stilted pose, her dark hair worn a bit too long for a woman of middle age, her smile a bit too bright. Or was she letting her feelings for her mother color the way she viewed her? Lainey wondered.

Irene had been beautiful in her youth, but not with the perfection that everyone agreed her daughter had in abundance. She'd wanted admiration and recognition, a dazzling career, and Edward had had only disdain for her needs. Highly intelligent and ambitious, already a successful CPA, he thought his wife frivolous and foolish. They fought constantly, separated briefly, then finally divorced, leaving ten-year-old Lainey floundering. Wiping the brass picture frame, she let herself remember those lost years.

Her mother had tried to profit from her looks, but it hadn't worked and she'd had to settle for a job as a typist. Living on too little money and struggling with too-big dreams gave Irene a frantic edge. She'd wanted a shot at the big time, and she came to realize that Lainey was her chance.

Lainey remembered the excitement in her mother's pale blue eyes as she'd talked Edward into paying for dance lessons for his only child, then horseback-riding instruction, followed by tennis lessons and finally an expensive modeling course. Lainey had hated it all, except being with the horses. But she hated disappointing her volatile mother more, so she'd gone along with Irene's lofty plans.

Soon there were small modeling jobs at local department stores and country clubs. As Lainey moved into her teens and her looks matured, there were beauty pageants where she always finished in the top three, dragging home useless cups to stack on her bedroom shelf. Then finally, in her last year of high school, she'd won a contest and a trip to New York, including an interview with Anne Blackburn of the Blackburn Modeling Agency. Lainey Roberts had the look they'd been searching for.

Her life had changed drastically, then. Back-to-back classes—makeup, wardrobe, exercise—endless photo sessions, work and more work. Lainey reached into the box and took out the first magazine featuring her on its cover. The seventeen-year-old girl who stared back at her with violet eyes looked confident and happy, but she knew she'd been neither. The only outlet, the only happy moments she'd had in those days, had been the few precious hours at a Long Island riding academy where she'd felt at home with the horses, who demanded nothing from her. She'd talked to them, brushed them down and ridden like the wind, forgetting the life she'd somehow gotten trapped into living. And she'd swallowed her tears.

Fortunately, Anne Blackburn had taken a liking to her and, along with several other young models, moved her into her huge apartment in Manhattan. But the long work hours left little time for friendships. Lainey had just turned twenty when the representative for an international cosmetics line, Temptation, had called, wanting to sign her to an exclusive contract. Suddenly she was launched and on her way.

Her dreams about to be realized, Irene moved to New York to be with her, renting a small apartment and insisting Lainey live with her. If Lainey hadn't been almost delirious from the hard work, the long hours and missing out on a more normal life, she could have believed her mother's assurances that, in time, she would have it all. But Lainey had gotten more than she'd bargained for....

She browsed through half a dozen more magazine covers, glancing at the girl she'd been. Innocent, hopeful, trusting. For years she'd lived fulfilling someone else's dream—until six months ago, when her life had spiraled out of control. So she'd run from New York and all the heartache she'd experienced there; run back to Detroit and her father's house.

Only he hadn't understood, either. Feeling defeated and desperate, she'd phoned her old friend, Dionne Keller, in St. Clair and received the warm, no-strings-attached invitation she'd been hoping for. Through the years, Dionne had been the only friend from her youth she'd kept in touch with. Not revealing her plans to anyone, she'd packed up her things and fled to Dionne's. That had been the best decision she'd made in years, Lainey thought.

Rewrapping her father's picture, she decided that Edward Roberts had never approved of her and probably never would. As for her mother, she'd been terribly disappointed in her daughter, too. No matter how hard Lainey had tried, she'd been unable to please either parent. Sighing, she set both wrapped photos aside, then reached into the box again.

Pulling out the last three items, she broke into a smile. As she unwrapped them, she heard a voice from the direction of the kitchen and tilted her head to listen.

"Lainey, are you there?" Zac yelled through the screen door. "I need to ask you something."

"In the spare room," she called back, too preoccupied to get up just now.

He found her sitting on the floor, a nostalgic smile on her face. Spread in front of her was a stack of magazines and some items wrapped in newspaper. Alongside an open cardboard box was propped a floppy-eared pink rabbit, a stuffed dog with one eye missing and a small doll with very little hair.

"I used to have tea parties with these three," she explained in a voice that sounded small in the nearly vacant room. "They were my friends." Clearing her throat, she straightened her shoulders and sent him a quick, apologetic look. "I must have been a strange child."

Zac felt something inside him turn over, something unexpected. No, Lainey Roberts had never been lonely. Of course not.

He stepped inside and stooped down beside her. "Not so strange. Somewhere in my attic in Detroit, I've got a box of wooden soldiers I used to spend hours with. I think it's called make-believe."

Lainey felt a rush of gratitude as she gathered up the mementos from her childhood. He hadn't laughed at her; had actually seemed to understand. "I guess so."

Zac reached to pick up the magazine on the top of the pile. *Stunning* was the first word that came to mind, though she'd been years younger. But the woman who sat before him, wearing a full cotton skirt and loose top, her dark hair pulled back from her oval face and with a touching vulnerability in her violet eyes, held a mature appeal that far surpassed that of the girl on the cover. "I'm impressed," he told her honestly. "I had no idea you were that famous—a cover girl."

Lainey took the magazine from him and placed it back in the box. "Don't be. That girl doesn't exist anymore." She quickly piled the rest of the items into the box and closed the lid. "What is it you wanted to ask me?"

Zac stood, wondering again what really had caused her to turn away from such an exciting and lucrative career. Could it be that she was hiding from something? None of his business, he reminded himself. "Tomorrow's Saturday and there's a horse auction being held on the outskirts of town. I was wondering if you'd like to go with me.''

Lainey rose to her feet thoughtfully. She'd spent a lot of time with horses, but had never attended an auction. "I don't know what to look for in a horse, or how an auction works. Trixie came with the property and I lucked out with her.''

"I can teach you. I breed them, remember?''

"I was hopeful I could buy a couple from you.''

"Mainly thoroughbreds are raised on my ranch, for racing and showing. You're better off with mixed breeds like Trixie, for your purposes. They're far more gentle and adaptable." He gave her a coaxing smile. "Auctions are fun. We could use an afternoon of fun, couldn't we?''

She did need more horses. And maybe she needed to prove to Zac—and herself—that she could spend an afternoon in his company without overreacting. She met his calm and patient gaze. When he was like this, she could almost let herself believe she could handle being with him, could think of him as brotherly. It was when he stepped too close, when his eyes darkened and made her blood heat, that the panic began inside her. But she wouldn't think about that. It would be a sunny afternoon spent in a crowd of people and horses.

"Is the barn ready, in case we find one or two?''

He nodded. "The stalls are all finished, and the loft is almost done. Next week I'll work on reinforcing that buckling back wall.''

"All right then, let's do it." She waited for that slow smile that softened his features, and finally he gave it to her. Funny how she'd come to look forward to those infrequent moments.

"Great. By the way, you did a beautiful job on the cupboards." He started down the hall toward the kitchen.

"Thanks," Lainey said, following him. She felt a sense of pride. Never before had she worked on something with her hands and been so pleased with the results. Maybe she could make a go of this ranch.

"If you ever get tired of teaching kids, I can put you to work in my company."

She shook her head. "I'm quite content right here."

Pausing by the back door, Zac took a pipe out of his pocket and tapped the bowl in the palm of his hand thoughtfully. "Are you, Lainey, really? Is this life so much better than the one you were living in New York?" After seeing her on the cover of several magazines, he had trouble believing her.

Her voice was very soft as she answered him. "That life for me is over."

Was that a wistful note he heard? "Well, I, for one, am glad you're here." Impulsively, he reached to touch the silk of her cheek in the lightest of caresses. "I'll pick you up at one tomorrow." He opened the door and skipped down the steps.

Lainey could hear him whistling for Willie as he walked toward his truck, along with the chirping of the small brown wrens that nested in her big maple tree. She leaned against the door, her hand touching her cheek where she still felt the faint imprint of his fingers. What a strange combination of virility and tenderness he was.

He wanted no involvements, he'd said. Yet his eyes sent different messages and his touch had a different feel than that of mere friendship. The problem was that while he was like a strong, magnificent eagle, she was more like a broken bird. And perhaps she always would be.

Lainey leaned back in her seat in the row of folding chairs set up in the cavernous building and checked her program. All around her was the buzz of excitement, horse fanciers mingling and greeting one another before the bidding began, and owners circulating and chatting. Zac had walked her past the stalls, pointing out the merits of several of the available horses, and telling her what to look for.

She opened the page to the picture of the black mare with the white markings on her forelegs and frowned. "I'm really drawn to this one," she said to Zac, who leaned closer to have a look. "Her name is Smokey and she's three. It says here that she's very adaptable and has no bad habits. What do you think?"

Zac stretched his long legs as he leaned back. "Did you ever hear the old saying that goes: 'One white leg, buy him; two white legs, try him; three white legs, deny him; four white legs, cut him up and feed him to the crows'?"

"No, I haven't. Do you believe that?"

He grinned. "Not a word. It's just an old wives' tale, probably conceived by someone who didn't want to spend extra time cleaning his horse's white legs. I think it's a nice touch. Are you thinking of bidding on her?"

"Yes. But how can the owner prove the horse has no bad habits?" As they'd strolled around, the comments Lainey had heard made everyone sound far more experienced than she, raising her doubts. Zac, however, looked very much at home and had been greeted by several ranchers, even though he spent very little time in St. Clair.

"Some bad habits, like a tendency to rear, can't really be discovered until you start working with the horse. Some horses bore easily and get restless, often chewing up their stalls, even injuring themselves. That's another one that's hard to spot until you get them home. Most owners aren't likely to point out these small annoyances. Only way around it is to put a contingency clause in your purchase agreement—say, a month for approval rights."

"Will a seller agree to that?"

"Sometimes. I can have my business manager from the ranch look over your paperwork, if you like." His eyes on the stage, he tapped her arm as a chestnut mare was led out. "There's one I spotted when we were out back. Her name's Juno and she's from the Chelsea Farms. I know Bob Chelsea—he's honest and fair."

Lainey leaned forward. "But she's pregnant, isn't she?"

"Sure is. You get two for the price of one."

"I don't know a thing about foaling."

"Dr. Davis does. And so does Charley Peters, my stud manager." Seeing her still frowning in concern, he shook his head. "You worry too much."

"I don't like to impose."

"You won't be. Besides, think how the children would enjoy a colt or a filly."

That made her smile.

She should smile more, he thought. He was glad he'd talked her into coming to the auction, as she seemed eager and pleased to be here; not as jumpy as she so often was. Glancing toward the stage, he held up his program. "Now, you remember how I told you to join the bidding?"

"Yes. Hold up my number and say 'here.' I hope I don't mess up and wind up with the wrong horse."

Several others sat down in their row, causing Zac to have to move closer to Lainey. His thigh was touching hers, but she didn't seem to notice or pull away, her attention riveted on the front of the room where the bid master was approaching the podium.

Her violet eyes shining, she sent him a quick look. "This should be fun."

Fun. For some reason, Zac had the feeling Lainey Roberts hadn't taken much time out of her life for just plain fun. Maybe he could change that.

"You've never been to a street carnival?" he asked, sounding incredulous.

Lainey stood looking up at the array of rides and booths in the small park they'd strolled to near the arena and shook her head. "No, never. There just never seemed time. I was always taking lessons or studying my schoolwork or being fitted for costumes."

He heard the regret in her voice and, taking her elbow, led her over. "What could be better after a successful afternoon at a horse auction than to let yourself go at a carnival?" He stopped at a booth under a striped awning where a man in a big white hat ran a paper cone around a machine that was spinning candy. "I don't suppose you've tried cotton candy then, either?"

"You're making me sound like I've just stepped out of a long-lost cave," Lainey remarked as she watched the fluffy mound grow. She couldn't deny that her mouth was watering.

Zac paid the man and took the cone, handing it to Lainey. For a moment she frowned, looking unsure just how to attack the silky pink strands. "Like this," he said, leaning in and grabbing a cottony wad into his mouth.

Following suit, she did the same, then laughed as the sticky stuff stuck to her lips, then her fingers as she tried to break off a section. "Mmm . . . Fun, but messy."

Zac bought a bag of peanuts for himself and they strolled off toward the rides, watching the kids jostle and shove as they climbed aboard the colorful cars. "So, are you pleased with your new horses?"

Lainey swallowed a sugary lump and nodded. "You were right. Juno's a real find. I wonder what kind of a foal she'll have?"

"You've got the papers on the sire. We can look him up one day at Chelsea's place. And, although Smokey's a little frisky, I think she'll settle down." Popping another peanut into his mouth, he tossed a handful of shells into a trash can. "If they're going to be delivered next week, I'd better make sure that pastureland fence is sturdy all around."

"Looks like you've got more work than you bargained for at my place. Are you getting weary of it all and anxious to get back home?" She walked beside him, trying to remember the last time she'd had such a nice day.

"No. Are you anxious to get rid of me?"

"Of course not."

Turning toward her, Zac leaned down. "You have a pink spot on your nose." With a finger, he rubbed off the candy, then shifted his gaze to meet hers. Her violet eyes darkened and filled with apprehension. She took a quick step back, just out of reach.

Frowning, Zac studied her face. So lovely, yet so often troubled. He'd never mentioned her jitteriness. Maybe it was time he did. "Why do you pull back from me, Lainey? That time by the ladder and just now. I mean you no harm.''

Lainey ran a nervous hand along her ponytail. "I'm just not comfortable being touched. It has nothing to do with you.''

"Is there someone special in your life, then? Someone you care about?''

She shook her head. "No, no one.''

He sighed, realizing that if he pushed, she'd back away even more. Thinking to bring the smile back to her face, he pointed off in the distance. "Look over there— a ferris wheel. You want to try it?''

Walking closer, Lainey looked up at the ride silhouetted against the evening sky, the lights blinking and whirling as the wheel turned. "It looks awfully high up there.''

But Zac was already moving to the ticket booth. "Come on. You can handle it.''

Everything came so easily to him, she thought as she finished her cotton candy. Standing in the slowly moving line zigzagging toward the cars, she sighed. Days like this, she realized how much she'd missed as a child and how inexperienced and wary it had left her. Even while living in New York, she'd often felt like a fish out of water, with everyone knowing the way to swim upstream except her. But Zac was so self-assured, such a calming influence. Why hadn't he come into her life years ago, when she'd been open and receptive?

She watched him joke with the ticket taker, a shy young blonde, and saw the way the girl looked at him. Even wearing what most other men wore—a denim shirt and jeans—he stood out head and shoulders above the crowd, and not just because of his size. There was an aura of strength about him, a lean-on-me look that was as appealing as it was somewhat disturbing. Lainey didn't want to lean on anyone, but rather wanted to build up her own strength so she wouldn't need to. Still, there were days . . .

"This car's ours," Zac said as he helped her in, then waited for the operator to fasten the safety bar in place.

Lainey felt the wooden car rock, then looked up. Lord, but it went high. Suddenly, they lurched as they started the upward climb, and she found herself gripping the bar, her heart in her throat.

"Look at that house way down there," Zac commented. "Looks like a toy. This is higher than when we were sitting on your barn." He noticed she was a little pale. "You okay?"

"Fine," she muttered, unwilling to show her unease.

Near the top, they stopped while the bottom car changed occupants. She tried to concentrate on the lights in the distance, but the swaying was unnerving. "Could we hold this thing still?"

"Not likely," Zac said with a grin. "Relax."

How could she? Clenching the bar, she sat back and closed her eyes, wishing the ride would end. They started back down, and the car bounced along while children squealed and the music of a nearby calliope ground out its repetitious tune. Not much longer, Lainey fervently hoped.

Perhaps she wasn't crazy about being touched, but this was an exception. Zac slid his arm about her and pulled her close, finding no resistance as she buried her face in his shoulder. "I guess the first time is scary," Zac said in an effort to console her.

She sat there, clenching the material of his shirt in one hand and the bar in the other, inhaling the distinctive masculine scent of him. She waited for the panic to begin and was surprised when it didn't. She took another deep breath, smelling rich leather, a slight after-shave and a hint of tobacco clinging to his clothes. His heart beat steadily under her ear, and she dared open her eyes only to find herself staring at the dark hair of his chest at his open collar. She kept her hand from moving to touch his skin only with the greatest of effort.

None of the dreaded feelings emerged, and she took a chance and let her head ease back on his shoulder. She met his eyes, which were dark and watchful and aware.

Zac's grip on her was feather light, nonthreatening; it was as if he were dealing with a skittish mare. The car lurched downward again as he continued watching her, wondering what she was thinking behind her hooded gaze. "It feels so good to hold you," he whispered.

She didn't know what to say to that. Oddly, it felt good to be held, too. But that edge of fear still lurked in the wings. Dionne had said it would disappear in time. Lainey wasn't so certain.

Then his head moved fractionally closer, lowering to her. Experiencing a flash of panic, Lainey broke out of his embrace and looked around. They were the next car to be released, and she took a deep, steadying breath. When the operator unfastened the bar, she climbed out and started walking briskly.

Damn! Zac thought, following her. Just when he thought she'd begun to relax. He caught up with her and positioned himself in front of her without touching. "Wait!"

She did, running her hands along her forearms as she shuffled restless feet. "I'm sorry," she whispered.

"Don't be. It's all right. But it's more than not liking to be touched, isn't it, Lainey?"

She dropped her gaze, knowing he'd already seen the answer there. "I don't want to talk about this." Stepping around him, she wound her way back toward the auction arena where his truck was parked, her footsteps echoing in the nearly deserted lot.

For a long moment, Zac stood watching her hurry from him. Whoever had hurt her had done one hell of a job. Maybe he should just back off. He had enough debris from his own past to sort through. But there was something about Lainey, something he could sense that seemed to cry out for the very touch she turned from.

Feeling as unsettled as she was acting, he walked after her.

Chapter Four

*I*t was dark, so very dark, and something massive was blocking her from seeing the light in the distance. There were sounds, everyday noises, but far off. Too far away to do her any good. The fear clutched at her, making her heart pound and her breathing quicken. She could taste fear on her tongue as she licked her dry lips and tossed her head. The smells were gagging her, city dust and trash cans and accumulated sweat. And up close now, cheap cigars and stale beer. She couldn't breathe!

Then she was falling, falling, and the snow was cold as she curled her fingers in it. She felt a scream bubbling up in her throat, but couldn't get it out. She tried to remember prayers from her childhood, but her mind wouldn't focus. Then, from somewhere nearby came the incongruous sound of a Christmas bell clanging. She fought to get up, the hysteria building, and her own voice echoed in the fearful stillness. "Help me!"

* * *

Lainey bolted upright in bed, her eyes flying open, her hands clutching the bedsheet as she tried to slow her racing heart. Her face was drenched in sweat, and then the trembling began. Lowering her head to rest her cheek on her raised knees, she circled her legs with shaky hands and hung on. It would pass, in just a few minutes. It always did, Lainey reminded herself. If only she could hang on and let the memory recede on its own instead of fighting it.

How long, she asked of no one in particular, would these terrible nightmares continue? How long before she could let go, forget, rebuild? Or would it always be like this?

Long moments later, she crawled out of bed and shakily made her way to the bathroom, removing her damp gown with a quick overhead tug. Turning on the shower spray, she adjusted the temperature and stepped under it. Was it the perspiration she was washing away, or the unclean feelings these dreams always brought to mind? Lainey was no longer certain as she rubbed fragrant soap onto her skin and inhaled the floral bouquet.

Her mother had advised that she could stop them by concentrating on more pleasant thoughts, as if willpower alone would do the trick. Her New York doctor had said she might never rid herself of her nighttime fears, for in dreams the mind roamed free. That statement had really alarmed her.

Lainey turned off the water and reached for her towel. Dionne's analysis was probably the correct one, she thought as she dried off. Her friend had told her that when she learned to accept what had happened to her and its consequences, not just physically but emotionally, then she'd be ready to rebuild her life. The problem, Lainey thought as she hung up her towel, was that she wasn't convinced that that day would ever come.

Shrugging into a clean gown and slipping on her robe, she strolled through the house in bare feet, rechecking each window and door to make sure the locks were secure, though she'd done that earlier. Next, she turned on the lights in every room, chasing away the uneasy shadows. There'd be no more sleep for a while for her, she knew from past experience. Another aftermath, she thought wearily. Caution was one thing, but paranoia quite another. Still, she needed to feel safe and would do what she had to do.

She put water on for tea and waited for it to boil. A glance at the clock told her it was just past midnight and here she was, wide-awake and fidgety. After the tea had steeped, she poured some into a dainty china cup with violets painted all around, a gift from her grandmother. In the living room, she curled her legs under her in the roomy bentwood rocker. Taking a careful sip of the hot brew, Lainey still felt chilled, though it was the middle of a hot June night.

Willie was restless. Zac set down the book he'd been reading and looked up to see the hound dog prowling the perimeter of the large glassed-in back porch for perhaps the tenth pass in as many minutes. Rising and stretching, he acknowledged that he was a shade restless, too.

"Come on, boy," he said, opening the back door. "Let's walk." Grateful for his freedom, Willie scampered on ahead, sniffing and pausing often along the way.

Moving to the side yard, Zac paused at the fence line of one of the smaller corrals, the one used for the young horses. Beyond that, in the moonlight, he could see the stable, the red barn and several more outbuildings, as well as the bunkhouse where the hands lived. Near the road was Charley Peters's small cottage, its windows all dark. But he could see a red glow near the stoop and guessed that Charley was probably sitting on his front step having a smoke. Zac felt lucky to have such a good stud manager, fair and honest.

Following Willie into the trees, he thought about his ranch. The spread pleased him, fulfilled him, gave him a purpose beyond merely making money. And the peace and quiet of this northern community soothed his soul.

Zac Sinclair had grown up on the rough side of Detroit, with hard-living men and their worn-out women. He'd been young and eager when he'd joined his father on a construction gang, and he'd learned to handle his liquor almost as quickly as the tools of his trade. He'd learned to fight, too, because the men he worked with— bigger, stronger, meaner—had forced him to defend himself.

He'd used his fists to win arguments then, until he'd realized that the bigger victories were won with the brain. So he'd worked days, gone to school nights and saved his money. There'd finally come the day when he owned the company. He was the boss, the final word, and he didn't have to use his fists anymore. But he never forgot the lessons he learned on the long road he'd traveled.

Finding the narrow path between their properties, his thoughts turned to Lainey and why she was so hesitant with him. Perhaps she'd had a father who'd been a bully, coloring her opinion of men. Or maybe she'd had a relationship that had soured, where the man had abused her, physically or emotionally. She was touchy and evasive, and gave the impression that she was running from some past hurt. But what? There were a lot of questions and few answers.

Willie leaped over a fallen branch, and Zac followed, stepping across. He found himself wanting to show her things she'd never seen, teach her things she'd never done, and he had a feeling the list would be long. His reasons, even to himself, were vague. Because after years of being needed, he found he missed someone needing him. Because she was lovely, fragile, needing someone. Because he wanted to be with her, that's why. Did a man need a reason beyond that?

Zac and Willie came within range of Lainey's house at almost the same moment, and both stopped as they saw lights ablaze at every window. Wondering if something was wrong, Zac lengthened his stride.

Lainey nearly dropped her tea when she heard the heavy steps on the wooden porch, then the firm knocking. Heart hammering, she set down the cup and stood. Then she heard Willie's howl and let out a relieved breath. Moving aside the blinds, she saw Zac standing in a splash of moonlight, fists bunched on his hips, his legs spread and a frown on his face.

Her hand at the throat of her robe, she opened the door and looked at him through the screen. "Don't tell me, let me guess. You were just in the neighborhood."

Zac felt a little foolish now that he saw she was just fine. He glanced down at Willie, to include him in his scheme. "Actually, we were out for a stroll when we saw your lights on. Everything all right?"

"Yes." She peered around his shoulder. "I didn't hear your truck."

"We came through the woods. The path's quite usable."

Wonderful. "Is there something you want?"

He'd noticed before that she was seldom aware of the double meanings that could be taken in her questions, as if she'd grown up missing the flirtatious years. He took in the softness of her features, her eyes defenseless with sleep, her hair hanging in a long braid down her back. Yes, there was something he wanted. He wanted to remove that high-necked, long-sleeved, floor-length robe from her, to unbraid her hair and run his hands over the feminine curves he'd been imagining for days now, and to kiss her until they were both breathless. Zac cleared his throat noisily.

"Just couldn't sleep, and when I saw your lights, I thought maybe you couldn't, either."

His square jaw, shadowed by a day's growth of beard, with that small indentation in the center that wasn't quite a dimple, was thrust forward somewhat challengingly. His dark hair looked as if it had been combed by his long, restless fingers. But his eyes were a silver reflection of the moon, and hinted of something she hadn't noticed before: loneliness.

Hoping she wasn't making a big mistake, Lainey stepped back and opened the door wide.

Zac walked in and strolled over to the fireplace, sitting down on the raised hearth, while Willie folded himself at his feet. Knowing how nervous she was alone with men, he knew it had cost her to invite him in, and wondered why she had.

"Would you like a cup of tea?" she asked. "I've made a pot."

"Sure." He watched her disappear into the kitchen, thinking he'd like to take her entire wardrobe, each baggy androgynous piece, and burn them all. Then he'd take her shopping—for silk underthings and a fitted, satin robe and jeans that clung to her curves. Strange that a former model would dress like . . . like someone's maiden aunt.

Lainey took down another cup with an unsteady hand. Dionne would never believe her if she were to mention that she entertained Zac Sinclair in the middle of the night, clad in her nightclothes. At the very least, Dionne would take her temperature. She poured their tea and took both cups back into the living room.

He was packing his pipe when she handed him the cup before returning to her rocker.

"Do you mind the smell of a pipe?" he asked.

"No, I rather like it. My father used to smoke a pipe, a tobacco that had a cherry aroma."

"I know the one." He held a match to the bowl and took several short puffs until the tobacco caught. Leaning back against the stone wall, he stretched his long legs in front of him. For several minutes he puffed on his pipe and they shared a comfortable silence. "Did you ever smoke?"

"No. Like so many other things, I was shielded from it. Might color my teeth or change my complexion, Anne Blackburn used to say." She smiled affectionately. "Plenty of time for vices when you get older, she often told us."

"I've heard of the Blackburn agency. They're big."

"Yes. Anne's wonderful. She made us each feel like we were a favorite niece. She's endlessly patient, constantly encouraging, always there for you. A rare lady." She smiled into her teacup, then giggled. "She has only one drawback."

"What's that?" Zac asked, pleased at her good humor.

"Her nephew, Phil Armstrong. He developed this huge crush on me. Even if I'd have had time to date much, he wouldn't have been my choice."

"What's wrong with Phil?"

She settled back in the rocker, her feet under her. "He's a New York stockbroker who comes from Old Money, waiting to step into Daddy's shoes when the old man retires. Phil's a very careful man, the kind who wears both suspenders and a belt. He writes down the punch line to jokes and carries them in his vest pocket. I found him boring while my mother found him fascinating, mostly because of his bankbook and his lineage."

Zac blew smoke into the air. "She'd dislike me then. I grew up on the wrong side of the tracks. We didn't have money, New or Old."

"But you have some now, and you earned it on your own. That beats inheriting. At least in my book."

"You've earned your own way, too."

She sighed, a ragged sound. "I'd give it all away if I could turn back the clock, do it all differently."

Zac understood, having thought the same thing during the past few years. He struck another match and fussed with his pipe. "I don't know why I mess with this thing, except that it's relaxing."

"Do you have trouble relaxing?"

"Not these days, not up here. But I was pretty uptight for a while back home. How about you?"

"I was on a treadmill for so many years that I find it hard to relax even here."

"You sound as if you have a few regrets."

"A few. Don't we all have some?" She watched him, thinking that there was something about this man that invited confidences. "I've always believed that if you make a commitment, you honor it, no matter the cost. That you don't quit when the going gets rough. But this one time, the going got too rough and I quit. I ran as fast and as far as I could." She stifled a yawn behind her hand. "Something I have to learn to live with, I guess."

Zac finished his tea and stood, realizing she was looking tired. "You left everything and came here. Pretty brave."

"Brave? Not really." He held out his hand, and after a moment's hesitation, she took it and let him draw her to her feet. She felt her breath flutter as his gaze dropped to caress her lips, a touch she could almost feel. Her heart picked up its beat, but this time it wasn't from fear. "Zac, don't make me regret inviting you in."

His voice was low and husky. "I hope you never regret anything you do with me, Lainey." Raising her hand to his lips, he turned it over and placed a kiss in the center of her palm. "I just want to be your friend."

Lainey felt her heart lurch at the gesture, wishing they could truly be good friends. In a short time, she'd gotten used to his comforting though occasionally unsettling presence. She hated the thought of losing him as a friend, which was only one reason why she hadn't been completely honest with him. The risk seemed greater than the reward.

"Sleep well, Lainey," Zac said as he opened the door. Willie ran out, and he followed.

She watched them until they gradually disappeared into the trees, then closed and locked the door. What defenses did she have against such an appealing man? She dared not give in to her longings, even if she could get past her fears. If Zac knew the truth about her past, he'd run as fast as she herself had run.

Concentrating on that thought, she turned out the lights and went to bed. But she knew it would be a long while before she would lose herself in sleep this night.

She was running late. Lainey hurriedly rubbed her hair dry, wishing she had kept a better eye on the clock. But she'd lost track of time this morning, helping Ben groom the two new horses and making sure they were comfortable in their refurbished stalls. When she'd checked, she'd been shocked to see that it was already three in the afternoon. Shelly's aunt would be dropping the little girl off for her lesson any minute.

Zac had been sanding pieces of wood near the barn door, and she'd asked him to keep an eye out for them, then she'd run into the house for a quick shower. In the bedroom, she rummaged through her closet for clean slacks and could find only an old pair of designer jeans she'd brought from New York. She really had to make time to do the laundry soon.

Pulling up the zipper, she glanced at herself in the full-length mirror. They fit her like a glove, clinging to every line and curve, which was not the image she wished to convey. Sighing, she grabbed an oversize sweatshirt and shrugged into it, pulling it low on her hips. Not much better, but it would have to do. As she reached for a piece of yarn, she heard the car pull in. Damn!

Zac would entertain Shelly for a few minutes, she decided as she pulled back her hair. The child had taken to watching him work while waiting to be picked up, her huge eyes following his every move. And he'd always stop and talk to her, sometimes walk her over to the garden and show her the new flowers beginning to push up through the soil, and vegetable plants already flourishing.

Shelly still hadn't spoken a word, but she'd progressed to being led around the corral on Trixie, in a position that was relaxed and unafraid. And she loved to help brush down the horse afterward, while Lainey kept chatting, teaching her how to groom. It was her philosophy, and Dionne's, that a child should learn that an animal was a responsibility as well as a pleasure.

Quickly Lainey pulled on her boots and ran outside.

Shelly's aunt, Joan Morgan, was just turning her car around and raised her hand in a wave as she started down the drive. Lainey waved back, sending a smile to the four little towheads in the rear seat. Not for the first time, she wondered how Joan and her husband, Mark, managed such a large family plus the added problem of caring for Shelly. The poor woman always looked tired and slightly harassed, but she maintained a cheerful attitude. Lainey greatly admired parents who enjoyed their children and provided a loving environment for them—maybe because she'd missed out on that kind of family herself.

Stepping off the porch, she saw Zac sitting with Shelly on the bench outside the barn. He was showing her a coin trick, finding quarters behind her ears and up the sleeve of her polo shirt. The child's eyes were wide with the wonder of it all.

What a shame that Zac and his Nancy hadn't had children, Lainey thought, pausing for a moment. He seemed so comfortable with them. Perhaps raising children without a mother would have been difficult for him, but somehow she was certain he'd have managed.

Because he was that kind of man—solid, caring, dependable.

If it weren't for that underlying attraction, she might even feel comfortable around him. Walking toward the bench, Lainey wondered if she'd ever feel truly relaxed around any man.

It was a hard-won smile, but he finally got one out of Shelly, and Zac couldn't help but be pleased. Four children came regularly for lessons now, yet this was the one his heart went out to more than the others. They'd buried her mother, and her father was still in a coma. Her aunt had told him that Shelly never cried, just sat and stared for hours out the window, sometimes not playing all day with the other kids. What was going on behind those sad eyes? he wondered.

Taking a chance, he hugged her lightly, and was surprised when she hugged him back fiercely, her small arms wrapping around him and holding on. He heard Lainey approach and looked up. Over Shelly's head, his eyes locked with hers, and they shared that special moment, the realization that Shelly was beginning to reach out.

"Is this the little girl who has quarters behind her ears?" Lainey asked as she stopped in front of them. She watched Shelly move back from Zac and nod shyly.

"And here's another," Zac exclaimed, bringing forth a coin from around Shelly's head. He reached for her hand and let four quarters fall into her small palm. "Why don't you place these in your pocket for safekeeping? We wouldn't want you to drop them from your ears while you're riding Trixie."

Solemn again, Shelly deposited the coins, then slid her hand into Lainey's.

"Ready to go riding?" She smiled down at her as Shelly nodded.

"I've got Trixie all saddled and ready," Zac informed her as he stood and picked up the wood he'd been working on. "Need anything else?" He tried to ignore the just-showered flavor of Lainey's scent, drifting to him on the still, afternoon air.

Lainey shook her head as she led Shelly into the barn. "We're fine, thanks."

Zac narrowed his eyes as they disappeared into the shadows. Finally, she'd put on something that fit. Her legs were long and slender, and he stood back admiring the subtle sway of her hips in the fitted jeans. Looking at her, he felt a restless stir of desire, one he hadn't felt in some time. Had his visit last night caused her to abandon those baggy slacks she usually wore, or was that just wishful thinking on his part? His mind took it a step further and imagined how soft, how silken her skin beneath the denim would be. He wanted to touch her, to taste her, yet he knew she'd likely send him packing if he tried.

Reaching for the sandpaper, he chastised himself mentally. With so many women in the world, why was he plotting how to get this one small female to allow even a kiss? He stroked the board, removing the rough edges left by the saw. The truth was that since Nancy, no woman had appealed to him. He knew he was attractive, in an untamed sort of way. And he also knew that his financial situation might appeal to a certain type of woman.

Setting the board aside, he picked up another. He'd seen women measuring him, in their eyes the look of a possible conquest. In Lainey's eyes, he saw a guileless innocence and a need she would deny. Despite his philosophy of noninvolvement, she intrigued him.

And the fact that she was sexy as hell didn't hurt, though she did everything she could to camouflage her looks.

Turning, he saw her lead Trixie out the side door to the corral with Shelly high in the saddle. The wind lifted and whirled a few loose strands of hair around her face as she smiled up at the child, and Zac felt something inside shift. Time to face a fact: he wanted her.

Ben stood alongside Lainey in a splash of late-afternoon sunshine as they watched Shelly leave in her aunt's car, her small, serious face staring out the window as she waved to them. He took off his cap and brushed back his thinning hair. "Don't believe that poor child will ever talk again," he commented sadly.

"Oh, now, Ben," Lainey admonished. "These things take time." Nobody knew better than she that people didn't get over traumatic events in their lives overnight. "She likes being here, she's learning to ride Trixie and to trust us all. That's progress."

"Maybe."

"Earlier I saw her give Zac a hug. And when he helped her choose a flower to pick for her aunt, she actually smiled."

"Yup, that man's nearly as good with kids as you." He returned his hat to his head and turned to her. "Hope you didn't forget about tonight. Clara's looking forward to seeing you."

Lainey sent him a puzzled frown. "Tonight?"

"The barn dance over at Donovans'. All for a good cause, you know. Raising money for the Nelson boy. Kidney transplant. They had car washes all week in

town, teens been selling candy door-to-door, and tonight the dance.''

She did remember now. Ben had mentioned the fund-
raiser to her several days ago, but it had slipped her
mind. She certainly wasn't anxious to go, but how could
she refuse such a worthy cause? Still, she hadn't been to
a large gathering in a long while. "I don't know, Ben.
I'm not much of a partygoer."

"Me neither. But folks got to help one another. Clara
and me, we'll watch out for you. Do you good to get out
a little.''

Trapped—by the good manners that had been drilled
into her, and by her desire to please this dear man who'd
been so nice to her; and by his wife, Clara, who was always sending over a jar of her pickles or a loaf of zuc-
chini bread. Lainey had never been part of a caring
neighborhood, but she knew there were rules about
happy coexistence.

She nodded, bringing a smile to Ben's weathered face.
"All right, Ben. I'll go. What time do the festivities begin?''

He nodded in satisfaction. "'Bout seven. They'll
have plenty of food and drink, too." He gave her arm a
fatherly pat. "You dress up real pretty. We'll come get
you and bring you home.''

"That won't be necessary, Ben," Zac said as he
walked toward them, wiping his hands on a rag. "I'm
just next door and I'll be glad to give Lainey a ride.''

Lainey tried to hide her sudden unease. "You're
going?''

"Sure. Ben asked me this morning. I couldn't refuse
helping contribute toward that boy's kidney transplant. It's the neighborly thing to do." He'd overheard
some of their conversation from the doorway and

wondered if she'd back down, now that he was going. "I just wish I didn't have two left feet." He gave her a disarming smile.

"Don't worry 'bout that," Ben said. "We don't dance fancy around here." He leaned closer to Lainey. "That be okay if he picks you up? 'Cause I can drive back if you—"

She placed a hand on his arm. "It's fine, really." Ben was kindly and protective, but she didn't want to be a bother to him. She'd ridden with Zac to the vet and to the auction. This was no different. She swung her gaze to Zac. "Around seven, then?"

"Right."

Still she felt the flutter of butterflies in her stomach as she waved to them and started toward her house.

"Oh, Lainey?" Zac called from alongside the truck. He waited until she swung back to face him questioningly. "See if you can rustle up a skirt, why don't you?"

"What makes you think I own any?"

"Gut instinct." With a grin, he got into the cab of his truck and started the engine.

Lainey marched up the steps and inside. She hated being maneuvered. But she hated being thought uncharitable more. So she'd go to the dance, and she'd have a little punch and chat with Clara and Ben. And she'd be friendly but discouraging to her neighbor, Zac Sinclair.

Just a simple country dance, she thought as she reached the bedroom. She hadn't danced in years—not since all those lessons her mother had insisted would teach her poise. Long ago, she'd given in to pressure and demand, and closed herself off from so much in order to focus on the world of modeling. Now that she'd left that, she felt somewhat of a social misfit, a little lost.

Tugging off her sweatshirt, she walked to the closet. The nerve of Zac, telling her what to wear. She frowned at her clothes, many in zippered plastic bags that hadn't been opened in months. Her New York wardrobe. Maybe she should get rid of it all, have a huge garage sale.

Shoving the hangers aside, she studied several pieces with a critical eye. It had been quite a while since she'd even attempted to dress up. She reached to touch a red cotton skirt, narrow at the waist and falling in soft wide folds to a midcalf hemline. She remembered the last time she'd worn it—with a white peasant blouse to an outdoor shoot on the Staten Island Ferry. A year ago. A lifetime ago.

Nervously, she withdrew the blouse. Not a low neckline. And the skirt had yards of material. She looked down at the white sandals on the closet floor, consisting mostly of straps. A softly feminine outfit, yet not provocative.

For months now, she'd cloaked her femininity in baggy clothes, feeling safer. Dionne had told her the need would pass, that what she'd been wearing hadn't affected things one way or the other. She knew that, intellectually. Emotionally was another hurdle to overcome.

Reaching for the skirt, she held both pieces in front of her and gazed at her mirrored reflection. What would Zac think if she put these on? Not that it mattered, for he was only offering her a ride. It wasn't as if they were going on a date.

A date. She'd had so few for a woman of twenty-seven, one whose face had appeared on national magazines. One whose life had undoubtedly been the envy of many a teenage girl. Ironic. She'd dated perhaps three boys in high school and had gone out with a couple of carefully selected and approved men in New York—usually to chaperoned events, group parties, with the press invited and an early curfew for that all-important beauty rest. Anne Blackburn had been strict with her girls. Kept busy around the clock as she'd been, where would she have met men she might have chosen for herself? The male models she'd found too vain, the photographers too artsy, the celebrities too intimidating. And men like Phil she'd found too boring, though she'd blamed the lack on herself.

And then there'd been Steven, with his blond, all-American charm and his fierce ambition. Steven and his shattering disdain. No, she wouldn't think of him tonight.

Lainey leaned closer to the mirror. Dare she take a chance on triggering her unsteady emotions into an unwanted and possibly embarrassing reaction? Must she feel this dreaded need to hide forever? Had she made any progress in all these months? Or, as Ben had predicted about Shelly, was she simply never going to overcome what had happened to her?

Shelly was coming for lessons, reaching out to people, trying. Shouldn't she be at least as brave as a small child?

Lainey placed the outfit on her bed and went into the bathroom.

She took his breath away—like a fast run on a sleek stallion, like a hard fist in the solar plexus. On her porch, staring through the door she held open, Zac stood mesmerized.

Her ebony hair was pulled back and held in place with a gold clip, and he wished she'd worn it down. The delicate material of her blouse hinted at curves far lovelier than he'd been imagining. The red skirt, a skirt made for dancing, flowed around her slim hips. In the flat, strappy shoes, she was shorter than in the boots she usually wore, and seemed even more fragile.

The scent of her perfume wrapped itself around him, and he found himself taking a step backward, feeling as awkward as a teenage boy on his first date. He guessed she'd had too many men in her life commenting on her beauty. Perhaps she'd appreciate a change of pace.

Affecting a nonchalance he was far from feeling, he leaned his arm on the screen door and nodded approvingly. "You clean up pretty good, Roberts. Ready to roll?"

She burst into laughter. He was a little awkward, a shade uneasy, shuffling his feet. That charmed her, drew her in and had her relaxing. If he'd said something sappy instead of silly, she would have shut the door in his face. She gave him an exaggerated perusal. "I guess you'll do, too, Sinclair."

His grin widened. Elbow bent, he offered her his arm.

Lainey grabbed her purse, set the door lock and put her arm through his. Together they walked to the truck. "What, no carriage, no horses?" she teased, feeling better than she'd dared hope she would after pacing and worrying the past hour.

"Carriage in repair and both horses sick in bed with colds." He opened the cab door for her. "Next time." He helped her up, then walked around and climbed in beside her. "Have you ever been to one of these country hoedowns?" he asked as he started down the road.

"No. Is there something I should know?"

"You bet." Zac swung the truck onto the highway before continuing. "There'll be two punch bowls—one spiked, one plain. Watch out for the former. There'll be a table spread with homemade food, an assortment like you wouldn't believe. There'll be a fiddler, probably an accordion player and, of course, someone pounding on a piano.''

''No one playing a washboard or a comb?''

''Hey,'' he said with a mock scowl, ''what do you think we are around here? A backward bunch?''

Lainey found herself smiling, and it felt good. Normal. This is probably what normal people did on an average Saturday night in a thousand rural communities across the continent. Perhaps if she pretended she was one of them she would become so.

In a few minutes Zac made another quick turn onto the rutted road that led to the Donovans' barn and came to a stop at the end of an uneven row of assorted vehicles.

''I can't believe the crowd,'' Lainey commented. ''There must be fifty cars.''

''Looks like it's the social event of the week. Hold on and I'll come around for you. There's a lot of mud here.''

''That's all right. I can manage.'' But he was already at her side, yanking the door open.

''No, you can't.'' He pointed down at the mud underfoot, then held out his arms. ''Come on.''

No big deal, Lainey told herself. A couple of yards, that was all. She angled her knees toward the door and allowed him to scoop her into his arms.

Zac bumped the door closed with his hip and shifted her more comfortably in his arms, his touch light, hoping she wouldn't freeze up on him since she'd seemed so relaxed on the way over. Gingerly stepping around several muddied rocks, he took a deep breath and got lost in the fragrance of her hair. Fighting the desire to bury his face in its silken strands, he walked toward the open barn doors.

She was fine, Lainey reminded herself, just fine. Her one arm was around his shoulders, the other resting lightly on his chest where she could feel the steady beat of his heart. Her eyes were even with his strong chin, and she noticed he'd recently shaved, a small nick still evident alongside his full mouth.

She wondered if he swore ripely when he cut himself, or if he took it in stride as he seemed to do with everything. She wondered if he'd chosen his shirt and the new-looking jeans with as much thought as she'd picked out her outfit. And she wondered why she was wondering such silly things. Probably to keep from reacting to his powerful male presence, she decided as he set her down just outside the door.

"Thank you," she said, straightening her skirt.

Zac stopped to wipe the mud from his boots on a mound of grass before glancing inside. "Looks like Ben's already here." He touched her elbow. "Shall we join him?"

The man at the door had a straw hat on his head and a coffee can in hand, accepting donations for the Nelson boy. "I've got it," Zac told her as he threw in a folded bill, more than generous from both of them.

"No," Lainey objected, reaching past him. She tossed in her own contribution.

Stubborn, Zac decided as he maneuvered them through the crowd.

Lainey looked around, trying to absorb it all. The barn seemed as large as a football field with the aluminum stall doors all closed off, bright overhead lights blazing from the high ceiling and sawdust sprinkled on the clay floor. The band, much as Zac had described it, was set up on a wooden platform at one end, with folding tables and chairs surrounding the small dance floor. Along the perimeter were picnic tables laden with food and drink. And there were people everywhere—all ages and sizes, laughing, talking, enjoying. She'd never seen anything quite like it.

As they reached Ben's table, the spry gentleman stood, introduced Zac to his Clara and insisted that Lainey have the first dance with him. They sidestepped a teenage boy being scolded by his mother for sneaking a taste of the spiked punch, and made their way onto the crowded floor. Never would she have guessed that Ben would turn out to do a lively fox-trot, Lainey thought as he swung her around, his reddened face beaming. He, too, had perhaps sampled the punch bowl, she decided.

"You looked lovely out there, dear," Clara commented as Lainey eased onto a chair after the dance. "What a pretty outfit."

"Thank you. I haven't danced in a while. I'd forgotten how much fun it can be."

"You should get out more," Clara said, patting her tightly curled gray hair. "Puts color in your cheeks."

Ben drained his glass of punch and glanced over at the bowl, obviously debating about having another. But Clara had other plans as she eased her rotund figure from the chair and took his arm.

"That's our song, Papa," she reminded affectionately. With that, she pulled him toward the dance floor.

Zac smiled as he watched them go. "Looks like she's got his number. They've been married forty years, she just told me."

"Hard to imagine," Lainey answered. She picked up the glass in front of her. "Is this mine?" He nodded and she took a sip, finding the punch too sweet but cold. She was warm from dancing, and nearly drained the glass thirstily.

"Go easy. It's got vodka in it."

She finished the rest. One glass, she could surely handle. The neighbor on the far side of Zac's place came up to their table, and Zac introduced Lainey, then stood to talk with him. Lifting her ponytail from the back of her neck to cool her skin, she turned to gaze toward the dancers moving around the crowded floor. The owner of the small grocery story she frequented stopped by to say a word, then wound his way to the refreshment table. Lainey followed, feeling warm and parched.

The white-aproned server filled her glass and handed it to her with a smile. Sipping, she stood on the sidelines, watching a young farmer's wife absently rocking her baby to sleep while she tapped her foot in time to the music, her free hand nestled inside her husband's. Lainey wondered what she'd be like if she'd grown up in a community like this, part of a neighborly group of people who looked out for one another. Different, she decided. But she was here now, and felt the beginnings of a warm acceptance.

The second glass was better than the first, she decided. Not as sweet. Accepting a third, she strolled back toward the table. Almost there, she ran into Joan Morgan, Shelly's aunt, carrying two plates piled high with desserts.

"I promised the kids cake if they'd finish their chicken," she explained with a laugh. "Are you having a good time?"

Lainey supposed so. "Mmm, but it's so warm in here."

Joan agreed. "Always is. Feels like rain in the air."

"Is Shelly with you?"

"No, she's spending the night with her grandparents in Detroit."

Lainey had met the older couple once, and recalled the worry lines etched deeply in their faces. "How's Shelly's father doing?"

Joan shook her head. "Still not out of the coma, I'm afraid." Shaking off the mood, she held up the plate. "I'd better get these to the table before the kids come looking for me. Good to see you, Lainey."

"Yes, you, too." Stretching, she saw that Zac wasn't at their table, nor were Ben and Clara. She took another swallow of punch and stopped to lean against a portable divider, trying to locate a clock. How long did these things go on? she wondered.

Feeling a hand on her shoulder, she turned quickly and looked up into Zac's gray eyes.

"I believe this is our dance." Taking her empty glass and setting it on the table, he led her toward the bandstand. Her eyes were suspiciously bright, and he wondered how much punch she'd had. It wasn't very strong, but if she was not used to drinking and hadn't eaten, she could be heading for trouble.

They were playing a wild Western romp with much stomping of the feet. "I can't dance to that," Lainey said as they reached the edge of the dance floor. But the tune ended abruptly, and in moments, the musicians swung into a slow ballad.

Zac held out his arms. "A sedate waltz. Can you do that?"

Of course, she could do that. She stretched to touch his shoulder as he took her other hand in his. He was so tall. Why hadn't she noticed before how tall he was? Their bodies weren't quite touching as he drew her around the floor. The steps came back to her easily and she let her mind drift, gazing somewhere over his right shoulder.

Zac felt her miss a step, but she caught herself and continued. More couples joined them, and he had to hold her closer in the crowded space. The top of her head came just to his chin, and he couldn't resist leaning down and inhaling the scent he now recognized as hers alone. His thumb rested on her wrist, and he could feel her rapid pulse.

His body was hard, lean and fit, the muscles under her hand shifting as his moved. She'd not been voluntarily this close to a man in months, and it was exciting and frightening at the same time. Lainey wished she'd kept a clear head, for she knew her blood was heating, her heart racing. She could feel his warm breath on her forehead and wondered what he was thinking.

His hand was firm on her back as he guided her around the floor. Lainey tilted her head back and met his eyes. She saw the silver darken to pewter, saw the desire he didn't bother to hide.

Breaking contact, she blinked and turned her head as she pulled back a fraction. She fought the panic, fought it down, taking deep breaths as she tried to follow his lead. For a moment there, she'd felt something she hadn't felt, had schooled herself not to feel, for a long while: that undeniable reaction of a female to an attractive male; that quick jolt of awareness, that reminder that she was still a woman despite her self-denial.

And she must not let herself feel it.

Through the open barn doors, Lainey noticed several people strolling around, getting some air. "I'm very warm. Could we go outside?"

Zac guided her through the crowd. Her face was damp and she was flushed. "How many glasses of punch did you have?"

"Two, I think. Maybe three."

Over her head, he waved to Ben. A young boy of about ten ran by them, nearly knocking Lainey off her feet. Steadying her, Zac kept them moving as he frowned in the direction of the boy.

Outside, the air wasn't much cooler—a typical humid Michigan summer evening. Zac nodded to a neighboring rancher who was puffing on a cigar. Mosquitoes buzzed about as they walked between the cars parked at crooked angles, avoiding the muddy ridges. "Are you feeling better?" he asked Lainey.

"Yes. I'm not used to drinking," she confessed as she took several deep breaths.

"I never would have guessed." He watched her shake her head, trying to clear the cobwebs. He'd been there a time or two and knew how she was feeling. "Are you going to be sick?"

She looked up at him, horrified. "I hope not."

"When did you eat last?"

She frowned, trying to remember. But suddenly her gaze fell on a rosebush growing in a patch of yard visible in the spotlight from the barn. She detoured to it, bending to inhale the marvelous fragrance. "Look, Zac. It's the color of the inside of a peach. Did you ever see anything so fragile, so beautiful?"

No, he hadn't, and he wasn't looking at the flower. She turned to look up at him, her eyes defenseless.

"Come touch it. So soft." She watched as he bent to stroke the delicate petals. "Did you ever feel anything so soft?"

He moved his hand from the rose to her cheek, then trailed his fingers downward to cup her chin. "Yes, I have. Something softer, more beautiful than any rose."

A flash of pain clouded her eyes, and she shook off his hand, then stood. "No, I'm not. Not beautiful and not sweet-smelling or delicate, either. Maybe I was once, but no more. It's over, all over. And you can't get it back."

It was the vodka talking, he was certain. But there was an underlying truth here. He took her hands in his, wishing he could ease her distress. "What can't you get back, Lainey?"

Shifting her gaze to the sky, she blinked rapidly while her fingers clung tightly to his. "Myself. What was inside me. He took it, he robbed me, and there's nothing left."

He felt the anger then, the fury at anyone who could do this to her. "Who? Who did that to you, Lainey?"

Her face, when she turned to him, was filled with anguish. "I don't even know his name," she said, a wrenching sound escaping from deep inside her.

Zac bent and picked her up into his arms, cradling her against his chest. "It's all right," he whispered gently. "I'll take care of you."

Turning on his heel, he carried her to his truck.

Chapter Five

The room was swaying. From beneath one barely raised eyelid, Lainey could see her bedroom walls moving, the drapes undulating, the furniture weaving. As was her stomach. With a groan, she closed her eye, afraid to move anything else.

She'd waited twenty-seven years to experience her first hangover, and wished she'd passed on this one. Probably wasn't better at any age, she decided as she dared to move one foot slightly. Not too bad. Maybe if she raised her head...

Oh, God! Why had she been stupid enough to drink those sickeningly sweet drinks obviously well-laced with vodka? Why hadn't she at least had the common sense to eat something first? Why had she even agreed to attend the barn dance in the first place? She could have sent her check to the Nelson boy without making a fool of herself at her first social event in St. Clair. If it hadn't been for Zac, she likely couldn't have found her way home.

Zac. He'd had a front-row seat to her humiliation, stumbling around the dance floor, all but weeping over a rose. No, it wasn't over a rose she'd carried on about, she thought with a frown, then flinched at the movement. He'd asked her a question, and she'd given him an honest answer, but the memory was hazy.

And he'd picked her up and carried her to the truck, driven her home and deposited her on her doorstop with a worried expression on his face. Glad to be rid of her, most likely, but wondering if she'd break her neck getting to bed. Lord, what a mess she was. And now Zac knew it, too.

She heard a car door slam and realized that it was probably Ben arriving to tend the horses. Well, she couldn't lie here all day. Time to see if her body was still functional. Gingerly she opened both eyes and grimaced, waiting for the room to hold still. She had to get a shower, a couple of aspirins and some water. She couldn't remember ever being so thirsty.

Moving slowly, she sat up, then stood. With no small effort, she made it to the bathroom. Hesitantly she looked in the mirror, then closed her eyes. That lady did not look well. She turned on the water.

The shower helped—a little. And the aspirin and two glasses of water revived her even more. By the time she'd put on her robe, the room was no longer moving, and Lainey supposed she should feel grateful. She was tying her hair back when the phone rang. Only a few people had her number, and she mentally ran through the list as she answered it.

"Lainey, is that you?" The caller's voice was strong and authoritative, with just a trace of a New York accent.

"Anne?" Lainey sat down on her bed, taking a moment to clear her oddly thick voice. "It's so good to hear from you." She pictured her former employer seated at her favorite Queen Anne desk in her nineteenth-floor uptown apartment overlooking Central Park, her red-tipped nails drumming on the polished mahogany impatiently.

"I've been wondering how you are," Anne Blackburn inquired. "You're not much of a letter writer, are you?"

"No, but then, I've been busy." Lainey stuffed both pillows against the headboard and leaned back against them. She'd last spoken with Anne shortly after buying her ranch over a month ago. With mounting enthusiasm, she told her about the horses she'd purchased, the renovations under way and the students who were slowly but surely progressing. "It's such a thrill, bringing about a change in a child, even a small change."

"It's always a thrill when you can touch someone's life and change it for the better. I just knew you'd do well working with children."

"There's this one little blond girl. She's seven and already been through so much." She told her about Shelly's background and how she was learning to trust again. "Dionne and I are very hopeful that in time she'll speak again."

"This is what you needed, Lainey. You've always had a caring heart, but after what happened to you, you relate even more to anyone who's been hurt."

She heard the warmth in Anne's voice and felt her eyes fill. She'd missed contact with this special lady and promised herself she would not to go so long without touching base again. "Thank you. Your belief in me means a lot."

"But how are *you?* Still having the nightmares, the black moods?"

Lainey let out a ragged breath. "Yes, though not as frequently."

"Have you made friends? Anyone besides Dionne?"

"There's an older man, Ben Porter, who helps with the horses. He reminds me of my grandfather. And his wife is always trying to feed me."

"That's all? Surely you're not doing all that work yourself?"

"Not exactly. The man who owns the ranch next to mine is really a carpenter by trade, and he's doing a great deal of the work. He's . . . very capable."

"I see." Anne was quiet a long moment. "You're not having any new problems, are you, dear?"

New problems? Like the fact that she got drunk last night and felt like hell this morning? Or that she was fighting this attraction that could very well lead her back to the psychiatrist's couch? Yes, perhaps those were a couple of new problems. However, this was not the morning to discuss them.

"I'm taking one day at a time, Anne. And how are things with you and the agency?"

Lainey listened while Anne updated her on several of the models Lainey knew, surprised when she felt not a pang of envy for her former co-workers. Then she hesitated a moment, wondering if she should open this particular can of worms, but finally plunging in. "Tell me, do you ever see Irene?" In her teens, her mother had insisted that Lainey call her by her given name, a touch of vanity Lainey had gone along with. She could imagine Anne's carefully controlled classic features moving into a disapproving frown at the mention of Lainey's mother.

"I run into her occasionally. She's working with this new young model, Dominique somebody-or-other. I wouldn't take her on, and Irene is furious with me. She's busily making the rounds of the other agencies, hoping the girl will hit it big, like you did. You haven't heard from her?"

Poor, sad Irene. Perhaps, she thought, she hadn't been fair to her mother, leaving abruptly like that. But for once, she'd had to think of herself first. "She doesn't know where I am, and I'd like to keep it that way."

"She won't hear it from me. Any chance you might consider a trip to New York? Just to visit me, of course. We could keep it quiet. I miss you, Lainey."

Lainey closed her eyes for a long moment, seeing herself back there in the warmth of Anne's comforting presence. Then her thoughts shifted to schedules and classes and hours under the hot lights. The discipline, the self-denial, the dedication. No, that was someone else's life, someone she used to be. Lainey knew she wasn't yet strong enough to go there and stroll through the minefield of her memories.

"I miss you, too, and I'd love to see you, Anne. But the timing's not right. My life is here now—my commitment to the children. I hope you understand."

"You know I do. Take care of yourself, Lainey. And remember, I'm here if you need to talk. Anytime."

"Thank you so much." Slowly, she replaced the receiver, her thoughts on the woman who was more like a parent to her than either of her own had been. It was good hearing from Anne, but they walked in different worlds now.

Rising, Lainey went to the kitchen. Maybe a cup of coffee would help her incredible headache. How did people who drank regularly ever learn to live with this?

The day was overcast and gloomy, in keeping with her spirits, she thought as she put on a pot of coffee. Peeking out the window, she nearly moaned aloud. Zac's truck was parked near the barn door.

She poured herself a glass of orange juice and dutifully swallowed her vitamin pill, a holdover habit from her early training. Glancing at the back door, she frowned. What would she say to him if he came in, which he probably would do? *Sorry I overreacted. Be grateful I didn't throw up in your truck. Next time, don't offer to drive me anywhere.*

Getting slightly tipsy in itself was no crime. It was the possibility of tears that she feared. Tears made a woman vulnerable, and that was something she'd vowed not to be in front of a man ever again. At least she hadn't gone that far. She closed her eyes, rubbing the lids with shaky fingers, wishing she were stronger.

She was on her second cup of coffee and chewing on a dry piece of toast she really didn't want when she looked up and saw Zac step onto the back porch. Time to face the music, Lainey thought as she waved him in.

"Would you like a cup of coffee?" she asked, rising to get down another cup.

"I'd love one," Zac answered as he pulled out the chair and sat down. He noticed that her back was very straight, her stance defensive, and her hands none too steady as she poured the coffee and set it in front of him.

Resuming her seat, Lainey studied the black liquid in her cup, searching for the right words she knew had to be spoken. If only her head would stop pounding. "I want to apologize," she began.

"There's no need."

"There is for me. I behaved badly. I'm not used to drinking, and I should have realized that even a small amount would hit me hard. I'm sorry I ruined your evening." Another damn good reason to stay away from alcohol—the necessity of these morning-after regrets.

"You didn't ruin my evening, and you didn't do anything so terrible." He took a sip of coffee, studying her. Her face was pale, and the tender skin beneath her eyes looked slightly bruised. "Are you always this hard on yourself?" When she didn't look up or answer, he set the cup down hard on the table and saw her flinch at the sound. "Will you please look at me?"

Slowly she raised her eyes to his, and they were filled with a plea for understanding that turned his heart over. He'd spent a restless night, hearing in his mind the words he'd wrenched out of her outside the Donovans' barn. He knew how much she disliked questions, yet he had to know who had harmed this fragile rose and made her feel so defenseless.

Her fingers were laced tightly together on the table-top, and he reached over, placing his hand over hers. "Who's hurt you so badly, Lainey?" She closed her eyes and shook her head. "Talk to me."

"It doesn't matter." She pulled from his grasp and got up, striding to the sink and standing with her back to him. Not today. Please, not today.

Zac had spent many an hour helping Nancy bear her pain. Not just the physical pain, but the pain of accepting a premature death, the sense of being robbed of her future, the unfairness. He was no stranger to women who preferred to suffer silently and privately. He had no idea what was bothering Lainey, yet his nature demanded that he try to share her burden and perhaps lighten the load she was carrying.

Zac went to her. "Of course, it matters." He placed his hands lightly on her shoulders and turned her to face him. Gently he slid his arms around her and eased her closer to the warmth of his body.

Her hands fluttered at her sides. "No, I..."

"Let me," he said quietly. "Let me hold you, just hold you. I won't hurt you. Sometimes, we all need to be held."

She stood rigid a long moment, then dropped her head to his shoulder with a trembling sigh. Her hands crept up his strong back and bunched in the material of his shirt as she let herself absorb some of his incredible strength. He was right. Everyone needed simple human comfort occasionally.

His hands moved gently on her back, his touch light, soothing. She reminded herself she had nothing to fear from this man, not *this* man. She'd forgotten there were people like Zac in the world, who would not force, who would not take without asking. Perhaps she'd known too many of the other kind and she'd lost faith.

He was so generous, so giving. But she had nothing left to give. Shakily she moved back from him. "Thank you. I feel better now."

She was avoiding his eyes again. "Do you?"

"Yes." Restlessly she pushed back a lock of hair from her face. If only he would go now.

"Do you know that, except when we danced, this is the first time you've let me hold you? Why, Lainey?

Why do you shy away from my touch? You must know I'm attracted to you.''

She leaned against the edge of the counter and pulled the folds of her robe closer about her throat. "Yes, I know. And I don't want you to be."

He took a step back so she wouldn't feel cornered. But he held his ground. "Too late. I've seen your eyes, Lainey, seen the way you look at me. You're attracted, too."

"No! Yes. I . . ." She rubbed the back of her neck, feeling the headache worsen. "Look, I'm not good at this man-woman thing. I haven't had much practice." She met his eyes finally. "All right, I'm attracted to you, but I can't let myself get involved. There are reasons, reasons you wouldn't understand."

"Try me. I'm fairly bright."

Frustrated, she balled her hands into fists. "I'm just not accustomed to playing games. I'm not a casual person."

"There's nothing casual about the way I feel about you." Zac ran a hand through his hair, facing a few hard facts himself. "I wish it was. I didn't mean for this to happen, but I can't seem to stay away from you, to stop thinking of you."

Her look of surprise soon turned to dismay. "Try. I'm not like the women you're used to. Too much has happened. I can't be that special person for you."

Impatience put an edge in his voice. "Women I'm used to! What women? I married at nineteen, and in the two years since Nancy died, there's been no one I've wanted. Until now."

She bent her head, covering her eyes with one hand. "Oh, God, Zac. Don't, please. I can't handle this. I've barely recovered from ... from something that nearly destroyed me."

He placed both hands on her arms, forcing her to look at him. "Whatever it is, it doesn't matter to me. You can lean on me."

Lainey shook her head. "No. Dionne told me—and she's right—I need to face this alone, to conquer it on my own. Or I'd never get over it. But I have no idea how long it will take, or even if it will ever go away."

He rubbed her arms under the wide sleeves of the robe and found her skin cool. He tried to warm her, tried to reach her. "Do you remember the day we talked about loneliness and you insisted you weren't?"

She sighed in resignation. "I lied."

"I know that. I've been lonely, too."

Lainey shook her head slowly, her expression sad. "Two lonely people reaching out doesn't mean they're right for each other. I would wind up hurting you. And you unnerve me, you confuse me. You already make me..." She fought against saying more, against getting in deeper.

"What? What do I make you do?"

Make me dream again, to plan, to hope. "You make me long for things I can't have."

His grip on her arms tightened. "Maybe you *can* have them. Maybe we both can."

"No." She pulled back, and he released her. Moving away, she felt the tears just behind her lids and took a deep breath. She would not cry in front of him. She would not. "Give up on me, Zac. Finish the work on the buildings and get on with your life. I have nothing to offer you but more pain, and you've had your fair share of that."

She swung back to face him as a rumble of thunder overhead warned of rain coming. "Thank you for looking after the horses, and for checking on me. I have to lie down now." She touched her forehead, trying to press away the pain. "My head is splitting."

He looked as lost as she felt. She sent him a pitiful version of a smile. "And thanks for seeing me through my first and last drinking spree." She paused. "I'm always thanking you for something. Have you noticed that?"

Zac watched her walk out of sight, the edge of her robe skimming the wood-plank flooring. He wanted to hit something—a feeling he hadn't experienced since he'd struggled against the inevitability of Nancy's death. He hadn't gained many points in their conversation today, but he hadn't lost them all, either.

Running a business with a staff of over two hundred, he'd learned to read people, and to read between the lines when they spoke. He'd also learned to be a tough negotiator. But most of all, he'd learned patience. He'd need all of what he'd learned to deal with Lainey Roberts.

He picked up his coffee cup and drank down the tepid remains. Plain and simple, she'd changed his plans. He didn't want to care, but she'd unwittingly snared him. With her soft, vulnerable eyes, with the need he could see in their dark depths, with the passion he was certain she'd deliberately hidden deep inside.

Moving to the screen door, he noticed that it was raining lightly. He'd go check the back of the barn where he'd been replacing rotted boards and make sure the tarpaulin covering was secure before leaving. And he'd be back tomorrow; back in Lainey's life, at least for the time being. He had a hunch that her past was tugging her back to New York.

Hands deep in his pants pockets, Zac stood gazing out his porch windows, watching the storm intensify. A flash of lightning momentarily lit the midnight sky, followed by a crack of thunder that shook the ground. It was shaping up to be a beaut, he thought as he walked restlessly to the opposite end of the room. The farmers would be pleased.

He'd never minded stormy nights. It was a cozy time to spend in a warm, dry place, listening to the rain on the roof, preferably in front of a roaring fire. Preferably on a couch, snuggled down comfortably with someone you cared about. He and Nancy had shared many such nights. And now there was Lainey.

Zac watched rivulets stream down the window, all but blocking the view of his backyard. It was really coming down. Just past midnight, and he wondered what she was doing, when her headache had finally eased, and if she was as restless as he. A storm like this could go on all night. He hadn't even attempted to go to sleep; he wasn't tired or sleepy. He was, however, fidgety as hell.

Was she sleeping? Was she sitting in her rocker, drinking tea and remembering the things they'd talked about? Was she thinking of him? This was crazy. Zac swung around and searched for his pipe and tobacco.

He had the pipe almost filled when he saw a light go on outside the foaling barn. Squinting through the glass, he saw Charley in his black slicker open the door and go inside. Probably checking on the pregnant mares, making sure they weren't spooked by the storm.

He wondered how Trixie and Smokey were faring, and the one whose time was nearing, Juno. She was probably a mite jumpy, due to her condition. He hoped the tarpaulin was holding, that the water wasn't leaking inside. Horses caught cold so easily. He wished he'd been able to finish repairing the back wall before this downpour. Maybe he should go check on them. Zac set down his pipe and stood. It would give him something to do besides pace.

In a matter of moments, he'd shrugged into his jacket, dashed to his truck and was on his way. Nearing Lainey's barn, he decided to park on the side so he could check the rear wall before going in. Grabbing his flashlight, he jumped down from the cab.

The heavy rain made it difficult to see, but he didn't think the wind had shifted the tarp much. He hurried to the side door and went in. The usual single overhead light was on, and he could make out the three horses in their stalls. Slipping out of his sodden jacket, Zac tossed it on a pile of straw and shook the water from his hair. The top of his shirt was wet, but he wouldn't be staying long. Rubbing his hands together, he walked toward Juno's stall.

"How you doing, girl?" he whispered, opening the gate and approaching her head slowly. She turned toward him, shuffling her feet restively. "Yeah, it's that kind of night." He smoothed her sleek hide, his tone reassuring. "You're just fine, girl, and so's your little one."

Convinced she was not unusually upset, he left her to say a word to the other two. Then he'd go duck under the hayloft and check the inside of that back wall before he left, just to be sure it was watertight. He opened Smokey's stall and heard her whinny a greeting. "Hi, there, lady," he said softly.

* * *

Electrical storms had always bothered her. Lainey stood at her front window and watched the rain gather in puddles around the base of the trees. A quiet summer rain was one thing, but thunder and lightning made her jumpy. She remembered an incident when she'd been a little girl. A house down the block had been struck by lightning and caught fire. The fire engines had roared down the street, and the neighbors had rushed outside in their nightclothes, huddled under umbrellas. There'd been police sirens and an ambulance. The memory had stayed with her, and she shuddered now as thunder reverberated through her small house.

Belting her robe tighter, she walked to the kitchen and peered out the back. She wished she'd left the light on outside the barn so she could see more than its vague outline. Were the horses as nervous as she? Another thunder roll and she jumped, wishing it would end.

Horses frightened easily, Lainey knew. She might as well check on them as stand here and worry. She hurried to the bedroom, pulled on her jeans and a cotton turtleneck, then sat to lace up her sneakers. At the door, she reached for the flashlight and arranged her raincoat tent-fashion over her head and shoulders. At least it wasn't cold, she thought as she ran toward the barn.

It was dim inside, the only sound coming from the rain hitting the roof and the snuffling of the animals. Tossing her coat aside, she shook her damp hair and smiled at Trixie. "Are you okay, Trix?" she asked as she opened the stall door.

Crouched down at the back wall, Zac heard a sound and straightened, cocking his head. Noises carried easily in the high-ceilinged building. He recognized Lainey's voice as she talked to the horses. He should have guessed she'd worry about them.

He took a few minutes to secure one flapping end of the tarp before walking back toward the stalls. He could see her leaning into Juno, murmuring softly to her as she stroked her muzzle. The jittery mare had quieted considerably. Noisily, he moved closer so she would hear him and not be frightened.

"Oh!" Lainey jerked back, then relaxed. "You startled me. I thought I was alone in here."

"So did I," Zac said, his hand on the stall door. "Guess we had the same idea."

"Yes." Absently she stroked Juno, but her eyes remained on Zac. His boots were muddy, his jeans stained dark from the rain. Even his shirt looked damp. His hair was plastered to his head, the wet curls falling onto his forehead. Why did he have to look so damn appealing?

She said another few gentle words to Juno, then left the stall. Zac stepped out of the way as she closed the door and secured it. "I couldn't sleep, so I thought I'd make sure the storm wasn't upsetting the horses."

"Yeah. Me, too." He pointed to the rear. "I wasn't sure if that tarp was holding. But I checked, and it is."

"That's good." She'd run out of small talk. She searched her mind for a good exit line.

A sound made Zac turn toward the haystack. "Look over there," he whispered as he pointed.

Lainey swung around. A light brown field rabbit had taken over his jacket and was sitting very still, her pink eyes watchful as her nose twitched. Close alongside her were two bunnies no more than a few days old, burrowing into their mother for warmth. "Oh, aren't they tiny? We no sooner cleared out the mice and now the rabbits have moved in."

"We can't turn out a whole family on a night like this."

"Certainly not." Smiling, she turned to look at him, then instantly forgot the rabbits.

He was much closer than she'd thought. She could smell the rain in his hair, the masculine aroma of tobacco that clung to his clothes. She could hear the sudden thundering of her heart, much louder than the thunder outside.

Zac ached to touch her, but was afraid she was as skittish as the rabbits. He raised a trembling hand to her cheek and couldn't believe it when she didn't move away. He struggled with his emotions, with his desires, wondering how to approach this fragile, sensitive, wounded woman. If she'd turned from him now, he might even have welcomed it. Yet she stood quietly, her violet eyes a little frightened, a little anxious.

Whatever had happened to her before, he could handle. If only she would trust him. If only he wouldn't blunder now and send her scurrying. Moving in slow motion, he lowered his mouth to hers.

She was frozen in time and place, unable to move, unable to think. As she'd watched the emotions flicker across his face, she asked herself how she could want something she also feared. Afraid of her reaction, yet unwilling to walk away, she felt his mouth touch hers and closed her eyes.

Sensations of tenderness, of hesitant seeking, almost of reverence, softened her. His lips moved over hers gently, unhurriedly, incredibly. He tasted warm and exciting and intensely male. She dared to return the pressure, and only then did he touch her elsewhere, sliding his arms around her.

More curious than frightened, more moved than aroused, Lainey let him align their bodies and draw her closer. Her mouth opened under his, inviting intimacy. He accepted, inching his tongue past her lips. She breathed in a sigh of surprise, then allowed him entry. Now there was more to savor, an underlying need held in check by a man who would never allow himself to race out of control. Curling her hands into his sleeves, she let him lead her.

She was sweeter than he'd imagined, softer than he'd dreamed. He hadn't known he'd been searching until he'd touched her; hadn't thought he was lonely until she'd come into his life and made him aware of empty places. He hadn't felt he could risk caring again until he realized that not having her was a greater risk.

The urge to take her deeper, to pick her up and move with her to the sweet-smelling hay and love her all night long raged within him. But he knew better, knew that this was only the first step on a long road he had to walk slowly. With that hesitant shyness he'd noticed before, she opened to him, offering the secrets of her mouth. But he knew it would take more than a kiss before she'd offer more.

Lainey had been kissed before, though not frequently. Boys first, clumsy as she in their inexperience. Later there'd been a few young men, confident and cocky, with hard mouths and eager hands, more repellent than exciting. And there'd been Steven—self-assured and somewhat arrogant. So how could she have known, how could she even have imagined, that there could be sensitivity such as Zac offered?

He moved his mouth to the corner of hers, kissing that tender spot, then tasted her temples, her closed eyes, before returning to claim her trembling lips—

endlessly soft, endlessly giving. But she mustn't make too much of this, she told herself even as she sighed with a pleasure she never thought she'd feel. Dionne had warned her that she might one day want again. But a kiss was only the beginning, and she had no way of knowing how much she could handle before the panic would begin, before the fear would take over.

He was having difficulty stopping—more difficulty than he thought he would have. He wanted her, true, but he wanted her untroubled and willing to trust him: with her secrets, with her body, with her feelings. Drawing back finally, Zac saw the confusion in her eyes and knew she wasn't ready for more just now.

Lainey lowered herself from her toes and trailed her hands down his arms, her eyes focused on the third button of his shirt. She had to hold on, for just a minute, until the trembling stopped. How could she tell him she'd just passed an enormous hurdle, actually enjoying a kiss, a man's touch, a moment of passion? She couldn't, and felt bad.

"I'm sorry," she said, her voice thick with emotion.

Why had he known she'd say those very words? "Sorry I kissed you? Or sorry you kissed me back?"

Lainey took in a shaky breath. She met his eyes and saw the patience, the caring. If only she could begin her life over this day, with this man, perhaps she would have a chance. But she'd stopped believing in second chances. "Neither. Sorry I'm such a mess."

Before he could protest, she grabbed her coat and ran out into the rainy night.

Chapter Six

Zac's face was grim as he watched the little boy hesitantly take Lainey's hand and walk with her to the corral where Smokey stood waiting, the child's saddle he'd placed on the mare's back gleaming in the afternoon sun. Realizing his hands were clenched into fists, he made himself relax before turning to the woman beside him.

"How do you stand it, Dionne?" he asked, his voice rough with a lingering rage. "Day after day, you see battered kids, physically handicapped kids, emotionally traumatized kids. How do you not let it get to you?"

Dionne let out a long trail of smoke. "What makes you think it doesn't?"

He leaned against the barn wall, crossed one dusty boot over the other and studied her. Neat and professional as always, wearing a yellow linen jacket over brown slacks and the high heels he'd never seen her without. Her red hair was unruffled even in a breeze, and her expression calm. Only the jerky way she drew on the cigarette hinted of a slight case of nerves. "You'd make a hell of a poker player," he told her honestly.

She laughed. "I learned a long time ago, Zac, to camouflage my emotions. I can't help my patients if I look horrified or upset, or if I rage, which is what I'd often like to do. Children, especially, pick up on moods."

"Not very healthy, hiding your feelings."

She sent him a mock frown. "Hey, who's the doctor here?" Dionne ground out her cigarette as she regarded Zac.

But Zac's eyes were on Lainey. A muscle twitched in his cheek as he watched her lift Bobby into the saddle for the first time.

"He's going to be all right," Dionne said matter-of-factly.

Zac saw the brave smile Bobby gave Lainey, as if he was determined to be a big boy about this new experience. She'd told him this morning that Dionne was bringing a new pupil—a boy who'd been abused for most of his six years by a drunken father and neglected by a mother who'd been beaten herself. Finally Bobby had been made a ward of the court and was living in a foster home, trying to forget, trying to heal.

Zac had just finished saddling Smokey when they'd arrived, and he hadn't been able to walk away after seeing those huge eyes solemnly watching the adults with a heart-wrenching wariness. Then he'd helped him off with his sweater and seen the scars on his thin arms, the way one small finger was crooked after having been broken too often to heal correctly. And he could have wept.

Turning away from Dionne, he eased onto the wooden bench alongside the barn and sighed. "*Is* he going to be all right? Are any of them? And how long will it take?"

Dionne sat down beside him and crossed her legs. "The body heals quickly, especially in children, but the mind is another matter. You have to have patience."

"I thought I did, but you have much more. You're able to celebrate each small accomplishment—like Shelly spontaneously giving us a hug now—and see it as a part of the whole, a step toward the final victory. I want to rush her along, to run through the steps with her, so she'll be well sooner, happy quicker."

Dionne shook her head as she leaned back. "I know, but these things can't be rushed. Each person progresses at their own rate. If you hurry them, you risk setting them back to step one. If you exhibit impatience, they stop trying."

"A little like walking on eggs."

"Sometimes, yes."

Zac frowned up at the blue sky, concentrating. "So if a child, or an adult, has been traumatized by something that happened to her, there's a natural progression of steps on the road to healing? A number of hurdles, say, that she has to overcome, one by one, until she's conquered the trauma?"

"Well, that's rather simplistic, but, yes."

"For instance, Bobby. He has to get over his fear that adults may hurt him?"

"He has to realize that *some* adults do hurt, but most do not," she emphasized.

"And he has to learn to trust people and his own instincts again?"

"Yes."

He turned to face her, his gray eyes anxious. "How do you get someone like that to trust you? Do you offer comfort when they remember the bad times, a shoulder to cry on? Do you force them to face their deepest fears? Or do you just let them know you care and wait for them to work their way through it all?"

Dionne rummaged in her bag for a cigarette. "We're not talking about Bobby or Shelly any longer, are we?" She quickly lit the cigarette before he could offer.

He sighed, having suspected she'd see through him. "No. We're talking about Lainey."

"Before I answer you, I need to know why you're asking. Is it simply curiosity, or something more?"

"I care about her. More than I'd planned to. More than I want to. Is that a problem?"

"It might be, for you." She inhaled deeply, and paused while she came up with a well-thought-out response. "Zac, you told me some weeks ago that you weren't masochistic enough to want another relationship that might end badly. I'm warning you now, this one might."

He nodded, as if he'd been expecting as much. "Another warning about Lainey. I'm getting used to them."

"Naturally, I don't want to see you hurt, but my patient is my primary concern. Lainey needs friends, support, occasionally comfort and understanding. But mostly, she needs time. I sense that as your feelings have intensified, your patience has flown."

Zac combed rough fingers through his hair, feeling frustrated. "You may be right." He swung to face her, hoping she would help him. "If I knew what has happened to her, I'd know how to proceed. I feel so helpless."

Inhaling, Dionne nodded. "I know, but I can't tell you more. When she learns to trust you—*if* she does—she'll probably confide in you."

"She told me someone had taken something from her, something she can't get back, and she doesn't even know his name."

Clearly surprised, Dionne just stared at him. "She told you all that?"

He looked a little chagrined. "She'd had a little too much to drink."

Fury jumped into her eyes. "You got her drunk?"

"No! She managed to do that all by herself. We went to the Donovans' barn dance. I warned her the punch was spiked."

She let out a long breath. "Lainey's not a drinker. Did she say anything else?"

"Yeah. A couple of things that might surprise you."

"Like what?"

"That she's attracted to me, but she can't get involved."

"Why should that surprise me? You're a very attractive man, and I'm sure you know it. Zac, I hope you're not looking on Lainey as something of a challenge. You could do a lot of damage if you lead her on, then go on to greener pastures."

"I told you, I care about her."

"And I told you, caring for Lainey right now is a crapshoot. Your being there for her might make the difference, or it might push her over the edge. She's been hiding her pain, denying her problems, and she's just coming around. I believe you're good for her, but I can't promise you'll come out unscarred."

He braced his elbow on the back of the bench. "I'm pretty resilient. This all goes back further than just one traumatic incident with this nameless man, I presume."

Dionne dropped her cigarette and stepped on it. "It usually does."

He swung his gaze to Lainey. She'd taken Bobby from the horse, sat him on the top rung of the fence and was pointing up into the apple tree, showing him the reddening fruit. The boy's arms were around her and he was nodding. If anyone could break through his fears, she could. Maybe because she'd been there.

"It's odd, you know," he said, still watching Lainey. "I used to look at a lovely woman like Lainey and think she had the world at her feet. And look at all she's dealing with."

"People are like icebergs, haven't you heard? Only ten percent visible to the naked eye."

Zac turned back to her. "But maybe they reveal a greater percentage to someone who really cares for them. Did you know she doesn't turn away from my touch anymore?"

Dionne kept her features even. Perhaps she'd underestimated Zac Sinclair and his quiet persistence. "That's good, but my earlier advice still stands. Go slowly with her. Her progress so far is tenuous at best. The wrong word, an upsetting person, a threatening situation could set her off and reverse the gain."

Lord knows, he was trying. "I hear you."

As Lainey turned to lead Bobby back to them, Dionne stood. "Looks like the lesson's over."

Zac got to his feet and smiled down at her. "Mine or the boy's?"

But Dionne wasn't smiling. "I wish you luck, Zac. You're probably going to need it."

"Thanks." He watched her walk over to meet Lainey and Bobby, wishing he felt as confident as he'd sounded.

Lainey dusted off her knees as she stood after weeding the small patch of flowers she'd planted alongside her porch. Dark red snapdragons grew along the back wall, purple and yellow pansies spread across the middle area and delicate moss roses curved around the front. The colorful array reminded her of Grandmother Nolan's flower beds that had decorated her large front yard. She'd bordered each with painted white bricks placed at precise angles. And in the center of the largest had stood a birdbath that her grandfather had painted a startling white.

Gathering up her garden tools, she let herself remember the Saturday afternoons she'd spent there in the company of those two dear old people before her mother had begun dragging her to the endless lessons. A few good memories, Lainey decided as she removed her cotton gloves.

She was about to go inside when she heard a car approaching from the road. The setting sun was low in the sky and bounced off the hood of the unfamiliar station wagon. So few visitors came, that this new arrival had her frowning as she watched the lone occupant stop alongside Zac's truck.

As he got out, she took an involuntary step backward. He was big, burly and unshaven, a stranger she was certain she hadn't seen before. His clothes were clean enough—overalls and a denim work shirt—yet he had an unkempt look about him. He glanced around the yard, then started walking toward her. Lainey looked past him, but couldn't see Zac anywhere, and she knew Ben had gone home an hour ago. The knowledge made her uneasy.

Squaring her shoulders, she held on to her pruning shears. "Yes, can I help you?" she called out.

The stranger stopped several yards from her and squinted toward the house. "You own this place?" he asked, sounding raspy.

She didn't like his voice. "Yes. Is it directions you need?"

"Nope. Are you Lainey Roberts?"

"Yes." He was making her nervous, and she wished he'd state his business and be off. Of all days for Willie not to be around.

"Fellow in town at the drugstore said you needed a handyman." He grinned, revealing a chipped-tooth smile. "I'm real handy."

She'd meant to take down those ads she'd placed at various bulletin boards. "I'm sorry, but the position's filled."

His small eyes darted toward the barn, then circled the yard and came back to rest on her. He stepped closer. "I do most anything. Clean out barns, groom horses, work in a garden, mend fences. What you need done?"

Lainey felt exasperation, and repulsion as the smell of cheap cigar smoke drifted to her. "I told you, I've hired someone else. You'll have to go."

He ran thick fingers over his unshaven chin. "Don't see no one around, and I need the job real bad." He waved toward the house. "How about painting? House sure could use it."

Lainey clutched the tools to her chest and fought down the nausea. He reminded her of someone, someone she'd been trying desperately to forget. His hair was greasy, and as he moved closer, the smell of beer had her stepping backward. "No, I don't need you. Please go."

The man smiled, looking pleased at her discomfort. "A woman all alone out here. Must be lots of things you need done." He kept walking as she stumbled onto the porch, the sudden fear in her eyes egging him on. "Maybe you should invite me in."

She froze, her back to her kitchen door. And then the trembling began.

"Trixie, you're getting ornery," Zac said as he passed her stall, carrying his carpenter's belt. The horse swung her big head in his direction and snuffled. "I think you're jealous of those other two." Trixie nodded as if she understood, then moved her nose to her treat box. Finding it empty, she looked back at him, her eyes sad. "Don't give me that. You've had enough sugar cubes for one day."

Shaking his head at her, he walked outside, and stopped. It took him only a moment to size up the situation. A station wagon he didn't recognize was parked next to his truck, and a man he didn't know was on the porch, backing Lainey toward her door. Even from this distance, he could tell the man was pressing and Lainey was frightened.

"Hey!" he yelled, then dropped his belt and ran toward them. "What's going on here?"

Startled, the man jumped back as Zac leaped onto the porch. "Nothin', buddy."

One look at Lainey's wild eyes told him differently. He grabbed a handful of the stranger's bib overalls and yanked him hard. "What the hell did you say to her?"

"I...I only wanted a job. In town, they told me she was looking for a handyman." He swallowed hard. "I didn't mean nothin'."

Zac thrust him down the two steps with one quick shove and watched him struggle to keep from falling in the dirt. "Get the hell out of here and don't come back."

"Okay, okay." The stranger hurried to his car and quickly climbed inside.

As Zac turned to Lainey, he heard the motor start and the squeal of the stranger's tires as the car swung around and shot down the drive.

Her eyes were wide and frightened as she stared at him unseeingly. She seemed rooted to the spot, holding her garden tools in an iron grip, leaning against the screen. What had Dionne said? That the wrong word or a threatening situation could set her off? God, he hoped not. If that son of a...

"Lainey," he began again. "It's all right."

She blinked rapidly, seeing another scene. "He smells like cigars, cheap cigars. And beer." She shuddered. "His eyes...His eyes are mean and..."

"He's gone." He dared to touch her, to take the tools from her and set them aside. Then he took her hands into his. "He won't be back."

She shook her head violently. "Yes, he will. He'll always be back. Always." With an anguished cry, she turned and ran inside, letting the door slam after her.

Zac sagged against the door frame a moment, then went inside. Twilight filled the kitchen with the colors of the fading sun. She wasn't there. He walked to the archway and saw the living room was dim and quiet. Though he hadn't repaired the flooring yet, she'd cleaned it, then spread an oval rug in front of the fireplace. The fresh, soapy scent lingered in the heavy air. Her rocker faced the hearth, and she'd tossed three overstuffed pillows on the floor. Perhaps the bedroom...

He heard a sound, like a whimpering, and ventured farther. He saw her then, huddled in the shadows of a corner. He moved nearer but stopped several feet away, afraid of startling her. She sat curled into herself, a low, keening sound coming from her.

Baffled as to what to do, Zac sat down facing her. Her fingers clenched and unclenched the material of her shirt. He wanted to reach out and cover them with his own, to offer comfort. But he waited.

For several minutes, she just sat, then a shudder moved through her. Finally she raised her head and opened her eyes slowly. As if coming back from a faraway place, she gradually focused on him.

"Lainey, I'm here."

"I'm so cold," she whispered.

Grateful for something to do, he stood. "I'll light the fire and make you a hot drink." He'd laid one for her days ago, but it had been too warm. Now, even he felt the chill in the old house.

"Yes, the fire." With shaky hands, she pushed stray tendrils of hair off her face. Would she ever be warm again? Lainey wondered. Ever be free, ever be whole again?

She heard him fuss with the fire, then go into the kitchen. She was so tired. She wished she had the energy to get her comforter. She would wrap herself in it, sit in her rocker and watch the fire. If she sat long enough, stared hard enough, maybe the flames would burn away the horrifying thoughts in her mind.

Zac came back with two steaming mugs and set them on the hearth. "Come over and sit in front of the fire. You'll be warmer."

Lainey doubted it, but she pushed herself up along the wall, avoiding his eyes. He meant well, but he should go. He couldn't help her; didn't he see that? When she was sure she could walk, she made her way to the fireplace. Wearily she sat down, picked up a blue pillow, hugged it close to her and again closed her eyes.

He sat alongside her for a long while, just letting her warm up, letting her calm down. A log shifted in the grate, and her eyes popped open. He seized the opportunity and held out her cup. "Try some hot chocolate."

She took a tentative sip and felt the warmth spread. "You don't have to stay with me."

"I want to stay with you."

She frowned. "Why?"

"I care about you, Lainey. Tell me why that man upset you like this. Tell me whatever it is that you're carrying around that torments you. I want to help."

Her eyes were filled with anguish and unshed tears. "I can't. You don't understand. I don't want to think or to feel or to relive it."

He was a builder and he knew about foundations. It was impossible to build a house—or a future—without first clearing the ground of debris, or hauling out the emotional rubble of the past. It was painful, but it was necessary. How could he convince her?

Slowly, he moved closer, propping his knee behind her, touching her lightly and letting her lean against it. He rubbed her shoulders then, finding tension knotting her muscles. Surprised she was allowing his stroking, he kept his hands impersonal. She sighed deeply and dropped her head forward.

It had to be said, and he had to start somewhere. "Did you recognize the man in the station wagon?" After a moment, she shook her head. "He reminded you of someone, then?"

She was gazing into the fire, unable to escape. "For a moment, I thought it was him. Same build, same smells—the cigar, the beer."

He continued kneading her neck under the fall of her hair. "Someone you knew in New York?"

"I didn't know him."

"I don't understand."

The revulsion washed over her again, followed by the heat of shame. Her head came up, her tortured eyes met his, and her voice gave a strangled cry. "He raped me. A stranger, in a cold, filthy alley."

Stunned, Zac hesitated, unable to find words. As the horror sank in, he pulled her to him, pressing her face to his chest. She was shaking uncontrollably. He stroked her hair as if she were a small child. She shed no tears, but dry sobs hiccuped through her small frame while the rage built in him, fierce and hot as the fire he stared at unseeingly. He thought of his earlier anger at the father who'd beaten Bobby, and knew that vulnerability wasn't limited to children.

Lowering his head to hers, he whispered soft, meaningless words to her, offering what limited comfort he could. How clear it all was, now that he knew—her actions, her fears. He'd read of rapes in the newspapers, seen the statistics on how one occurred every three minutes in this country alone. But he'd never been touched by one of the victims, not like this. The wrath he felt toward men who hurt innocent children and un-suspecting women had him curling around her, his protection, sadly, too late.

How long she stayed that way, Lainey couldn't have said. She hadn't cried after the rape had happened, nor in the months that had followed. You have to get it out, to weep, the doctor in New York had told her. But she'd been unable to. It's critical to your recovery, he'd said. What did he know? she'd thought. He was a man first, a doctor second.

She'd hated all men for a while, then feared them, then chosen to ignore them. Natural reactions, Dionne had told Lainey when she'd finally come to live with her. The doctor had patched her body, but Dionne had mended her mind. But who would heal her soul—the part inside that the man in the alley had taken from her?

With a trembling breath, Lainey eased away from Zac. Surely he'd be anxious to leave by now, eager to escape her near hysterics, trying to think of a polite exit.

But, no. Tenderly he framed her face with his large, callused hands while eyes filled with compassion met hers.

"It's all right," he said, his voice husky with feeling. He remembered holding Nancy the few times she'd given in to despair, remembered how she'd hated to break down in front of him. "You survived, and that's the important thing. I can only imagine the horror of what happened to you. But you're strong and you're healing."

She blinked rapidly. "Strong?" She shook her head. "Until someone touches me unexpectedly, and it all rushes back. Until a stranger gets a little pushy and I whirl out of control. I'll never be like I was before. Never."

"No, you'll be different. Each day, you'll make a little more progress. You'll learn to trust your instincts, to realize that only a few twisted men are like that rapist and that you have nothing to fear from the touch of a friend, even a male friend." Zac brushed a wisp of hair from her forehead.

"Give it time, Lainey." He shifted, putting his arm around her, his touch light, friend to friend, very conscious that he might still frighten her. He felt her take a jagged breath and relax a little. "Who knows about this, other than Dionne?"

"The doctor in New York, Anne Blackburn and my parents." A sigh trembled from her. "And a man I'd been dating, Steven Becker."

Her fatigue was obvious to him. "You don't have to tell me any more," he said. "I know how hard this is for you."

Friendship had a price tag, she'd always known. Earlier, Zac had gotten rid of the stranger and just now, he'd held her and not seemed anxious to leave, even when she'd finally told him her darkest secret. He hadn't looked vaguely accusatory and deeply disappointed in her as Irene had. Or angry, then impatient, and finally annoyed with her as Steven had. Nor openly condemning as her father had been. She wanted to tell Zac, wanted desperately for him to understand.

Finding a tissue in her pocket, she blew her nose. Zac's friendship had become important to her, more than she'd planned, but she wondered if it was strong enough to absorb all of the truth. Even people who'd claimed to care for her had turned from her. Maybe it was time to find out.

She swallowed more hot chocolate as she gathered her thoughts. "It was last December, the week before

Christmas. I remember the stores were all decorated and the Salvation Army Santas were clanging their bells on every corner. There'd been snow the day before, but you know Manhattan—all those marching feet—and by evening there were only dirty gray remnants along the curbs. It was dusk, just before the streetlights were turned on, and I was walking home from a late class. Aerobics, Thursday, four to five.''

"You were still taking classes?"

"It never ends for models, especially as you get older. At twenty-seven, I was up against twenty-year-olds, remember. I had to stay in top shape." She took a breath, taking herself back. "Irene and I shared an apartment off Sixth Avenue, though I wasn't there much. I was only about four blocks from home, taking my time, gazing in the shop windows. I remember I'd stopped to look into this travel agency advertising a windjammer cruise, a getaway vacation. I was thinking about that, about how I'd like to just pack it in and sail away. I didn't notice anyone following me or hear anything unusual.''

"The street was crowded?"

"Not crowded, but not empty, either. The next thing I know, this man was behind me, very close up against me. He muttered something into my ear, his arm circled my waist and he kind of shoved me into this alley. Maybe if someone had been watching all along, they'd have guessed what was going on. Maybe not, because he made it look like we knew each other and we were kind of wrestling. Then he pushed me farther along into the alley, back where it was darker. I tried to stop him, but he was so strong. I started to yell, but his other arm was around my throat. I couldn't breathe. Then he swung me around and I saw his eyes. And I knew.''

He heard the pain in her voice and tightened his grip on her arms.

She forced herself to go on, to get it over with. "I was wearing leotards and leg warmers and boots, and this heavy jacket. And I had this scarf around my neck. He tightened the scarf around my throat while he yanked at my clothes. I tried to get my knee up, to slam it into him, but he was so heavy. I almost got out a scream, but he was fast. Then he got mad and put his dirty hand over my mouth. Oh, God, the smell."

Lainey swallowed hard, the memories crowding in on her. "Sometimes I can still smell that alley when I wake up late at night. Cheap cigars and stale beer. I started to gag, but he held me down. Finally I managed to bite his hand, but I paid for it. He gave me two backhanded slaps and . . . and I must have passed out for a few minutes."

Zac took deep breaths, fighting back the anger. Suddenly he realized he was squeezing her arms and forced his fingers to unclench. In his wildest thoughts, he hadn't imagined the inhumanity. He caressed her arms patiently as she sat staring into the fire.

"When I came around, he was running down the alley toward the street. It took me a while to sit up, even longer to stand. My clothes were torn, I was wet and dirty. Somehow I made it home to face my mother."

"To face her?"

She made a bitter sound. "Yes. Her first words were 'He didn't mar your face, did he?'" Good old Irene, Lainey thought. Mustn't wreck the career.

Zac ground his teeth at the insensitivity, then tried to soften her pain. "She was probably just upset for you."

Lainey nodded knowingly. "She took me to the hospital, and they brought in the police. It was a hideous night." Wearily she ran a hand over her tired eyes. "They kept asking questions, like was I absolutely certain I didn't know the man, and how long had he been following me, and why did I suppose he'd picked on me. They made me feel like I was somehow responsible."

He'd heard about the guilt of the victim, how it stayed with them long after the physical effects of the attack had healed. And he knew a little something about guilt. Zac cupped her chin and turned her face toward him. "I hope you know you're not responsible, any more than Bobby is responsible for the things that happened to him. You were both just in the wrong place at the wrong time."

How did he know to say the perfect thing, to address the question that hadn't been resolved in her own mind? Intellectually she knew she'd never been flirtatious with strangers or invited advances indiscriminately. But so many others had believed she had left herself wide open for just such an attack.

Lainey looked down at her drink and realized it had grown cold. "When something like this happens, you can't seem to stop asking yourself questions. Did I do something inadvertently so that this man picked me out of a crowd? Irene often called me a daydreamer. And she was right. It was the only way I could handle the monotony of the long hours under the lights. She said if I'd had my wits about me that evening, if I hadn't been careless—"

"That's ridiculous!" He remembered calling her careless at the vet's office that day and how upset she'd become. Now he knew why. "Just because you glanced in a store window and thought about a trip doesn't mean you weren't aware of your surroundings. Hadn't you walked down that same street at basically the same hour many times before?''

"Hundreds of times, and I never once thought to be afraid. I'd lived in New York for years, and I knew where I could walk safely and what streets were dangerous. None of us at the agency had ever had even one serious encounter.'' She sighed deeply. "But all it takes is one. I just wish I could be sure that there wasn't something I could have done to prevent it.''

"Lainey, I know something about guilt and self-blame.'' Scooting around to face her, he took her hands into his. "I told you my wife died, but I didn't tell you all of it.'' It was his turn to gaze into the fire, feeling that dormant rush of pain. "I grew up without many extras. My folks loved us, but my dad was a construction worker and there were layoffs every winter, sometimes for months. I vowed I wouldn't raise my kids like that, getting shoes resoled instead of buying new ones, my mother mending socks, patching jackets. So when Nancy and I married, I insisted we not start a family until we were financially secure.''

Zac turned back and found her watching him intently. "She hated doctors and never went for checkups. When finally I said we should think about having a baby and for months nothing happened, she decided she'd better make an appointment. That's when they found the cancer.''

She squeezed his hands. "You can't blame yourself for that.''

"If I hadn't been so stubborn, if I'd agreed to a baby sooner, she'd have gone in for an exam earlier. Maybe they'd have caught it in time. Maybe she'd still be alive today.''

"Oh, Zac, don't do that to yourself. Certainly cancer isn't anyone's fault. It just happens."

He brought her hand to his lips. "I want to believe that as much as I want you to believe that attack could have happened to anyone unfortunate enough to be in that man's path that day."

Her eyes were dry and clear. "You're saying it was fate?"

"I'm saying that some things are out of our control, no matter how we wish it weren't so."

Unconvinced, she dropped her gaze. "Perhaps."

There was so much more he wanted to say, so many questions still unanswered. But he could see she was worn-out and knew she'd said far more than she'd planned, as it was. He rose and drew her to her feet, his hands still holding hers.

"You need to rest. Can I fix you something to eat before I go? Or if you're uneasy about staying alone tonight, I can sleep out here, so you won't be alone in the house."

Lainey struggled with a rush of emotion. Her mother had never understood, her father's reaction had bordered on cruelty, and Steven had turned from her. How was it that this man she'd known for only a few weeks could so easily empathize?

Her voice was whispery with disbelief. "I've told you such terrible things about me, and you're still here. I've never known anyone like you."

He reached to touch the ends of her hair lightly. "I care about you, Lainey, not because you have a lovely face and a beautiful body. Because of what's in here." He tapped her forehead. "Your mind—where you think and live and exist. And in here—" he touched the spot nearest her heart "—where you feel. The packaging is nice, but the contents are far more important. Despite what you fear, nothing that's happened has changed what's inside you. You're brave and intelligent and beautiful *inside,* where it counts.

She blinked back the moisture that threatened to overflow. ''Thank you.''

He wanted badly, so badly, to take her in his arms, to kiss away the pain and the unshed tears. ''Let me help you. Let me teach you to trust again.'' He saw a look of sadness, of despair on her face as she shook her head.

''Don't count on me, Zac. Despite all we've shared tonight, I feel broken inside. No one should have to put up with my black moods and the dreadful nightmares, least of all you. You deserve more. I'm not comfortable being touched or held. And the thought of more makes me shake with fear.'' She thought of Steven, who'd insisted his lovemaking would erase the dark pictures in her mind. Remembering, she cringed and wrapped her arms around her trembling body. ''I'm not good for myself, much less anyone else.''

''I disagree. And you'll find I'm a very patient man.'' He heard her sigh and decided it was time to leave. ''Will you be all right, now?''

She nodded.

Quickly he checked all the windows and locks, then walked to the door. ''I'll be back tomorrow to start on the floor in here, okay?'' The firelight cast a halo about her hair as she nodded again. ''You're safe now. Good night, Lainey.'' He closed the door behind him with a loud click of the lock.

She stood a long while, staring at the place where he'd stood. Safe now. But was she? Would she ever feel safe again? She thought he'd understood and maybe he had, a little. But he thought he could fix her, make her whole again. Not out of arrogance, like Steven. Out of kindness. Only it still wouldn't work.

"Good night, Zac," she whispered into the stillness of the room.

Chapter Seven

His favorite breakfast consisted of hot coffee and croissants, fresh from the oven. Zac placed the bakery bag on the seat and started the truck. Driving toward Lainey's, he wondered what kind of night she'd had, and if perhaps he'd pushed a little too hard last evening, finally wrenching the story out of her. And he hoped she wouldn't feel uncomfortable around him after having told him such personal things.

Leaving the highway for the road that bordered her ranch, he slowed, admiring the cloudless summer morning. He'd never lived anywhere but Michigan, and he loved the rolling hills, the clean smell of the nearby lake and the tranquillity he always felt here. He couldn't imagine ever living in the New York that Lainey described, yet wondered if maybe, after she felt more confident, she wouldn't return there. Return and leave him.

He'd vowed not to get involved again, not seriously. Yet from the beginning, Lainey had been so easy to care about. Her hesitancy had challenged him, her gentleness had captivated him, and her strength had drawn him in further. She was a special woman, yet he doubted if, once totally well and confident again, this quiet life would be enough for her. She'd been a cover girl, glamorous, sought after. She was hiding now, but one day that need would leave her. And he'd lose someone else he cared for.

Frowning, Zac swung into her drive. These feelings had snuck up on him. He didn't welcome them, nor did he deny them. Lainey wouldn't acknowledge them, and might even run if she knew how he felt. So it was his problem, Zac concluded as he drew the truck to a halt near the barn door. Not an easy one, either, he thought as he swung down from the cab.

With a wave at Ben who was tending the horses, he headed for Lainey's back door. From the porch, he saw that she was on the side lawn, hanging clothes on the line. She sent him a quick glance, then bent to her basket of wet things.

"I'll be in soon," she called. "Can you get started without me?"

"No." He held up the bakery bag. "I need help with these."

She shook out a damp towel. "What's that?"

"Breakfast. Has to be eaten warm."

"I'm not hungry."

"You didn't eat dinner last night. I'm putting fresh coffee on, so hurry up." Without waiting for the rest of her argument, he went inside the kitchen.

With a frown, Lainey set a clothespin in place with a bit more force than necessary. Since Zac had an-

nounced he would start in her living room today, she'd
planned to work outside. Obviously, he was a man who
enjoyed rearranging other people's plans. Now if she
didn't go in and share his breakfast, he'd think she was
afraid to face him after last night. She wasn't, really. A
shade uncomfortable, but not exactly afraid.

Hanging up the last item, she hoisted the empty basket. The trouble with sharing confidences was that it
added a dimension of intimacy to the relationship.
Which was exactly what she'd been trying to avoid.
Walking toward the house, she wondered if he would let
sleeping dogs lie.

Lainey let the screen door close behind her as her eyes
moved to the center of the table and a huge platter of
temptation. "Croissants. Oh, my!"

Smiling at her expression, he poured hot coffee. "I
take it you like them."

"No," she said, setting the basket aside and sitting
down. "I *love* them." She reached for one, inhaling its
buttery fragrance. "Do you know how many calories
are in one of these?"

Zac helped himself. "Do you know I don't even
care?"

Savoring a mouthful, Lainey all but purred. "To
those of us who've had to watch our weight, this is truly
forbidden fruit. The last time I had one was when Anne
brought a bag to the hospital. I was feeling so de-
pressed I wasn't eating, but I ate that morning."

Surprised she'd led into this subject, he kept his eyes
on his plate as he divided his croissant. "Were you in
the hospital long?"

"Several days."

"Until your bruises healed?"

"No." She took a hot sip of coffee, then slowly set down the cup. Whatever had made her start this? "To make sure I wasn't pregnant."

He heard the flat tone of her voice and searched about for a less dismal subject. His eyes landed on the ancient washing machine. "When you're ready for new appliances, maybe you'd like to add on a laundry room. Hanging clothes out in the winter might be a little rough."

She chewed thoughtfully. "I'd thought of that. Then again, I don't know if I'll be here next winter."

His heart skipped a beat. Hadn't he guessed she'd leave? "I thought you said you were finished with modeling, that you wanted to make a go of this."

"I am finished with that life and I do want to succeed here. But what if I can't? I've got only six students, and who knows how many more Dionne can refer, and if in fact learning to ride and work with horses will help any of them?"

Zac felt himself relax a little. Insecurities, he could handle. "You're new at this. It's only natural to worry about it all working out. You know, there are other doctors who might want to use your services, or maybe just a family coping with a problem child. You need some exposure, some publicity. Not enough people know you're here or what you offer."

Finishing her croissant, Lainey wiped her buttery fingers on a napkin. "I've had all the publicity I can handle in one lifetime, thank you."

He got up for more coffee. "I don't mean a billboard advertisement. Maybe a newspaper article focusing on the ranch, on how the kids are responding to the animals."

"Dionne had mentioned the possibility of an open house, to invite the parents to see their children's progress."

"Yeah, that kind of thing. And you invite the local press."

"The press. I don't know."

"Are you afraid you'll be recognized?"

She glanced down at herself, in faded jeans and a baggy cotton top, her hair in a long braid down her back, and grinned. "Do you think anyone would pick me out as a fashion model?"

Her skin was morning fresh, her eyes a mischievous violet and her mouth, as usual, full and inviting. Her kind of beauty was hard to hide, but she'd never believe it. He sent her a lazy grin. "You're right. Ugly as a mud fence."

She laughed, and the sound warmed him. "You're great for my ego, Sinclair." Quickly she cleared the table. "I suppose you want to get started on that floor. I can roll up the rug and—"

"*I'll* roll up the rug." He carried his cup to the sink. "And what are your plans for the day?"

"Oh, I'll be around." She ran hot water into the sink and squirted in soap.

He took a step closer. "I like having you around." With a touch on her arm, he turned her to face him. "Very much." He saw her eyes darken with that ever-present wariness.

"Zac, I—"

"I know. You're not comfortable being touched. Perhaps if you let me touch you more, you'll find you enjoy it, that you're no longer afraid."

"It's not a matter of enjoyment or of fear."

"Then what is it?"

She gazed at her hands buried in the soap bubbles in the sink. "I'm well aware that touching is only the beginning. It leads to kissing and to...to more."

"Lovemaking, you mean?"

"Sex, yes."

"Lovemaking or sex, Lainey? There's a difference." She looked up at him, her eyes filled with confusion. "Can you live the rest of your life without ever making love?"

"Lots of people do." Her tone was defensive.

Zac leaned against the counter, crossing his ankles. There had to be a reason why she felt like this, and he was beginning to think it hadn't been just the rape. "This man you said you'd been dating back there, Steven Becker. Where is he now?"

Lainey shrugged. "In New York, going places, I imagine. Steven's tall, dark and handsome, thirty years old, an attorney on the move. Up-and-coming, I think we call it."

"And you were close?"

A sigh slid from her parted lips. "I thought we were."

"How did he react?"

She reached for the towel. "At first, he was angry. Angry at the man and at me for wandering about the streets of New York without a bodyguard at my side or a pistol in my purse. Then he was impatient that I wasn't snapping out of it faster."

"Did you love him?"

Leaning alongside him, she gazed out the window. She'd been so desperate for *someone* to love her, when nobody really had, she'd read far more into her relationship with Steven than a more experienced woman would have. But she couldn't bare her soul quite that completely to Zac and risk having him pity her.

"Thinking about Steven since arriving here, I've decided he wasn't as fond of me as he was of being seen with a model, someone who dressed well and looked good. It's the proper image for a young attorney on the rise. I'm sure he had no trouble replacing me. As for me, I was very naive for my age."

Zac bit back an ugly remark. "And he let you go, just like that?"

"No. I left when he tried to...when he wanted to..."

"To take you to bed."

"Yes."

"You'd been lovers before?"

"Yes, and he couldn't understand why I couldn't just put the attack out of my mind and be as before. We hadn't exactly had this great love affair. But I thought he'd at least try to... Never mind." She whirled back to the sink, feeling suddenly embarrassed. She never should have told him anything, because now he was going to keep interrogating her. "Look, I don't want to talk about this anymore. Don't you have work to do?"

The haughty routine. Watching her profile, he could well imagine her in full makeup, in front of the lights and camera, splendidly regal in some expensive gown. He wasn't buying it. "You're beautiful when you're angry," he said quietly. She didn't react, except for a small twitch under her eye.

It was time for a change of pace. Moving fast, Zac dipped both hands in the sudsy water and quickly smeared soap bubbles on her cheeks.

"What! Are you crazy?" she sputtered.

"And beautiful when your face is wet." He scooped more suds and coated both her bare arms. "And beautiful when your arms are wet." As he bent for more, her hands gripped his arms.

"Stop this! What's gotten into you?" But her lips were fighting a smile and her eyes joined in.

Outmaneuvering her, he dabbed a generous handful of soapsuds on her forehead and then her chin. Standing back to admire his handiwork, he grinned. "Yup, just plain beautiful."

He certainly knew how to defuse someone's anger. Lainey struggled with an uncharacteristic impulse, then she gave in. Cupping her hands full of water, she doused the front of his shirt. "You, too, can be beautiful."

Laughing, Zac grabbed a final handful of suds and plopped them onto her head as she scooped more water, splashing his face and shoulders. "You're making a mess in the kitchen," he warned unnecessarily.

"The floor needed washing anyway." She giggled as her last shot brought his hair dripping onto his forehead.

He grabbed her then and swung her around, feeling her shake with the effort to control her chuckles. "Oh, Lainey, Lainey," he said, setting her down and capturing her eyes. "I'd forgotten what fun two people can have just being silly." He rearranged a wet curl near her face. "I haven't laughed like this in a long time. Too long. It feels good. I need to thank you for that."

Lainey wasn't quite certain how to react to his simple statement. Her fingers on his upper arms moved restively as her thoughts sobered. She inhaled his strong masculine scent mingled with the soapy aroma, and found it didn't frighten her.

His arms drew her fractionally nearer. "Lainey," he whispered as he lowered his head toward her. He moved in slow motion, watching her eyes, waiting for that hint of fear that would halt him. When he saw only a warm response, he closed his eyes.

"Hey!" A hard banging on the door was followed by another shout. "Anyone home?" asked the deep voice from the porch.

Pulling back, Zac reluctantly let go of her with a sigh of regret. "That man's timing has always been lousy." Brushing back his wet hair, he walked to the door. "I thought you were going to call before you came."

Colby Winters stepped in, his alert blue eyes surveying the disheveled twosome and the wet floor. "I did call, but you're never home." He looked pointedly at Lainey, who was toweling her arms dry. "Now I see the reason why."

Zac clasped him on the shoulder. "Good to see you, buddy. Lainey, this is Colby Winters. Colby, meet Lainey Roberts."

He'd told her about Colby, the boyhood pal who'd turned into his best friend and partner in the construction company. Every bit as tall as Zac, with muscular shoulders and arms and a head of unruly blond hair, Colby grinned at her and offered his hand. She reached out and found her fingers lost in his big grip. "Hello, Colby," she said, responding to his friendliness.

"I hear you're doing some great things up here, Lainey. I'm glad to finally meet you." He nodded toward Zac. "He been doing a good job for you?"

"Yes, he has." She glanced around at the mess in the kitchen. "We don't usually... That is..." Appalled to find herself nearly blushing, she grabbed the towel to dab at her damp hair. She'd never really been playful with a man and now found herself flustered at being caught. How much, she wondered, had Colby seen through the screen door?

Colby's shrewd gaze swung to Zac. "Didn't know you were such a cutup, Zachariah."

Zac coughed, knowing he was in for some heavy questioning whenever Colby used his full name. "Did Charley tell you I was over here?"

"Sure did. He also told me you only go home long enough to change clothes these days." Only a friendship that went back twenty-five years allowed him to throw Zac a few jabs. Both of them looking like two kids caught with their hands in the cookie jar told Colby far more than their awkward answers. Colby hid his grin with a cough and swung his gaze to the cupboards as he strolled over to inspect the workmanship. "Say, you've really done a beautiful job on these."

"Lainey refinished them," Zac corrected.

"No kidding?" He turned to the first woman in years who had Zac nearly stuttering. "Where'd you learn to do this kind of thing?"

Inordinately pleased, Lainey joined Colby at the counter. "I read a book on refinishing, that's all."

Zac stood back, watching the two of them discuss wood finishes while he struggled with his thoughts. Colby was really more her type, he ruefully admitted. Despite having grown up much as he had, on the wrong side of the tracks and dirt-poor, his friend had an aura of sophistication that Zac had never achieved. Nor had he wished to, until possibly this minute. He could picture the two of them, one so fair and one so dark, dressed in formal clothes, strolling down Fifth Avenue. The image had him balling his hands into fists.

He knew more about Colby Winters than any man alive—knew of his troubled past—yet none of it showed on Colby's tanned all-American face. A ladies' man, that was how he thought of Colby, a love-'em-and-leave-'em guy who'd been badly burned once and was cautious and wary under that easygoing charm. Still,

Zac could see where his raw-boned, rugged good looks and his restless nature might appeal to a woman.

But, he reminded himself, Lainey wasn't in the market for a man. Zac saw her look up at Colby and laugh at something he said, and felt a sudden and unexpected tightening in his gut. He'd never been a jealous man—not with Nancy, certainly. It was not a feeling he was comfortable with.

Colby swung around to Zac. "We could use her in the company, eh, Zac?"

Lainey shook her head. "Thanks, but I've got my hands full right here."

"I think you probably do, at that."

Zac decided it wouldn't be a bad idea to get Colby the hell out of Lainey's kitchen. "Did you bring those papers you wanted to go over?"

"I left them back at your house."

"Lainey, I'm going to go with Colby, but I'll be back sometime this afternoon and get started in the living room."

"Fine. Whenever you're free."

Colby took her hand and gave it a quick squeeze. "I'm really glad we met."

Just weeks ago, she'd have been intimidated by this vibrant, masculine man. Was it Zac's influence that had her smiling back at him so easily? "Are you staying a while?"

He shot Zac a questioning glance. "Doubtful. But I'll be back, now that I know how lovely the scenery is around these parts."

With a hand on his shoulder, Zac guided Colby out, waiting until they were well into the yard before speaking again. "I'm surprised you didn't kiss her hand."

"I thought about it," he said with a grin, "until I saw your face. I gather you two are more than just friends?"

Zac stopped, his face suddenly serious. "I care about Lainey, but she's got some problems to work through. Go easy around her, will you? She's coming off a bad time."

Immediately Colby matched his mood. "Sure, no problem."

Zac resumed walking, then turned as he heard the sound of a powerful engine approaching. Dionne's red Corvette cruised to a stop on the graveled apron. "I want you to meet the doctor I've been telling you about, the one who refers the children to the ranch."

Colby's eyes widened as a striking woman wearing a Kelly-green cotton sweater over white slacks emerged from the low-slung sports car, her green strappy sandals crunching on the stony drive. She slammed the door shut, ran a slim hand through her short red hair and aimed her whiskey-brown eyes at him. She was short—nearly a foot under Colby's own six two—small-boned and unsmiling.

"That's a doctor?" Colby asked, deciding that the long drive up from Detroit had been worth it.

"Yeah. Come on and try not to drool." Zac walked closer to where Dionne stood alongside the Corvette. "Good morning. You missed breakfast."

Dionne shifted her gaze to Zac. "I didn't know I was invited."

"Fresh croissants. There may be one left, if Lainey hasn't beaten you to it."

"I know she loves them." Pointedly, she looked back to the tall blond giant whose eyes had never moved from her.

Zac introduced his partner and stood back as Colby offered her his hand. Somewhat hesitantly, he thought, she shook it. He could almost see her busy mind sizing him up. He'd love to know her conclusions, but knew he never would.

"I've heard a lot about you, Dionne," Colby said. "All good, I might add."

She placed the strap of her bag over her shoulder carefully. "You have me at a disadvantage, then, for I've heard nothing about you."

"Oh, I doubt if anyone has you at a disadvantage for long, Dionne."

Zac watched her eyes frost over at his friend's practiced charm. He shuffled his feet uneasily.

"Where's Lainey?"

"I believe she's mopping the kitchen floor." He gave her an easy grin as he held out the front of his wet shirt. "We had a kind of water fight."

She smiled at that. "Looks like you lost." Dionne moved around them. "Nice meeting you, Mr. Winters. See you later, Zac."

Sticking his hands in the back pockets of his jeans, Colby watched her walk away, the smooth sway of her hips capturing his attention. "Runs hot and cold, doesn't she?"

Zac opened the door to Colby's Jeep Wagoneer. "She's got a quick temper, but she's a good friend and a very caring doctor."

"If you say so." Colby climbed behind the wheel.

"So, what've you got for me?" Zac asked as Colby made a wide turn and headed down the drive.

"A few things that need a signature, the electrician's contract renewal and the problem that won't go away: too much absenteeism due to drinking problems."

"I've been thinking about that last one since we talked on the phone, and I've got a couple of ideas to kick around."

"Great, because I'm fresh out. It's costing us a bundle and other companies are struggling with the same thing. I really don't think firing them is the solution."

"Nor do I." They'd have to come up with a plan soon, and see if they could help their men, to get through to them. Much like he was hoping he could get through to Lainey. Zac smiled, wishing he were a fly on the wall in her kitchen right now, listening to Dionne's impression of Colby.

"A bit arrogant, wouldn't you say?" Dionne asked as she finished her last bite of croissant. "Not at all like Zac."

"Did you think so? I thought he was charming, and he has nice dimples." Lainey took a last swipe at the floor nearest the door and set the mop onto the porch to dry. Crossing to the sink, she washed her hands, then poured each of them fresh coffee before sitting down across from Dionne.

"Children with dimples are charming. Men who have them are lethal, and they damn well know it." Dionne took a sip of coffee, ready for a change of subject. "I understand you and Zac had a water fight this morning."

Elbows propped on the table, Lainey smiled. "Yes, sort of. He said something that irritated me and I clammed up. The next thing I knew, he was rubbing soapsuds from the sink on my face. We wound up dousing each other, then giggling like two kids." Her eyes softened in remembrance. "He thanked me for making me laugh again. Funny, eh?"

Dionne leaned forward. "Not funny. Very nice, I think." She studied her friend a long moment. "You're falling for him, aren't you?"

She never beat around the bush with Dionne. "Yes. And it scares the hell out of me."

"You told him what happened."

Lainey had long ago stopped wondering how Dionne could read her so easily. "Yes."

"And how did he react?"

"Very well, all things considered. But he thinks he can fix me. He told me he cares about me, that I have no reason to fear him, that in time I'll get used to his touch. Meanwhile we work on developing a good friendship."

"How do you feel about what he said?"

Lainey shrugged. "Ambivalent at best. Certainly not hopeful. There are times, I admit, when he touches me that I find I want him to hold me, to kiss me, then other times when I literally freeze, when I shrink back from him. I get so afraid of my own reaction, and of the fact that I know he'll want to move to the next plateau eventually. And that thought terrifies me." She shook her head in puzzlement. "I'm surprised he doesn't just walk away and never return."

Dionne chose her next words carefully. "Do you want him to? It would take the pressure off and you wouldn't have to face your fears every day."

Lainey sat quietly staring out the window, searching her heart for the honest answer. Finally, she shook her head. "No, I don't want him to leave, even if it would be easier."

Dionne let out a sigh of relief.

"But I worry about him," Lainey went on. "It's not fair, stringing him on with the slim possibility that one day I might be what he wants. I feel like I'm using him to get over my problems. He could be investing his time in someone who doesn't need fixing.''

Dionne reached out to touch Lainey's restless hands. "It would seem he wants you and that he doesn't consider time spent with you a waste.''

Lainey looked out the window again, her eyes troubled. "I thought I could avoid this, you know. I thought I'd bury myself in working with the children and the horses—no threats, no hard decisions. I'd gradually forget, and one day I'd wake up and be ready to have a normal relationship without strain.''

"Nothing is that easy, Lainey. Give it time.''

She sighed. "That's what Zac said.''

"Sounds like a smart man to me.'' She reached into her oversize bag and pulled out two manila folders. "Time to get down to business. I have two new students for you, if you can fit them in.''

Lainey leaned forward eagerly. "You bet I can. And I also want to talk with you about that open house for parents you mentioned. Zac thinks it's a good idea, one that might generate a little publicity for the ranch, let people know we're here and what we're trying to accomplish. What do you think?''

"Sure. How soon can you get ready?''

Zac pushed up from his squatting position and checked his watch. Three o'clock had to be the hottest part of a July day. He'd been working on Lainey's living-room floor, replacing damaged boards for over five hours, and he felt hot and sticky. He'd removed his shirt and now used it to wipe his damp face and chest. The two windows were open, but not a breath of air was stirring. Maybe the smart thing to do would be to quit for the day and return in the cooler early-morning hours.

Shoving his tools back into their case, he decided to do just that. He'd worked through lunch today because he'd never gotten back at all yesterday. His conference with Colby had taken them to the dinner hour, and Zac had felt the least he could do was to feed Colby before he started back to Detroit.

Zac closed his tool chest and set it out of the way in the corner. He felt good about Colby's visit. They'd gotten a lot of work done and agreed on several new undertakings. And his partner would be looking into some possibilities for an alcohol rehab program they needed to implement. They were losing too many good men. Colby's father was an alcoholic, so he had first-hand knowledge of that particular road to hell.

Walking outside, Zac looked around. Ben's old Dodge was still there, but he didn't see Lainey anywhere. He'd called her yesterday to let her know of his change in plans, and she hadn't seemed to mind. This morning when he'd arrived later than usual, Ben had told him she'd gone shopping. She'd popped in for a brief few minutes to put away her purchases, then had hurried out to work in the garden. That had been hours ago. He hated to leave without a word, so he went looking.

No one in the garden or the corral area. Only the three horses were in the barn, semidozing in the heat. Damn, it was hot, he thought, slapping at a buzzing fly. A sudden thought occurred to him, and he grinned. Yes, that was the answer to this scorcher.

Moving to Smokey's stall, he unlatched the gate. "Come on, girl," he whispered. "Let's go for a ride."

* * *

It was her favorite spot on the ranch. Lainey sat on a patch of thick grass under a weeping-willow tree, its long leafy arms dangling into the cool stream that crossed her property at the southern end. She lifted her heavy hair off the back of her neck and let the breeze dry her damp skin. Heavenly.

A fish jumped high in the air, silvery in a patch of sunlight, then dived back into the frothy water. She should have brought her suit, she thought, as she lay back peering through the branches at the blue of the sky. But she was too lazy to move and too contented to want to. It was so peaceful here.

She'd spent a hot morning running errands, then a busy afternoon weeding the garden. Ben had told her to leave it for him, but she'd wanted the exercise. And it was a great excuse not to be in the house with Zac's undeniable presence distracting her from any chores she might have considered. But by midafternoon, she'd felt hot and itchy and very much in need of a break.

It was a good half-mile to this point, but she'd enjoyed the stroll, most of it under cover of a variety of trees. Now she lay back and let her mind float free, thinking about the open house she and Dionne had organized yesterday. It was to take place the following Saturday and now that it was in the works, Lainey was getting excited.

She needed to work a bit more with Danny so he'd be ready. And Bobby could use more encouragement; then perhaps he'd try riding on his own around the corral. One of the new ones, Laurie, who at eight years old was in her fifth foster home, was a natural and loved riding. And even Shelly had made great progress with Trixie, though she still wasn't talking. However, the child was bright, cautiously affectionate and even smiled occasionally, mostly when Zac stopped to talk to her.

Hearing the unmistakable sound of a horse's hooves, Lainey sat upright. Peeking through the curtain of willow leaves, her eyes widened.

Speak of the devil. He was on the other side of the narrow creek, downstream a few feet and in full view. Zac looped Smokey's reins over a branch and, as she watched, he peered up and down. Then he began stripping off his clothes.

Grateful that he hadn't spotted her through the thick foliage, Lainey pulled up her legs and propped her crossed arms on them. She should leave, creep quietly away and sneak back to her house. But she sat riveted to the spot, admiring the sun dappling his broad shoulders. Clad only in his briefs, he walked to the water's edge, stooped down and tested the temperature. Standing again, he stretched his arms high and rolled his shoulders, as if easing a cramp. Then he shoved off his briefs and threw them onto the pile of clothes.

She almost gasped aloud. He was beautiful, strong and well proportioned, with a flat stomach, slim hips and muscular legs. Lainey's heart was in her throat as she watched him wade over the rocks into the gently rushing water. Her mouth went dry as he neared the middle, closer to her now, the water only up to his knees. Abruptly he sat down and splashed water on his shoulders and over his head. Lainey wiped her damp hands on her jeans without tearing her eyes from him.

Would he be angry if he knew she was watching him? Perhaps not. Perhaps he'd rise, reach out his hand and draw her into the cool water with him. She felt herself tremble as she pictured herself running her hands over his smooth skin, free to touch him with her hands, her lips. She would lean closer and kiss him, leisurely explore his mouth. And then he would reach out and unbutton her blouse and . . .

Breathing hard, Lainey closed her eyes and hid her cheek on her bent knees. She had no problem thinking of touching him. But when she thought about his hands on her, removing her clothes, touching her intimately, the anxiety returned. She seemed unable to carry the fantasy that final step forward.

Taking a deep breath, she looked back toward Zac. He was nearly prone, his head bent back, obviously enjoying the cool water. How she wished she had the courage to jump up and join him, to see his eyes light up when he saw her, to anticipate with joy a union she both craved and feared.

She'd had but one lover, and Steven had been clinically adequate but lacking in warmth, in passion. Lainey had suspected during those months that she had untapped passion hidden inside her, and that the right man could set it free. But now, she was less certain. Perhaps it had only been wishful thinking and she was one of those people who was destined never to reach the heights she'd heard so much about. Had the man in the alley taken that from her, too?

Zac shook the water from his hair and slowly stood. He glanced in her direction, almost as if he knew she were there, and Lainey held her breath. Then he turned and walked to the shore. She slumped to the grass, totally drained.

By the time she looked up again, he was dressed and untying Smokey's reins. With a fluid movement, he

swung atop the huge black horse and nudged her toward the path through the trees. Lainey listened to the
receding footsteps as she waited for her heart to slow its
pounding cadence.

Chapter Eight

The cameras were clicking. Zac leaned against the fence and watched the proud parents snapping pictures of their children. The open house was going well.

He watched as shy little Bobby gave an honest-to-goodness big smile as he rounded the bend in the corral atop Trixie, to the applause of several onlookers. A bright blue long-sleeved shirt covered his thin arms with the scars that would never go away, but Zac could still see them. Everyone here knew that each child demonstrating new skills was special; that they'd been through a great deal in their young lives and that each accomplishment had been hard won. So relatives, friends and foster parents were generous with their praise and their smiles. The kids in turn were flushed with pride—a new feeling to most of them. Zac felt a knot of warmth spread deep inside as he saw Lainey help Bobby dismount.

She'd worked tirelessly for the past week and a half preparing for this event. She'd spent extra hours with each child, guiding, reassuring, building up their confidence. She'd told Zac to forget working on the house for now, and had kept both him and Ben busy adding finishing touches to the barn, the yard and the fenced areas.

This morning, she'd had him stringing colorful balloons around the barn doorways and hanging streamers along the fence. She'd hired two teenage girls from a nearby riding academy for the afternoon to help with the horses and children. And Ben, minus his bib overalls and plug of chewing tobacco, was in charge of directing the parking.

Smokey, Trixie and Juno had been scrupulously groomed, though Juno's participation would be limited, due to her condition. Lainey had added the final embellishment by deftly twining bright ribbons in each horse's mane. After all, they were all females, she'd explained, and a female feels better when she feels pretty.

If that was the case, then Lainey must feel very good indeed, Zac thought as he propped a booted foot on the bottom rung of the fence. She had on a yellow one-piece jumpsuit that wasn't two sizes too large for her for a change. It wasn't baggy or too snug, hinting at the soft swelling of her breasts and outlining the sweet curve of her thighs. His imagination easily removed the outfit, and he wondered if she wore silk or lace beneath, or nothing at all. No, not Lainey. She wasn't that confident—at least not yet.

She caught him studying her as she sent Shelly and Trixie around the track, and her eyes were shiny and bright. He kept his gaze steady, letting her see the pride he had in her, and saw a rosy blush creep into her cheeks. The look held, and for Zac, the horses and people disappeared, and there was only Lainey staring at him across a green field; Lainey with her jet-black hair, Lainey whose eyes told him what her lips could not. Slowly, reluctantly, she turned back to watch Shelly, and he felt his breath tremble.

He was lost. Lost to a woman he'd known only a few weeks and kissed only twice. Lost to huge violet eyes and small, hesitant hands. Lost like a teenager staring across a crowded room at the prom queen he didn't know how to win over. Patience, old man, he told himself. Entire wars were won by patient strategy. Intellectually, he was patient, but physically his all-too-frequently aroused body was quickly growing impatient.

With an exasperated sigh, he tore his gaze from Lainey and found himself being scrutinized by Dionne's thoughtful brown eyes. In direct contrast to Lainey, her friend wore a severely cut black suit, looking a shade schoolmarmish. He waited while she pushed away from the fence and stepped closer.

"You two have done a marvelous job on this open house," Dionne said with admiration.

"Lainey did most of it."

She gestured toward the refreshment table offering cold soft drinks and a variety of cookies. "Even goodies. Do you hire out?"

Zac laughed. "Can you imagine Lainey, who hates to cook, baking ten batches of cookies?" He shook his head, visualizing her last evening as he'd helped her mix the dough, flour dots on her nose and her cheeks flushed from the heat in the kitchen, cursing the temperamental old stove and vowing to replace it very soon.

Afterward they'd sat on her newly refinished living-room floor and munched on chocolate-chip cookies while sharing a glass of milk. He hadn't touched her all evening, not once; yet she'd touched him, inside where it counted more. She'd told him about a young school-mate named Dolly, a girl she'd envied with the intensity of the very young. Dolly had come from a real family, one where the mother baked cookies and the father came in to steal a couple while they were warm. A wide-eyed eight-year-old, Lainey had watched them smile and share a hug right there in the kitchen in front of Dolly and her. And she'd wondered why she'd never seen an affectionate gesture pass between her parents.

And Zac had wanted to gather her to him and kiss away the hurtful memories. But she'd changed the subject quickly and told him a funny story next, about a play she'd been in at school, when her costume had split down the back as she'd taken a bow, and how mortified she'd been as she'd backed off the stage. She'd had him laughing again, and it had felt good. But then, just being with Lainey felt good. Perhaps too good to last.

Zac brought his attention back to Dionne and realized she was frowning as she searched his face. He cleared his throat. "It's going well, don't you think?"

"Yes," she agreed distractedly, worry lines creasing her forehead. "So, is your work here pretty well finished?"

"There's still a lot to do in the house."

"I thought perhaps, when your partner was here last week, that he was trying to convince you to return. I mean, you must have a lot of work piling up back at your office."

Zac watched Lainey stretch her arms out to Shelly as she dismounted, saw the child hug her in that fierce way she had. "I'm not ready to leave just yet."

"Because of Lainey?"

He turned back to Dionne. "You don't approve?" Not that it would stop him, but he was curious.

"As a matter of fact, I do. With reservations."

"Which are?"

"She's falling in love with you."

Zac raised an eyebrow, afraid to let his hopes soar. "She told you that?"

"She didn't have to."

"You're clairvoyant? Comes with the job, I suppose."

"I don't believe Lainey's admitted it to herself yet. What are you going to do about it?"

Zac shook his head as he turned his back to the fence. "Damned if I know."

Dionne turned away to watch Lainey, who was chatting with several of the parents at the far end of the fence, her arm around one child while she held another's hand. She looked more confident, even happy.

"Lainey's made great progress, with your help, but..."

"But she has a long way to go."

"Yes. Will you run out of patience before you run out of time?" As he shook his head, she raised her hand. "Don't be too quick to answer. I told you before, these things take a while, and we don't know how long. The wrong move, and she could still backslide."

He nodded, knowing she was right. "If only she would trust me."

"We all have difficulty deciding whom to trust."

Zac ran a hand through his hair in frustration. "I just wish I knew how to reach her, to break down all her barriers." He sent her a look of appeal. "Any advice, Doctor?"

Dionne waved to the parents of one of her patients, then shifted her attention back to Zac. She liked this man, liked his openness and his honesty. If anyone could get through to Lainey, he would be her first choice. "My educated guess would be that Lainey will reach out to you when her fear of losing you is greater than her fear of her reactions over becoming close. She has to be willing to risk again, because all reaching out for love is a risk. How good are you at waiting?"

"I care too much to give up on her."

"Good, because it may take all you have to give." She smiled up at him warmly. "I want to say I think you're quite a man, Zac Sinclair."

He guessed that compliments didn't come too easily from this careful woman. "Thank you for that. I happen to think you're quite a woman, too. And Colby couldn't keep his eyes off you."

She felt her back stiffen and dropped her gaze. "He's not my type, thanks all the same."

"Who is your type, Dionne?"

She shook her head and ran a hand through her wind-tossed hair. "We've done enough analyzing for one day. Let's save me for another time."

It was the answer he'd expected. Zac glanced over at a tall man he'd noticed earlier, snapping pictures with what looked like a very expensive camera. "Say, which child's relative is that man over there? He's taken a ton of pictures today."

Dionne followed his gaze, then frowned. "That's Tim Collins from the local paper. Did Lainey invite him?"

"I suggested it wouldn't hurt to get a little press coverage, so she might have. Why? Is he a problem?"

"Mmm, I don't think so. It's highly doubtful that he'd connect Lainey to her New York persona. It would upset her if he did, if her mother learned where she is."

"I'll go talk to him."

She stopped him with a touch on the arm. "Perhaps we should just let it go. Something you say may pique his interest and send him poking around for answers."

"You're probably right," Zac agreed.

Suddenly Shelly appeared at Dionne's side. "Hi, sweetheart," she said as the child's hand slipped into her own. "I was watching and you did beautifully." A shy smile appeared on Shelly's wan face. "Zac, I think we're going to go over and sample the cookies."

"You go ahead," he said, his eyes on the dark-haired woman walking toward him. "I'm going to wait for Lainey." He walked along the fence to the gate and met her just inside. Taking her hands in his, he squeezed both. "You did a great job. I've heard some wonderful comments."

"I'm glad," Lainey said, releasing a nervous breath. "Glad the parents are pleased, and glad it's over."

Unable to resist, he raised her hands and kissed her fingertips.

Wrinkling her nose, she made as if to pull away. "I smell like leather and horses, I'm afraid." Embarrassment warred with pleasure as she felt his warm mouth on her skin.

But he wouldn't let her go. "You taste terrific, better than chocolate-chip cookies." Zac watched her face soften and knew she was remembering last evening when they'd shared cookies and confidences. He wanted to recapture that intimacy, and he wanted her all to himself. He nodded toward the crowd gathered around the refreshment table. "How long before this is over? I'd like to take you out to dinner tonight. Someplace quiet, to celebrate your fine showing."

A dinner out. It had been so long. Lainey found the thought very appealing. "I'd like that, if I can shower and change first."

He held her away while his silver gaze slid down the length of her. "Only if you wear something that fits as well as this."

Feeling the heat move into her face, Lainey took back her hands. "I think I'd better mingle awhile before everyone leaves." At his nod, she started to walk away.

Warm. She felt very warm, in a good way, and it had nothing to do with the heat of the late-afternoon sun. Giving in to a smile, she joined the crowd at the table.

Lainey came out of her bedroom and found Zac sitting in her rocker exactly where she'd left him when she'd gone in to shower and change. "I've been thinking about what you said, and I don't feel that Tim Collins would think to connect me with modeling. I mean, a middle-aged man working on a small-town weekly paper wouldn't read fashion magazines, would he?"

She had on a simple white cotton sundress and low-heeled shoes, and he couldn't take his eyes from her. "You look terrific."

He had a way of stopping her in her tracks. "Thank you." She took in his tan slacks and short-sleeved black shirt, admiring the combination and the fit. "I've never seen you in anything except jeans." Except the afternoon she'd seen him in nothing at all. She felt her cheeks flame at the memory. "Very nice." Made clumsy by her own thoughts, Lainey gathered her hair back and slid a pin into place.

"Don't," Zac interrupted. Questioning eyes swung to him. "Don't pin it up. Wear it down, please." He remembered the first day on her porch when she'd whipped off her scarf and let the wind take her hair, stunning him from across a hundred yards.

Ever more nervous, Lainey removed the pin and shook back her hair. Maybe this dinner hadn't been such a good idea, she thought. In the flush of excitement over the success of the open house she'd accepted, and now wondered if she'd been wise. His eyes were a deep gray and a shade too serious for comfort. But how could she back out now, without hurting his feelings?

"About that reporter," she began again.

Zac stood and walked to the window, suddenly thinking it was awfully close in the small room. "I think he'll do a good article along with pictures on the ranch, and do you no harm."

"Yes. Me, too. He seemed very nice. I'll get my purse and we can go." As she headed for her room, the bed-side phone began to ring. "I'll just be a minute."

But it was more like five before she returned, white-faced and trembling. Zac took her arm and led her to the rocker. "What is it?"

"That was Anne Blackburn. My father's had a heart attack." She sat back, clasping her hands together. "The only number they had for me was Anne's phone. He's in a hospital in Detroit and he's critical."

Zac crouched beside her, covering her hands with his. "What do you want to do?"

"Anne said he's asking for me. Oh, God." Lainey closed her eyes. Why did this have to happen now?

"Do you want to go to him?"

She let out a shaky breath. "No. But I have to."

Zac rose. "Get your things. I'll drive you."

"You needn't bother. I—"

"You're in no shape to drive. Where are your keys so we can lock up?"

She didn't protest further, nor again when Zac said that her Mustang would make better time than his truck. Seated alongside him, skimming along the highway at dusk in the powerful little car, Lainey felt a weary numbness settle over her limbs. Yet her thoughts raced frantically.

She looked so pale, so dazed, Zac thought as he glanced over. She was shredding a tissue in her lap and staring straight ahead. He wondered what she was seeing, certain it wasn't the road before them. "Would your father have had the hospital try to find your mother, as well?"

"I doubt it," Lainey said softly. "I don't even know why he wants me there. He all but threw me out the last time I saw him."

"When was that? After you left New York?"

"Yes. After the hospital released me, I guess I thought it would take a week or ten days and I'd be all right, like getting over the flu. I was wrong. My body healed, but mentally I sank into this depression I couldn't seem to climb out of." She remembered how she'd been then, without the energy or inclination to get out of bed.

"They put me on some pills, but they didn't help. I couldn't eat, I didn't sleep. My mother dragged me out for walks, telling me the fresh air would do me good. But I was terrified outside, looking over my shoulder, seeing that awful face on every passing man. So I went back to bed.''

"But you didn't stay there?"

"I couldn't. My mother tried to be patient, I suppose, but it simply isn't in her. I couldn't face going back to work so I turned down the jobs Anne offered. I hated disappointing everyone, but I couldn't stay."

Zac reached over and took her hand. She held on, feeling as if she might shatter into a million pieces. "I left New York and went back to my father's house. I hadn't been there in ten years.''

"But he'd visited you in New York?"

"No, never. He didn't approve of the work I did. Never had. He'd hated the way my mother had groomed me for that life, and I'm sure that had a lot to do with why he divorced her. And when I came back and told him about the attack, he felt justified in his opinion.''

"I'm sure a lot of parents don't approve of things their kids do. But surely when they're hurt, when they need them . . ." He found her story incomprehensible.

"Not necessarily. My father told me that he wasn't surprised about the attack, that I should have known that a woman who made her living capitalizing on her looks instead of using her brains would end up regretting it.'' Swallowing the rush of emotion, she turned to his profile almost defiantly. "So there you have it, the rest of my heartwarming story. Why would you want anything to do with a woman who could inspire such loyalty and devotion from her very own father?''

Zac heard the pain and he heard the challenge, and he needed to stop both the only way he knew how. A quick glance in the rearview mirror told him no cars were close behind him. Swiftly he pulled over onto the shoulder of the road, rammed the gearshift into park and turned to her.

He saw his hands tremble as his fingers framed her face and drew her close to him, so close he could see in the dim light from the dash that her pupils had widened. "So your parents aren't perfect and Steven isn't worth your trust. You can't change any of that—not by dwelling on it, nor by looking for flaws in yourself as to why they acted that way. None of what they did was your fault. We're not responsible for the actions of others. They are."

He noticed a small tear gathered in the corner of her eye and smoothed it away with his thumb. "They're not worth even one tear. You are decent and loving and bright and beautiful. And you deserve every happiness this life has to offer."

He could see she wanted desperately to believe him. "You're going to be all right, Lainey. No matter how many rotten people have touched your life, you're going to be all right. And I care about you."

"No, Zac . . ." She started to struggle.

"Yes, Lainey, yes." He cursed the gearshift as he tried to draw her closer. "Don't tell me not to because it's too late." He bent his head and touched his lips to hers.

He wanted to go easy, not to frighten her, but adrenaline pumped through him in his anxiety to convince her. His hands at her back pulled her toward him as his mouth moved over hers in a kiss that would not be denied. She held herself rigid for a long moment. Then, to his surprise, she sighed and opened to him.

Passion rose, hot and insistent, while desire had him tightening. He thrust his hands into the thickness of her hair, running his fingers along her scalp and feeling her answering shiver. His mouth pillaged, plundered, ravaged, and still she held on.

Now she was kissing him the way he'd dreamed she would, her tongue tangling with his, her hands on his shoulders, bunching his shirt. Her heady scent teased him, spurring him on as he took her deeper. This was what he'd know was lying dormant inside her. This was what he'd been hoping to set free. This was what he'd lain awake nights longing for, since the first time he'd sampled the sweetness of her lips.

Lainey was flying high and wide, racing along on a rush of newly awakened desire. Some other woman had gotten inside her and was now in control. And that woman wanted this man, needed his kiss, to warm all the dark places inside her soul. That woman longed to taste again the flavors of his mouth, the ones she'd been craving since that first brief encounter in the barn. That woman was passionate and loving, and that woman was also Lainey Roberts—maybe the best part of her.

Zac's lips traveled over her face, and she heard herself moan softly. Her eyes, her cheeks, the pulse point in her throat—there was nowhere his heated mouth didn't linger. How had she thought she could live without this; this wondrous feeling that had her skin heating and her blood racing? How had she lived so long without ever knowing there was this?

Finally, breathing hard, her chest heaving, Lainey drew back. She saw that his hands were none too steady, either, as he struggled to catch his breath. A long moment later, she raised her eyes to his. Her lips felt thick and they trembled, but she gave him a small smile. "You have a unique way of making your point."

Zac searched her face for signs of fear, or of anger, and found none. "I didn't mean to frighten you, to be rough—"

She raised her fingertips to his lips to stop his unnecessary explanation. "I've never been kissed like that. Never. I wasn't frightened. More like overwhelmed, but not afraid."

Gently he kissed her fingers. "I'm glad I don't scare you. I know we have to go, but could we maybe take this up where we left off a little later?"

"I'd like that," Lainey said, and found she meant it. For a few minutes, she'd almost forgotten their reason for being on the road. She had to face Edward Roberts.

As Zac pulled back onto the highway, she reached into her purse for her mirror, thinking to repair her face. In the patchy light, the woman who looked back at her was someone she'd not seen before, not quite like this. Hair disheveled, cheeks rosy, lips swollen from kisses she could still taste. But it was the eyes that mesmerized her—still dark with lingering arousal, sensually eager.

Oh, God, could it be? Was she finally going to be all right?

She'd always thought of him as big—tall, lean and tan, rigid and unbending, wrapped in a cloak of authority. The man lying in the hospital bed, hooked up to an endless array of beeping and blinking machines, was pale and nearly gaunt, his cheeks hollow and sunken. The hands lying so still on the stark white sheets were almost bony, the freckled skin taut and dry. Only the mouth was the same: thin and disapproving.

Lainey took her father's hand in her own and leaned down, struggling with a rush of garbled emotions. Ten years. Not so very long, yet a lifetime ago. This unbending man had given her life, yet she hardly knew him. Had he felt joy at one time, known spontaneous laughter, experienced love? Or had he always felt secure with only his righteous indignation to keep him warm? She wished she felt more, felt something other than pity.

As she studied his face, his eyes slowly opened, pale blue and watery, and he blinked several times. The harsh lighting of the intensive-care unit took a moment to get used to. The nurse in the glassed-in cubicle had warned her that she could stay only ten minutes and that he might not respond to her. She'd also told her that the doctor would discuss her father's prognosis with her afterward.

Lainey squeezed his hand as he focused on her. "Hello, Dad," she whispered softly.

He tried to speak, but the tubes in his nose seemed to bother him, and she heard only a raspy sound.

"It's all right. You don't have to talk."

Edward Roberts frowned and tried to clear his throat, but the effort seemed too great. He saved his strength for his speech instead. "Wasn't sure you'd come," he finally managed.

Lainey blinked, recalling how strong, how vibrant his voice had always been. "I'm here." What did he want of her? she wondered. Even in the best of times, they'd never been close. He'd always kept himself apart from his wife and daughter, as if neither quite measured up to his expectations. Yet now, he seemed anxious to say more. She leaned closer.

"Not your fault," Edward said, gripping her hand tightly. "The unhappiness in our house. Your mother and I, we were wrong for each other. The life I offered her was never enough for Irene. She always wanted more. When she took you from me, I learned to hate." He took in a shaky breath.

Emotions churning, she patted his hand. "That all happened a long time ago. Don't tire yourself now."

He moved his head, clearly annoyed. "No. I...I need to say this. I hurt you recently when I didn't mean to. I wanted to lash out at Irene, for dragging you away, and instead, I harmed you. You needed me and I wasn't there for you. When someone we care about reaches out to us and we turn away, it's like sticking a knife in them. I know that now. I'm sorry, Lainey. So sorry."

She saw tears on his cheeks and fought back her own. "It's all right, Dad."

"Forgive me, please?"

Overwhelmed, unable to speak, she nodded, clutching his hand in both of hers.

"Pride, Lainey. It's a terrible thing. And so is stubbornness." He coughed, and the sound seemed filled with pain. "I was wrong and too stubborn to admit any of it. If I had it to do over..."

"We all make mistakes." Lainey dabbed at her own eyes, absorbing words she'd never thought she'd hear from her father.

"Too late now, I know," Edward whispered. "Too late."

"No." With a tissue, she dried his sallow cheeks. "It's never too late to start over."

"Watch out for your mother, Lainey. She's a viper. I'm not the father I should have been, but that woman will devour you."

He'd been hurt, Lainey knew. It was the bitterness talking. "Don't worry about me, Dad."

"But I do." His trembling hand touched her face lightly. "Did we mess you up too badly, Lainey? I hope not." His eyes drifted closed. "So tired."

"You rest now." Hearing the nurse approaching, Lainey leaned down and kissed her father's cheek. "I'll be back." Gently she laid his hand back down. Straightening, she thanked the nurse and turned toward the door.

She needed some air and to find the doctor. And she needed Zac.

Twenty minutes later, having taken care of the first two, she went looking for the third. She found Zac in the ICU waiting room, sitting in a chair, his long legs stretched out, his head leaning back, fast asleep. Smiling, Lainey walked close and paused for a moment to just look at him.

It had been an emotional day, from the nervous energy of the open house, to the stunning encounter while parked at the side of the highway, and winding up with her father asking for forgiveness. And here sat the best part, a man the very sight of whom sent warm waves through her. Sleep softened the lines of his face, made him look younger, his hair curling boyishly down onto his forehead. But there was nothing boyish about him—not the way he accepted responsibility or the way he handled himself. Or the way he kissed.

His mouth was slightly open, his full lips inviting even in repose. What would he do if she leaned down and kissed him? No, she wasn't quite that bold. Not yet. But perhaps one day. Zac was shoring up her confidence daily. She touched his arm lightly.

Zac's eyes flew open, and he straightened. "How is he?"

Lainey took the chair next to him and sighed. "He looks terrible, sounds worse and he...he cried. But the doctor says that amazingly enough, if he follows orders, he should recover."

"A second chance. Sometimes we get lucky."

"I'd stopped believing in second chances." She raised her eyes to his and let them finish the thought for her. *Until you.*

"Don't stop. Anything's possible." He stood. "Ready to leave?"

"Yes. Take me home, please."

Reaching for her hand, Zac led her to the elevators.

Lainey swallowed the last bite and licked each finger. "Mmm, that was the best sandwich I've had in ages."

Zac smiled. "You're a junk-food junkie," he told her as he gathered up the papers from their take-out dinner and stuffed them into the sack. Leaning back against her living-room wall, he arranged the pillow more comfortably and sipped his milk shake.

"If you'd been told since you were twelve not to even walk through a fast-food restaurant—bad for your complexion, clogs your arteries and loaded with calories—you'd relish junk food, too."

"You don't relish it, lady. You revere it."

She shrugged, stretching out lazily. "Everyone's got a weakness." After such a tumultuous day, she was surprised to find herself lazily content. She'd slept on the ride home, hardly aware when Zac had pulled into a drive-in restaurant for their dinner, and now felt rested, sated and lethargic. Her thoughts, still restless, returned to her father.

"I wonder if he's going to include Irene in his need to mend fences," she mused.

Zac didn't have to ask who she meant. "Hard to say. From what you told me of your conversation, he doesn't sound like he has any kind thoughts of her."

"I guess not. So many mismatched people wasting their lives chained together, messing up their kids, spending a lifetime holding grudges."

He moved closer and took her hand, still somewhat surprised when she inched closer and twined her fingers with his. "Then you honestly have forgiven him?"

"Yes, but it's not the noble act you seem to imply. Forgiving is easier than forgetting. But I've come to realize that people can't be what you want them to be, even if they're your parents. We have to accept them for what they are, imperfections and all."

"That's a two-way street. Do you think your father will now accept you and the life you chose to live?"

"Maybe. Now that I've left that life, he'll probably approve of what I'm doing here. Surprisingly, it doesn't matter all that much to me whether he does or not. Isn't that odd? When I stopped needing his approval, he came around."

"A brush with death can do that to a person—cause them to take a long, hard look at their values."

Lainey thought of her mother and had her doubts. "Some people. Others simply aren't capable of admitting their mistakes, not ever." She felt his lips trailing up her bare arm and shivered, not having noticed he was so near. "What are you doing?"

"Contemplating dessert." He leaned forward and pressed his face into the fragrance of her hair. "Remember what you said in the car, that you'd like to pick up where we left off?''

It seemed like such a long time ago. "I don't know, Zac. It's getting late."

Moving her hair aside, he nuzzled her neck. "Not yet midnight. Even Cinderella wouldn't end her day just now."

Decision time, and she'd invited it. Ambivalence had her twisting her hands together.

It was time, Zac decided. Time to press, just a little, and see what she would do. With a lithe movement, he had her lying on the floor, her head on the pillow, and himself stretched out alongside her. "Let me love you, Lainey. Let me show you how it can be between two people who care about each other."

"Zac, I don't know."

Angling toward her, he touched his lips to hers, gently but firmly cutting off further comment. Where before he'd devoured, now he worshiped with gentle pressure, brushing back and forth, lingering at the corners, coaxing the sensitive flesh to respond. Bracing himself with an elbow on the floor, he touched only her mouth. With his tongue, he traced her lips, up and around, his movements unhurried. Teasingly he nipped her lower lip, then placed a healing kiss on the spot.

He moved his tongue into her mouth and coaxed hers into a breathtaking dance. Lainey moaned, and her hands left the floor, curling around his back. Only then did Zac lean lower and slide his hands into her rich hair, as he'd been longing to do. Heart racing, he took his mouth from hers and trailed along her smooth chin, then down the lovely curve of her throat. He tasted the pulse pounding there, pounding for him.

Languid and lazy, Lainey drifted as he rained kisses on her neck, sending shivers shooting through her with his wet tongue in her ear, then traced the width of her collarbone with the same drowsy pace. She raised her knees, unable to lie still any longer, pleasure and need mingling to make her body restless.

Lifting from her, his hands moved to the row of buttons down the front of her dress as his mouth came back to hers. The kiss started off gentle, then he sucked in an impatient breath and took her deeper. So lost in feeling was she that she was unaware he had her dress open until she felt hard fingers close around one aching breast.

"Oh," she murmured into his mouth, pulling away.

Immediately he eased back, his touch growing lighter, and she let out a relieved sigh. But her traitorous body seemed to grow fuller, to reach out for the hand that no longer was pleasuring her. Lainey made herself relax, take deep breaths, tamp down the shiver of fright that beckoned.

"It's all right," Zac whispered. "I'll slow down."

Was that what she wanted? She wished she knew. She wanted his hands on her, she wanted the fulfillment her body craved, yet already she was having trouble breathing. She closed her eyes, warding off the memory that would start the trembling.

He seemed to know, contenting himself with stroking her arms while she calmed. She had to do this, she *could* do this. Reaching up, she pulled his mouth back to hers. This kiss was long and soothing, then gradually shifting and building. Not fully distracted this time, she felt his hands move inside the opening of her dress. And felt herself stiffen again.

"No, please." She pushed, then struggled to sit up, her hands drawing together the front folds of her dress. "I can't do this, Zac. I just can't."

Disappointment had him moving slowly. "It's all right." He sat up and away from her, giving her the time she needed. What had he done wrong? he asked himself. He struggled with impatience, with frustration, with a churning need.

Unable to meet his eyes, she finished fastening the buttons. "No, it isn't all right. I hate doing this to you." She choked back the sob that wanted to break through. "I'm so sorry."

From behind her, he touched her shoulder briefly, then stood. "It's been a long day and you've been through a lot."

Eyes downcast, she shook her head. "It's not the day. It's me. Don't you see?"

"Maybe after a good night's sleep, you'll . . ."

"No, I don't think so."

Swinging about, Zac hit the wall once, very hard, the sound reverberating through the near-empty room. He saw her flinch, but he was past caring. Rubbing his knuckles, he cursed under his breath. "All right, Lainey. You win. You'd rather stay here and wrestle with your demons alone than let me help you beat them. I care about you, but I won't take the lead again. If anything happens between us, *you*'ll have to come after *me*."

He walked to the door, his footsteps echoing hollowly. Hand on the knob, he turned back to her. "If you change your mind, you know where I live." And then he was gone.

She sat there a long while, huddled on the floor, her arms wrapped around her legs and her head resting on her knees. She tried to keep her mind blank, but it wouldn't work. Pictures of Zac kept intruding, as he'd been the first day she'd met him in the barn, confident and a little arrogant. She remembered how tender he'd been with her when she'd gotten herself drunk and rambled on about lost opportunities and a fragile rose. And she saw him at her sink, dripping wet and playful, thanking her for making him laugh again. And she felt again his mouth on hers this evening in the car, the rush of need he brought to her, the desire she saw in his gray eyes. For her. And she'd sent him away.

She cared for Zac. She was certain, and the shock of admitting it stunned her. But she'd let fears keep her from him. And perhaps pride and a streak of stubbornness. Terrible things, as her father had told her tonight, and he should know. Would she need a life-threatening illness before she would admit she'd been wrong?

When someone you love reaches out to you and you turn away, it's like sticking a knife in them, Edward Roberts had also said. She'd stuck a knife in Zac, all right, and twisted it. He'd had every right to expect her to at least try to get past her fears and let him show her how to love again. But at the first uneasy sign, she'd frozen and stopped fighting. Just go slowly, Dionne always said, and you can conquer this, if you want to badly enough. Did she?

The answer was yes. She hadn't know how badly until today. Quickly, Lainey jumped up and went to the bathroom to rinse her face and comb her hair. Grabbing her keys, she hurried to the Mustang, hoping she wasn't too late.

The house was dark. He'd gone somewhere else, to someone else. She'd put him off once too often. Pushing aside her irrational thoughts, she ran around to the back.

A light was on in the enclosed porch as she stepped hesitantly onto the stoop, but she could see no sign of life. Did he have a housekeeper who would turn her away? Where was Willie? If only Zac would be home, she'd try to make it up to him.

Gathering her courage, she knocked hard. It seemed an eternity before she heard footsteps approaching. Wearing only a towel tied around his middle, his hair still wet from his shower, Zac swung open the door. His expression was more curious than annoyed, and she took strength from that.

Swallowing hard, Lainey looked up at him. "I care about you, but I'm so afraid. Please help me."

Chapter Nine

Zac held out his hand, and she put her own in it, allowing him to draw her inside. Lainey heard him close the door, but kept her eyes downcast. He hadn't said a word, not one; or had she simply not heard over the hammering of her heart? *Please, God, don't let this be a mistake.*

"I was just going to pour myself a brandy," Zac said, watching her clutch her keys in a white-knuckled grip. "Would you like some?"

Maybe it would give her the courage she needed. "Yes, please." She followed him through the archway into the kitchen, where he snapped on a light and moved to the counter.

"I didn't hear your car," he said, getting down two snifters.

Nervously she set her flashlight and keys on the edge of the counter. "I parked out front."

Zac frowned. "Not such a good idea, out past midnight all alone."

She hadn't thought of her safety, only of finding him. "I needed to see you, to tell you." She took a deep, bracing breath. "I'm ready for you to make love to me. Right now."

He set down the brandy bottle and looked into her pale, determined face. Like a woman facing the guillotine. Very flattering. "Right now?"

"Yes, please. Could we get it over with?" Her lips trembled in her haste to rush him.

Zac moved to her. "I'm afraid I can't make love on command."

At last, Lainey raised her eyes to his. "You're making fun of me." She gave a shake to her head. "I shouldn't have come."

"No, I'm not, and I'm very glad you're here. But making love isn't something we need to get over quickly. It's not bitter medicine, but more like a reward. We need to go slowly, not rush things." He held out her glass. "Drink some of this." He watched her take a cautious sip, then make a face.

"Not as good as your grandmother's, but it's all I have," he said as he wondered how to play this new hand he'd been dealt.

He'd been angry, disappointed and frustrated when he'd come home from her place. He'd tossed down a splash of brandy, then jumped into the shower, trying to put things into perspective. She'd been trying, and he felt angry with himself that he'd lost patience with her. He should have had more control; yet holding her, touching her, letting his need build only to have to put the brakes on still again was taking its toll on his mind and body.

Coming out of the shower, he'd been asking himself if maybe he shouldn't just back off for a while. Perhaps he'd overestimated Lainey's feelings for him. Then he'd heard the knocking at his back door.

"Your house is nice," Lainey commented, looking around, trying for normalcy.

"Thanks."

"Where's Willie?"

"Down at Charley's cabin, I think." Small talk. He wasn't in the mood for it. "What changed your mind?" he asked softly.

Lainey twirled the brandy snifter between both hands, staring into its dark contents. "I don't want to lose you."

It was the closest she'd come to saying what was in her heart. Setting down his glass, he stepped closer. "Lainey, you won't lose me, and you don't have to make love with me if you don't want to."

She raised eyes, dark blue and troubled, to his. "But I want to, I really do. It's just that I...I..."

"You're afraid."

"Not in the way you think. I'm afraid of how I'll react, of scaring you off. I'm worried I'll disappoint you."

"You won't. You couldn't." He set her glass aside, then reached to tenderly stroke her cheek. "Did you mean what you said at the door?"

"That I care about you? Yes. I didn't realize how much until tonight when you walked away." She reached for his hand, noticing the bruise where he'd smashed it into the wall. Absently, she caressed the darkened skin. "Dionne and I had a lot of talks about my wanting to bury any sexual feelings I might have in order not to face my fears. She told me that one day I'd be ready, that my fear of losing someone I cared about would be stronger than my other fears, and that I'd be willing to take a chance. I feel I'm ready to take that chance, if you are."

His answer was to take her hand and lead her down a dim hallway. Heart pounding, Lainey thought it was the longest walk of her life. Spotty moonlight drifted in through the two windows and onto a huge four-poster bed of dark pine. The light from his bedside lamp was soft and inviting. The room had warmth and a kind of restless energy, like the man watching her.

She ran her hand along the smooth wood of the bed-post. "This is quite a bed."

Zac stepped close to her. "I've spent a lot of hours in that bed, thinking about you, picturing you here. You can't know how many times I've awakened from a dream—a dream where I've been making love to you, and you wanted me as much as I want you."

His words gave her the freedom to touch him, and she placed her hand on his chest, over his heart. She felt the strength there, the steady beat. "I've lain in my bed, too, wondering what it would be like if you were to walk in suddenly. Wondering what it would be like if you were to touch me and I would be unafraid."

"Are you afraid of making love?"

"I'm not sure I've ever made love at all. I've had sex but, as you pointed out once, there's a difference." She raised her other hand to his chest and took a step closer. "Being with you feels very different from anything I've known."

He slid his arms around her, but held her loosely. "Being with you feels better than anything I've known." Lowering his head, he kissed her, fighting the urge to crush her to him.

His mouth was so soft, so giving. He was tasting, teasing, and she grew impatient. Sending her tongue past his lips, she found his and drew it into her own mouth. She felt his arms tighten around her then, and felt the hard evidence of his desire move against her as their bodies became aligned. Unable to prevent her reaction, she stiffened in his arms and he immediately pulled back.

"We'll go slowly, I promise," Zac assured her. "I won't hurt you."

"I know," she whispered, taking a deep breath.

"You can stop me anytime if I frighten you."

She looked at his face, his dear face. How could this man ever frighten her? *I want this more than anything in the world. Please don't let me fail.* With shaky hands, she touched both his cheeks. Rising on tiptoe, she gave him a quick kiss. "You're so tall. You make me feel fragile, almost delicate."

"You *are* fragile and delicate, and so lovely. I haven't told you how lovely I think you are because I know you've heard it countless times, probably since you were three or four."

"Not so many, and never from someone I cared for."

"Then let me tell you." He raised his hands and eased them into the thickness of her hair. "I love your hair, the way it looks in the wind, wild and free." He buried his nose in its dark fragrance. "And the way you smell—like a sweet summer day, like a field of flowers, like the morning after a spring rain."

He was romancing her—something no one had ever bothered to do. She was nearly purring inside as his words washed over her.

"Your eyes are the most incredible colors. Violet in the daylight, and a stormy purple when you're riled.

And now, now when I stand close and touch you, they're an inky blue, dark and aware of every move I make.''

Lainey was trembling slightly, but not with fear. Could he really mean all he was saying? Or were they just words meant to tame and to pacify? Steven had always been so eager, so ready, that he'd never bothered with words.

With his thumbs, Zac caressed her lips slowly. ''And your mouth. Sometimes when I'm talking with you, I can't keep my eyes off your mouth. When I kiss you, I forget everything. You taste so special, like no one else, a taste I can't get enough of.''

His words had worked magic on her senses. Reeling, Lainey moved closer and invited his kiss. Her arms circled him, drawing him nearer as his mouth on hers blotted out the world around them. She felt shock waves of pleasure shiver up her spine while the knot of need inside her began to unfurl. Again she felt his arousal press against her, but she didn't freeze this time. This was Zac who would teach her to reach out for the passion.

Breathing deeply, Zac stepped back, needing a moment to regain his pacing. He touched the neckline of her dress, remembering earlier when he'd unbuttoned her only to have her hands stop him. ''Do you think we could take this off?''

Her hands moved to the top button.

''I could maybe help,'' he offered.

She dropped her arms and stood waiting.

His fingers on the buttons were clumsier than before, and there were so many. In the dim light, he could see her chest move as she breathed. The dress fell, and he tossed it onto a chair. She stepped out of her shoes and stood before him wearing only a lacy bra and silk panties. He wanted to take the rest off, to explore every beautiful inch, but he held on to his control.

Zac walked around to the other side of the bed and pulled the comforter back, revealing pale gold sheets. Then he lay down on the far side, the towel still knotted at his waist. "Come to me, Lainey."

She hesitated, feeling suddenly uncertain. "I don't know what you want me to do."

"Do whatever feels right."

Cautiously she lay down beside him, leaving a generous space between them.

He wanted to cry out to her. *Touch me. Learn me. Show me you care. I've been without a woman's touch for so long, and I need you.*

Lainey lay still while her mind raced. Men should make the first move. What did she know about pleasing a man? But soon, she felt foolish just lying there, so she inched her hand over and touched his. Warm fingers laced with hers, and she felt better. Slowly she rose on one elbow and angled toward him.

Beautiful. He was strong and beautiful. His skin, bronze from the sun, his chest liberally sprinkled with dark hair disappearing into the white towel at his waist. She moved her eyes back to his face and found his solemn gaze watching her.

"You said you used to wonder what you'd do if I suddenly appeared at your bedside. Well, here I am. Go with your feelings."

She placed her free hand on his chest. "I want to please you."

"Everything you do pleases me."

She had fantasized the day she'd seen him in the stream, had ached to touch him. Sliding closer, she bent to place her lips to the smooth skin of his chest, his throat.

The dark curtain of her hair fell forward, grazing him, sending shivers of delight along his sensitive nerves. Zac lay as still as he could, his expression encouraging.

Lainey trailed her lips farther along, rubbing her face in the soft fur of his chest, pausing to place a soft kiss on his nipple. She felt him shudder and, made bold by his reaction, moved over him and caressed the strong muscles under his flushed skin. It was exciting to be able to do as she wished with this beautiful specimen of a man, to feel him tremble under her fingers as she ran her nails lightly along his sides.

Trusting more, she inched up farther and touched her breasts to his chest. She closed her eyes and heard a soft moan of pleasure, uncertain if it had come from him or her. Lying half atop him, she rubbed gently, feeling the friction spread heat throughout her body. As he eased toward her slightly, she moved in to kiss him, needing the contact.

He tasted familiar and oh, so good, as she gave herself freely to the kiss, letting his strong arms draw her nearer. His hands caressed the bare parts of her back and she felt her pelvis shift and rotate, seeking his heat. Surprised at her body's reaction, she pulled back.

Zac touched the fastening of her bra. "Can I take this off?" he asked, his voice thick with passion held in check. She nodded, and he did, then pulled the lace down along her arms. He eased up on an elbow, letting his eyes feast on her.

"Perfect. You're absolutely perfect." Moving slowly, so she could stop him anytime, he lowered his head and placed his wet tongue on one swollen tip. There was no mistaking the groan that came from her this time. Encouraged, he took it into his mouth, kissing her flesh the way he'd so often dreamed of doing.

Her body was moving restlessly now, and she shoved her hands into his hair, pressing him closer as he moved to her other breast. She couldn't remember that this had ever felt this good before. There was no pain, no fear, and no shame. Lainey arched her back and closed her eyes.

Raising his head, Zac struggled for control. He'd promised himself and her that he'd let her lead the way. "Tell me what you'd like me to do, how I can make you feel good," he whispered as he kissed the satin of her throat.

"I already feel good."

He moved his hand then, slowly downward along her belly, then trailed a finger along the top band of her panties. He felt her sharp intake of breath and held still for a heartbeat. He kissed her, then placed his palm over her intimately. Changing the angle of his head, he deepened the kiss as he began a rhythmic kneading, hoping she wouldn't pull back. When she began to move against his hand, when he could feel moist heat radiating from her, he breathed a sigh of relief and continued.

A long moment later, she looked at him, her eyes dark with awakened needs she couldn't put a name to. "Zac, oh, Zac." She buried her face in his neck, struggling with the desire infusing her.

"It's all right, honey. Just go with it." Bolder now, he pulled the panties from her and tossed them aside. She turned into him, trembling slightly. "It's all right. I'm not going to do anything you don't want me to do."

She waited until her heartbeat slowed and she felt in control again. Gently she eased back from him and saw his worried frown. She desperately wanted to erase his anxiety and her own. Hesitantly, she placed her hand on the knot of his towel. "Isn't it time we took this off?"

Zac lay flat on his back. "Go ahead," he said, giving her back the lead.

It took her several moments, but finally she freed the material. He lifted his hips, and she pulled the towel away and dropped it to the floor. Her eyes were riveted on him, strong and powerful and throbbing with life. Her hand was damp as she reached to touch him. As her fingers closed around him, she heard him make a sound deep in his throat and looked up to see his eyes smoky with passion.

Reaching over to the nightstand, he removed a foil package from the drawer. She let go of him as he set about protecting her. Then he reached for her hand. "You set the pace."

Her moves a bit awkward, she straddled him. For a moment she felt the panic begin, felt her body tighten, but she pushed back the feeling. Her eyes never wavering from his, she shifted and took him inside her. This was Zac, she reminded herself, and he wouldn't force, wouldn't push. She adjusted her body over his, taking more of him. Trembling now, she leaned forward, her mouth a breath away from his. The feel of a man inside her was unfamiliar, unnerving, as if her body had forgotten. "Help me, Zac."

His arms closed around her as he arched and filled her completely. He began to move then; slowly at first, then deeper and faster, watching her face. She was concentrating, her hands tight on his shoulders, her eyes closed.

It was going to be all right, Lainey thought, and relaxed her grip. Sliding her arms around his neck, she tried to stay with him. Tears of relief sprang into her eyes. She wasn't going to bolt and run. She cared for this man, and she was going to be able to please him. With that thought, she pressed her mouth to his.

He wasn't sure just when he lost control, but suddenly Zac felt the change. "Lainey," he groaned. "I can't..."

"Shh, it's all right," she said, stunned at the absence of fear. She could feel her tension dissolving at her need to satisfy him.

It was too late to stop. He'd been without so long. Zac closed his eyes and thrust upward, then felt the explosion begin.

She held on, feeling him deep inside her, and she clung to him. She'd done it, at long last.

Feeling relieved, yet disappointed in himself, Zac smoothed the damp skin of her back as she lay atop him. "Lainey, I'm sorry."

"It's all right."

"It's *not* all right. Nothing happened for you."

She raised her head, and her eyes were shining. "Maybe not in the way you mean, but I just climbed a very high mountain and I feel wonderful. I wasn't afraid, Zac." She gave him a soft, tender kiss and curled into his side.

"But I want—"

"I want you to hold me, Zac. Please, just hold me."

He gathered her to his chest, settling her head under his chin, his hand caressing her hair. He heard a sigh tremble from her as she closed her eyes.

Zac stared out through the slanted blinds at a sliver of moonlight. Damn! This wasn't the way he'd meant for things to happen.

She was drifting on a gently rolling sea, the warm waves caressing her arms, her stomach and her legs. Lainey sighed and let the languid feelings permeate her senses. Whisper soft and feather light, the touch on her arm then trailed along the swell of her breast. She shifted and arched as her swollen flesh reached out toward the lingering caress.

Sensations skittered along her ribs, and her skin tingled. She found herself squirming as the warmth spread to her thighs, moving higher. A circling motion centered there, creating a restless urgency.

Her eyes opened, and she found Zac lying on his side, studying her face, his hand resting on the curve of her inner thigh. In the soft light of the bedroom lamp, she saw him lean closer.

"What time is it?" she asked suddenly.

"About two." He leaned down for a slow, lingering kiss. "You're very beautiful when you sleep."

The heat rose in her face, and she brushed her hair back. She wasn't used to men watching her sleep. No man, in fact, ever had. She became increasingly aware of his hand moving lightly, his fingers stroking her leg. Raising her head, she frowned. "Could we pull the sheet up?"

"We don't need the sheet just now." He lowered his head and settled his mouth over her breast.

The quick arch of her body was totally involuntary. "Oh!"

"Something wrong?" he asked, barely pausing in his ministrations.

"I . . . I didn't think you'd be . . . interested again so soon."

He smiled at her phrasing. "As a matter of fact, I am interested again. But this one's strictly for you."

Before she could protest, his hands and lips began a slow, tortuous, maddeningly exciting journey over her body, kissing, tasting, exploring every secret place. She couldn't speak, couldn't think, could scarcely breathe, as expertly he had her soaring higher than she'd dared hope.

His mouth trailed along the soft skin of her arm, then shifted to nibble just behind her ear before moving to sample the delicate underside of her breast. Magic. His touch was magic, and she was afraid to move, afraid to break the spell.

Returning to her waiting lips, he stroked her side, then slid his hand up her inner thigh. His tongue moved into her mouth as his fingers moved deep inside her. Lainey clamped her legs together and eased back from him, her hand stopping his.

"No!"

He held very still. "Why not?"

"You don't have to. I'm all right."

"This isn't about *have to.* It's about *want to.*"

A breath trembled from her. "Look, I've come a lot further than I thought I would tonight. I'm just one of those women who can't seem to . . . who may never again . . ."

"And I'm one of those men who says that's a lot of bull. Lainey, let me try."

For a moment she debated, then she drew back her hand. He was wrong, as he would soon discover. She'd been feeling so good at having pleased him. Now he was going to spoil it. She shivered as his fingers began to stroke her.

Zac moved his mouth close to her ear, whispering soft words while he caressed her. She was fighting him all the way, moving restlessly, her hand clutching the sheet. "Just relax, sweetheart," he murmured. "Let it happen."

It wasn't going to, didn't he see? She wasn't like she'd been. She couldn't . . .

Then suddenly, things began to shift. She hadn't given her body permission to move with him, to move against him, had she? Her blood was churning, the sound a roar in her ears. She was having trouble breathing. Her voice sounding foreign to her, she called to him. "Zac!"

"I'm right here, sweetheart. Let go."

And finally she did as the waves rolled in on her and bright, shimmering colors exploded behind her tightly closed eyelids. And through it all, Zac was there, holding her, murmuring to her, rocking with her.

As the powerful feelings receded, she clung to him, unwilling to lose the pleasure so quickly. She felt cherished, she felt loved, she felt *normal*. The tears that fell cleansed her, washing away the shame she'd carried for so long.

Lainey felt strong hands frame her face and sweet kisses brush away her salty tears. She opened her eyes, her heart filled with so much emotion. "I didn't think I'd ever be able to feel again. Thank you."

Humbled, Zac kissed her tenderly, then wordlessly pulled her close into his arms. He held her that way for a long while, with her soft breasts cradled against his chest and her long legs wrapped around his. They'd broken through a lot of barriers tonight and, though there was still some hesitancy in her, she was reaching out. Soon she would be whole again, confident again, ready to face the world.

When that happened, would she leave him? Zac wondered as he lay there feeling her heart beat against his. Or would the quiet life he wanted to offer her be enough to hold her?

Zac awoke, finding his arms empty, as well as the space beside him. He sat up, then breathed a sigh of relief as he saw Lainey standing at the window, looking out. She was wearing his blue shirt that he'd draped over a chair, the hem skimming the backs of her knees. She had slanted the blinds, and he could see the beginning of dawn lighting the sky in the distance through the trees. He wondered what she was thinking.

Rising, he found his towel and draped it around himself before going to her. Sliding his arms along hers, he hugged her from the back, nestling his face in her hair.

"It's going to be a beautiful day," Lainey said, leaning into him. She'd expected to feel awkward, with the morning-after jitters. Perhaps she was still too moved by what had happened.

"Yes, a beautiful day." He heard a horse whinny from the direction of the barn and knew the men would be rising soon. He turned her in his arms and looked down at her. "Are you all right?"

"I don't think I've ever been so all right."

His smile was tinged with relief. "I was worried that you might have regrets."

She put her hands on his shoulders. "How could any woman regret lying with you, being loved by you?"

He opened the shirt she wore so he could feel her breasts against his chest as he pulled her close. "You sure know how to make a man feel ten feet tall."

She nuzzled into his neck. "I've never been with a man I could be myself with. I was always busy being this *person* he expected me to be. Thank you, for letting me be me."

He had no answer, just held her closer. Their bodies fit so well together, Zac thought, as if made for each other. He rubbed against her, and the sweet friction had the peaks of her breasts hardening against his chest. "Does that feel as good to you as it does to me?"

"Mmm, yes." On tiptoe, she pressed closer, not recognizing the woman who longed for more.

Angling his head, Zac took her mouth in a kiss that started out lazily, but swiftly escalated. "I want to make love with you again, Lainey."

Feeling the hard swelling against her stomach, she smiled. "So I noticed." But he wasn't smiling, and she sobered quickly. She wished she could tell him what he wanted to hear. She did the best she could. "Can you make me feel like that again?"

His eyes darkened to pewter with the challenge as he lifted her into his arms and carried her to the bed. Her hair cascaded over his arm like ribbons of black silk. He kissed her with something bordering on desperation, wanting her to know the depth of his feelings. She returned his kiss with a passion that left him breathless.

Mouths still locked together, he let her slide down the length of his body, and sighed with pleasure. Her hands moved to pull off his towel, then she pressed close to him, and Zac thought he would die with the beauty of having her here in his arms, his to love.

His hands were impatient with the shirt she wore as he quickly pulled it from her, then eased her onto the mattress. He followed her down, his mouth moving to envelop one taut nipple. Her cry of startled pleasure urged him on, and he shifted his attention to the other. Her skin was already hot and flushed as he continued to taste, to savor, to excite.

Unable to lie still, Lainey was moving under his questing mouth. Unable to be quiet, she murmured his name and foolish words that made no sense. Unable to be patient, she drew his face back up to hers. This time, it would be different. This time, it would work. "I want you," she whispered. "Now, Zac."

But he only smiled and sent his wandering hands where his lips had been. Lainey arched as his fingers found her, then moaned as he captured her mouth with his. She was a need pounding in him, she was an ache making him throb, she was a hunger in his soul. He hadn't known he'd been empty and lonely until he'd found her, an answer to his unspoken prayer. Now he would give to her and hope to make up for the lost years when she'd known no love, no passion. And in the giving, he would receive more than he'd dreamed possible.

It was wrong to take so much and not return the favor, Lainey thought as she shifted and pushed him onto his back. Unlike last night, her hands were sure and steady now, seeking all the vulnerable places she'd missed in her more innocent search. Her long hair trailing over his hot skin, she explored and pillaged and plundered with fingers and lips until his breathing was as frenzied as her own. He had freed her from the bonds that had held her passion captive, and now he would pay the price.

He'd loved before, but not like this. He thought of no one but her, remembered no one before her, needed nothing but this woman and this moment. When at last he shifted her to her back and lifted himself over her, he paused to look into her luminous eyes, waiting.

She raised her hands to his shoulders. "Yes," she whispered. "Oh, Zac, yes." She kept her eyes on his as he filled her, gently, sweetly, and Lainey knew it was the first time. No other man had ever touched her, not really. When he leaned down to her and his fingers laced with hers on the pillow, she was certain she'd never experienced a moment so perfect.

And then he was inside her, and she was moving with him, and the climb was fast, so fast. The rapid ascent was dizzying. Lainey felt herself straining, momentarily afraid she might not reach the summit, after all. But suddenly she was spiraling out of control, and she clutched Zac to her. She shuddered, her face in the hollow of his throat, and she felt him let go and join her.

The slide back to reality was slow and tender. He made as if to ease his weight from her, but she held him fast, unwilling to lose the closeness so soon. As her breathing slowed, Lainey knew that this was the first time she'd ever made love with her heart and body and soul.

Zac held her, needing no words. He knew their bodies had spoken the same language. Maybe one day Lainey would leave him, but at least he'd been able to give her this, this night he would never forget.

Lazily, she reached to caress his face. "I've never had such a magical night."

"Nor have I." He snuggled closer.

Lainey glanced toward the windows and the lightening sky. "I should go. If Ben doesn't find me there, he'll be scandalized, to say nothing of what your men will think if they see me leaving here at dawn.''

"We'll dress you in my clothes and you can sneak back along the path.''

"Yes, your clothes fit me so well.''

"Then we'll tough it out. I'll go with you, bold as brass. We haven't done anything wrong, Lainey.''

"I know that." She kissed him tenderly. "Nothing that feels this good could possibly be wrong. But this is a small town.''

Zac sighed. "All right, you can go. In a minute." He skimmed his hand along the curve of her hip and felt her shiver.

"Mmm, Zac, I . . .''

"Maybe two minutes." Wrapping his arms around her, he took possession of her mouth.

Chapter Ten

Lainey turned the Mustang into her driveway and hurriedly parked in the carport. Traffic on the way home from Detroit had been heavier than she'd anticipated, and she was running late. Jumping out, she rushed toward the porch where Zac was working on rebuilding the railing. Seeing him glance up, then stand and give her a warm smile, she waved.

Two days and nights since she'd first lain with him, days of sweet smiles and long looks and lingering kisses. Would she ever get used to the heart-stopping pleasure of just looking at him, of being free to touch him, of the wonder of having someone care that much for her? She hoped not, for she'd never been happier.

"I'm late, I know," she said as she ran up the steps. "I've got to change because Shelly will be here for her lesson soon." But she didn't go in, walking instead to his side. His welcoming arm slid around her. "Maybe I have time for one kiss."

"I was hoping you would." He pulled her close and kissed her, his mouth hot and urgent. He'd missed her and didn't mind letting her know. She opened to him, and Zac reveled in the recent change in her.

"Mmm, I'll have to go away more often," she said, smiling up at him.

"I'd rather you didn't. How's your father?"

"A little stronger. He's an old war-horse, all right. He asked if he could come visit, when he's out of the hospital."

"And you said?"

"I said we should take it one step at a time. He's not even out of intensive care." She reached up to brush his hair off his forehead, the need to touch him still surprising her.

"I suppose he wants to make it up to you—the way he treated you after you left New York."

"It's more than that, though. There were years that he never called or wrote me. It's hard to forget all that." There was regret in her eyes. "It would seem I'm not the sweet, forgiving person I wish I were."

"Don't go blaming yourself." Zac nodded toward her car. "By the way, the man from the leasing company dropped by. He wants to know if you want to renew the lease or buy the Mustang."

Lainey stepped back thoughtfully. "Buy? I don't think so. I've never owned a car. Besides, who knows how long I'll be here?"

Zac's worst fears weighed heavily in his chest, but he kept his expression calm. He turned his attention to sliding the replacement board into place on the railing, giving himself a moment. "Are you planning on leaving?"

"Not planning to, no. But what if this venture isn't a success? Then my plans may change." She studied his profile, wondering why he was so solemn today. "Is anything the matter?"

"No. Except that I missed you."

She smiled at that. "I missed you, too." She leaned over, intending to kiss his cheek. But he turned from his work and slanted his mouth over hers almost roughly. The kiss was long and deep.

At the honking of the Corvette's horn, Lainey stepped back, but her eyes stayed on Zac's face a moment longer. He looked the same as he smiled softly at her. Still, she had a feeling of unease. "I'd better go change."

Lainey waved to Dionne and Shelly. "Be right with you," she called as she scooted inside the house.

Zac watched her go with a troubled heart. Where would she go if she left here? Back to New York, back to modeling? But her business here was doing well. They'd picked up three new students since the open house. Still, he had to admit that teaching children to ride couldn't compare with having your picture on a magazine cover.

"Now you slip your fingers under this strap like this," Lainey instructed, helping Shelly attach the leather straps of the brush to her hand. "Then you make long strokes down her side to get the excess water off her hide." She guided the small hand to demonstrate. "That's it. Try not to get too wet yourself."

She'd attached ropes to Trixie's halter, then tethered her securely. After bathing Trixie down, she was showing Shelly how to groom her—part of their program to teach the children how to care for the horses. Developing the feeling of responsibility for an animal was part of their training.

"That's it. Now you've got it. Just remember to never stand behind her. Trixie's gentle, but you never know when something might frighten her and she would kick with her back legs."

Solemnly, Shelly nodded as she scraped more water from the horse's side, reaching as high as she could.

"I'm going just inside the barn door to get the clippers. I'll be right back. Stay right here, okay?" Again Shelly nodded, and Lainey hurried to get the grooming tools. Ben did most of the work on the horses, but she liked to keep her hand in, especially when instructing the children.

Coming back outside, she paused when she heard an unfamiliar voice. Cocking her head, she stopped to listen.

Shelly stood near Trixie's head, her small hand, strapped in the brush, reaching up toward the horse's thick neck. "It's all right, Trixie," she murmured gently. "We'll be done soon. Baths are a bother, but you feel better now, don't you?" Trixie poked her large head around, and Shelly patted her muzzle. "Sure you do."

Dumbfounded, Lainey stood in the barn doorway. Shelly was talking, whispering to Trixie the comforting words she'd heard Lainey herself say so many times. A breakthrough at last. Wouldn't Dionne be thrilled?

She waited there, not wanting to interfere with the moment, letting Shelly go on. Dionne had driven off before Lainey had had time to change clothes, but Zac had said she'd be back for Shelly around four.

Finally, not wanting the child to think she'd been left, Lainey rejoined her, pretending she hadn't heard. "You doing all right, honey?" she asked, hoping she'd answer. But Shelly just nodded and went around to the other side of Trixie. Lainey wished Dionne would hurry.

"Yes, of course it's important," Dionne said with a nod as she and Lainey stood by the fence, watching Shelly play with Willie near the porch where Zac was working. "But it's not over yet for Shelly." She turned to look into her friend's disappointed face.

"But she hasn't said a word in months. I thought surely..."

"There's more to Shelly's trauma than not speaking. She's dealing with a lot of buried emotions. Until she can accept what has happened to her, she won't be truly over her ordeal. Not speaking was her outer problem, which usually heals first. The inner problem may take longer and be more difficult for her to overcome."

Exasperated, Lainey shook her head. "How will she solve this deeper problem?"

"I'm not sure. Something may happen to trigger it, or something someone says may affect her deeply, emotionally, and it will become clear to her. No one can say. It varies with each individual." Impulsively she squeezed Lainey's arm. "But this is good, her talking to Trixie. It's a beginning."

"You surely have more patience than I could ever imagine having."

"Oh, I don't know. I think Zac runs a close second." She angled her head and smiled. "Was that you he was kissing on your front porch when I drove up today?"

Lainey felt her face flush, and she raised her hands to her cheeks. "Look at me, reacting like a teenager." She squared her shoulders. "Two evenings ago, I spent the night with him and, Dionne, it was all right. It was *more* than all right."

Dionne cocked her head to the side, her look thoughtful. "I like your hair loose this way," she commented.

"Thanks." There was that near blush again. Lainey tossed her hair back and tried to verbalize her relationship with Zac. "He says he cares for me, really cares."

"And how do you feel about him?"

"We had words that evening, and he walked away. I was so afraid of losing him, so I went to him and...and everything worked out." She smiled, feeling the relief. "I don't feel I have to hide anymore. With Zac, I feel strong."

"That's good, because—" Dionne reached for the newspaper stuck into the side pocket of her oversize purse "—you may not be able to be invisible much longer."

Hesitantly Lainey opened the folded paper. The reporter had done his homework. The first picture was of Lainey standing alongside Trixie, with Bobby in the saddle. Zac was holding the reins, and her eyes were on him. The second was of her as the Temptation model— a photo that had appeared in several magazines, a close-up of her face. Lainey let out a ragged breath as she scanned the article. "Looks like the cat's out of the bag, all right."

"The likelihood of the Associated Press picking it up and your mother seeing it in New York is slim," Dionne commented.

Lainey's expression was grim. "You don't know Irene the way I do. She has an uncanny sixth sense." Deliberately, she shrugged off the feeling of impending doom. "But, as I said earlier, I'm finished with hiding. If she learns I'm here, if she contacts me, I'll handle it somehow."

Dionne's look was assessing. "You *have* come a long way. Just don't rush things, Lainey."

She watched the wind ruffle Dionne's red hair. "Are you worried about me?"

Shrugging, Dionne slipped her arm around her friend as they walked toward the porch. "More like concerned. When we progress slowly, it usually lasts. I've never believed in instant cures."

"It's been nearly eight months," Lainey reminded her. "That's hardly instant." Her eyes went to Zac and met his, her reaction a spontaneous warmth. "For the first time in a long while, I feel optimistic when I think of the future."

"Then I'm glad."

Lainey waited until after Dionne and Shelly had left before showing Zac the newspaper article. Sitting on the porch stoop, she watched his face as he read it and studied the pictures.

The woman in both pictures were stunning, Zac decided. The professional one showed her smiling into the camera, the makeup so well-done and artfully applied that she looked natural. Lainey conveyed the impression of fresh beauty with a subtle sensuality that was unmistakable. In the second picture, she was smiling, with a look of contentment, of serenity. He wondered if Lainey had noted the contrast.

He handed the paper back. "It's a good article, honest and fair. Should generate some interest in the ranch." He stood, picked up his hammer and hunted around in his pouch for the right nail.

Lainey frowned up at him. "Is anything the matter?" she asked for the second time. "I get a feeling of deliberate distance here."

Was there? Zac asked himself as he pounded the nail home. The answer probably lay more with her than with him. Though the last few days had been idyllic in many ways, he had the uneasy feeling that Lainey was somehow preparing him for a goodbye scene—little things she'd said; nothing big that he could put his finger on.

Distance, she'd said. Yes, maybe they needed a little. "I got a call this morning from Colby. There're some problems at the office that need my attention. I'm going to have to go back to Detroit for a while. I just wanted to finish this porch before I left."

Odd how quickly she felt empty at just the thought of his leaving. Lainey swallowed down the feeling. Hadn't she known one day he'd have to return? Perhaps it was best. She'd been dependent on far too many people for far too long. She would manage. "How long will you be gone?"

He shrugged, trying for nonchalance. "Four or five days."

"I see." She twisted a lock of her hair as she gazed off into the woods leading to his house. Such a beautiful, peaceful place. A haven, a refuge, a new beginning. She hadn't realized that subconsciously she'd been weaving Zac into the fabric of her dreams about this place.

He'd said he cared for her; but had his vision been clouded by passion? She'd had so little experience with caring deeply for another. Perhaps he did care, for the moment; but on careful consideration, did he want to return to the life he'd had before they'd met? It would be best if she found out now, before more words were said. She'd adjusted before to living without love. She probably could again.

Lainey rose and dusted off the seat of her jeans. "I'll go make dinner." Hand on the doorknob, she turned back to him. "Unless you have other plans."

He saw the hurt in her eyes and wondered what he'd said to put it there. Was she dreading the thought of his leaving, as he was, or was that too much to hope for? He was selfish enough to wish that she'd miss him like hell.

Setting down the hammer, he went to her and pulled her close up against his body. "I do have other plans. Dinner isn't going to appease the hunger I feel."

Lainey felt her heart lighten, wanting to believe him, needing to. She leaned into him. "You know I'm always glad to postpone cooking." She glanced toward the barn where Ben's car was parked. "But it's still daylight."

"Do you need it to be dark when I make love with you?"

"No, but Ben's around here someplace."

"Ben'll leave when he's finished, whether you're out here or inside." He picked her up into his arms and entered the house. "And I much prefer you inside." Reaching down, he clicked the lock on the door.

With a weary sigh, Lainey poured the bucket of water into Juno's trough, then leaned down to check her again. The waxing of the teats had started, and delivery would be soon. Charley had told her what to expect. Straightening, she stroked the chestnut's long neck. "Don't worry, girl. We'll get you help when the time comes."

Leaving the stall, Lainey put away the bucket and gazed about the barn, making sure she hadn't forgotten anything. She was comfortably tired after working with four students today and seeing after the horses herself. Ben was home with a summer cold, and she'd missed his help. But more than ever, she missed having Zac with her.

Five days and he still hadn't returned. He'd phoned twice, but somehow their conversations had been strained and unnatural. Hanging a forgotten bridle onto the wall rack, she had to admit she hadn't realized how much she'd come to rely on Zac—not only to do the renovating, but to help with the kids and the horses. They'd drifted into a comfortable routine, one she'd appreciated. But perhaps he'd resented doing so many things they hadn't actually agreed upon. Maybe that's why he'd gone away: to think things over.

The time apart had given Lainey time to think, too. And she decided she missed him—not for the work he did, but for the pleasure of his company. Missed the warm touches, she who'd only recently learned to enjoy a man's hand. Missed his sense of humor, his optimism, his honesty. Missed him in the dark silence of her lonely bed.

He'd made her feel like a woman again. Correction—he'd made her feel more of a woman than she'd ever dreamed possible. It was a feeling she loved. Did that mean she loved the man? She thought so. But how could she be certain?

"Good night, ladies," she sang out to the trio of horses, then walked out and closed the barn door. The late-afternoon sun was still bright, and she felt hot and sticky. A shower would feel good.

The car coming down her drive was a late-model economy sedan that bore rental license plates. Lainey felt a flash of momentary fear, one that might have caused her to panic a few weeks ago. But she fought it back and walked toward her rebuilt porch as the car swung around and stopped. When the driver stepped out, she felt her heart lurch.

The woman was tall, wearing a stylish if not recently purchased suit of pale gray, and leather heels that matched. The scarf at the neckline undoubtedly hid a throat that would have hinted at aging. The hair, once lush and full, was now thinning and dyed a black that contrasted starkly with her pale skin. Her small blue eyes took in the modest house, coming to rest on its owner, who stood quietly waiting.

"So this is where you've wound up, Lainey," Irene commented in the New York accent she'd cultivated so carefully.

"Hello, Mother," Lainey answered, marveling at the even tone of her voice.

Irene Roberts narrowed her gaze and glanced at the barn, the corral, the garden just beginning to flourish, and turned back to her daughter. "I never would have guessed you were so...rural. When I saw the pictures in the paper, I thought that surely someone was playing a cruel joke. My daughter, a top fashion model, choosing to live in a backwoods shack—never!"

With difficulty, Lainey held her ground, and her temper. "The joke's on you, Mother. This is exactly where I choose to live."

"Incredible." Irene patted her damp brow. "I don't suppose you have air-conditioning, but you could ask me in out of the sun. I'd forgotten how dreadfully humid Michigan summers are."

Lainey decided not to mention that New York summers were equally humid. She moved to the porch and held open the door. Why had Irene come, and what was she after? She surely hadn't dropped in for tea or merely out of curiosity. Lainey had told Dionne that if her mother showed up, she'd handle her somehow. Now that she was here, she felt less certain as she watched Irene move inside, a look of barely disguised distaste on her face.

Irene halted at the sight of a lone rocking chair in front of a rustic fireplace and nothing else. "How very primitive. Tell me, do you sleep on a straw mat and eat only nuts and berries?" She made a dismissive gesture before Lainey could reply. "I blame myself for this. As a teenager I never allowed you to go through your rebellious stage."

Lainey crossed her arms over her chest, recognizing it for the defensive posture it was. She could have explained that she was nearly ready to order furniture, had even gone looking at appliances yesterday, but decided not to waste her breath. "As a teenager, I seemed to have missed several stages, as I recall." Like the time to make real friends, hayrides in high school, trying out for the cheerleading squad. Irene had dismissed those activities as frivolous and a waste of valuable training time. Lainey kept her expression blank as she offered her mother a glass of iced tea.

Irene nodded and followed Lainey into the kitchen. Pulling out the wooden chair, she sat down gingerly.

Lainey saw that her hands shook only a little as she poured tea into two frosty glasses and joined her mother at the table. The need to get this uncomfortable visit over with burned in her as she met Irene's eyes. "Just why have you come?"

Irene put on her most persuasive smile. "Darling, to take you home, of course."

She'd been foolish to think, to hope that Irene would simply state that she'd wanted to see her, had perhaps missed her. "I *am* home."

"We've all missed you," Irene stated firmly, then paused to take a dramatically deep breath. "Anne was just saying to me the other day how much she wished you'd come back. No hard feelings—she'd put you right back to work. And Steven. The poor man's devastated by your rejection, phones me all the time asking where you are."

Liar! Reality shocked Lainey. She'd spoken with Anne only last week. And as for Steven, he'd been glad to be rid of her and was probably on her second replacement by now. She took a long, cooling sip of the tea. "How's Dominique working out for you?" she asked, knowing full well from Anne that Irene's new protégée hadn't been able to get anything but a few minor shoots.

Irene's eyes turned cool. She leaned forward. "She's doing well but, to tell the truth, she can't hold a candle to you. No one can, Lainey. Come back where you belong." She waved a manicured hand to include the entire house. "Leave all this . . . this craziness."

"I *like* it here."

Irene was honestly incredulous. "How can you? It's living below the poverty level, for heaven's sake. And look at you. Your hair needs a good cut, you're dressed like a farmhand, your nails are neglected and your beautiful skin—it's getting freckled." She forced herself to brighten. "But we can fix all that. We can afford to hire the best. You can check into a spa somewhere for a week's rest and a beauty makeover. I'll tell Anne you'll report to her in, say, ten days. I've moved to a small place in the Village—for convenience. But we can get a larger apartment, in a better neighborhood, miles away from where your accident happened."

"No." Lainey set down her glass carefully. "I didn't have an accident, Mother. I was raped, violated and humiliated. It's not a minor thing you get over in a week or a month. I'm feeling better, but I'm not completely over all that yet." Not that Irene had asked.

"You're over it enough to be mooning over some cowhand in the newspaper picture. Honestly, Lainey. I hope you haven't shacked up with some drifter who—"

Lainey banged her fist down on the tabletop. "Stop it! You don't know anything. You don't even know me. And Zac—he's good and he's kind and patient."

Irene's expression was laced with disgust. "You *have* fallen for him. My God! You're so trusting, Lainey, so inexperienced. Can't you see a farmhand like that is after only two things: he wants to get into your bed, then into your bank account. I won't have it. I won't let my daughter be taken advantage of. At least half of that money's mine. If it weren't for me, for all the sacrifices I made all those years, you'd have been nothing. Less than nothing. You'd have truly wound up in a place like this."

In her anxiety, her voice had grown shrill, and she scarcely seemed to notice that Lainey had gone perfectly still. "But it doesn't have to be like this. I forgive you this...this little sabbatical. I suppose it was unnerving having that filthy man come at you in that alley. But it's over now, and we can go on. You have a great future ahead of you, if you come back now. You can't wait too long, because there are always more and more young women waiting to take your place. You're special, the Temptation girl. They'll take you back. I know they will. Lots of models work into their thirties, even later. One day, with my guidance, we'll be on Park Avenue, Lainey. Not on some smelly horse ranch.''

Lainey tried to swallow, but the lump wouldn't go down. She thought she might be sick, so she took several long breaths. Unnerving. Her own mother thought that her rape had been "unnerving." Not devastating and disastrous, not crushing and defeating. Unnerving. Finally she forced a sip of tea past her dry throat, then raised her eyes to her mother's.

"You never cared at all about me, did you?"

A small muscle twitched under Irene's eye. "Of course, I cared. I still do. Why else would I be here if not to rescue you?" There was an edge of impatience in her voice.

Lainey choked back the pain of realization. "All those years, the lessons, the pageants. They weren't for me, to make me happy, to answer my needs. You didn't give a damn about what I needed. You never once asked if I was happy. They were for you—for your ego and your wallet. Anne tried to tell me that you'd been skimming my earnings for years until she taught me to manage my own money. Even after that, I paid for everything and you let me. I made excuses for you, telling myself that you did care, you just couldn't show it.''

"I was your manager, guiding your career and—"

"My career didn't need managing or guiding. I was under contract to the Blackburn agency. They handled all the details." She ran a trembling hand over her eyes. "All that time, I thought you *wanted* to be with me, that you loved me at least a little. How could I have been so stupid?''

The chair made a scraping sound as Irene stood, her face suddenly hard and cold. ''You *are* stupid if you think I'm letting you get away with this. I know you've got plenty of money stashed away, Lainey, and I'm entitled to half of it. Lord knows how much you threw away on this worthless ranch, but I'm going to get the rest if I have to take you to court. I've inquired about your bank holdings, though the fools wouldn't tell me much. But I'll get an attorney, a court order. You'll see.''

Lainey raised her head and looked at her mother with bleak eyes. ''Get out of my house.''

''You call this dump a house?'' She made an ugly sound. ''You'll be sorry you didn't listen to me, my darling daughter. When I get finished with you, this *will* be all you can afford.''

''Do what you want. Just stay out of my life.''

Her mouth a thin red line, Irene grabbed her handbag. ''You're just like your father—shortsighted, weak, dull.'' Her heels clattering on the wood floor, she stomped to the front door. ''You'll be hearing from my attorney.''

Her head was throbbing, throbbing. Lainey laid her cheek on her arms resting on the table. She would not cry. She would not.

How long she sat like that, she wasn't certain. Her jumbled thoughts raced furiously around in her brain, denying the pain, finally accepting the inevitable.

Irene had used her—not once, but for years. She'd used her own daughter to get what she wanted. And when she'd lost her meal ticket and Dominique hadn't panned out, she'd come after Lainey the only way she knew how: with both guns blazing.

Lainey sat up, rubbing her forehead. *Watch out for your mother,* her father had warned from his hospital bed. *She's a viper.* Why hadn't she guessed sooner than this? Because Irene was very good at getting her way and making it seem as though it was in the other person's best interest. She'd been manipulating so long she didn't know any other way. Her father had caught on and divorced her. Too bad you couldn't divorce a parent, Lainey thought wearily.

A sound penetrated her musings. It was coming from the barn, a horse whinnying—not as usual, but with a frantic edge. Jumping up, Lainey ran to the barn, switched on the light and opened Juno's stall door.

She was lying on her side with sweat beading her hide, a look of pain in her brown eyes. What timing, Juno! Quickly she grabbed a blanket and spread it on the mare's distended belly.

"I'm going for help, lady. Hang on." At a dead run, she headed for the phone, praying Charley was available.

She glanced up at the evening sky streaked with color. *Zac, Zac, where are you? I need you.*

Chapter Eleven

He had the top down and his foot firmly on the gas pedal. His powerful Mercedes 560SL had made good time, which was why Zac had chosen it over his truck. After days of endless meetings, he was finally on his way, not even stopping for dinner or to change clothes before starting out. He was a man in a hurry, racing back to the woman he loved. Rolling his shoulders to release the tension, he left the highway and headed up the exit ramp.

Love. The realization had come to him slowly. Not like a thunderbolt out of the blue, or a sudden flash of insight. With Nancy, it had seemed as if he'd loved her always, having grown up with her. But with Lainey, he'd fought the feeling, afraid to let himself care that much again. His struggles had been in vain, for she'd been taking over his heart from the beginning. The problem would be in making her believe that his feelings were real and lasting.

It has been a long five days, but he felt good about all he'd accomplished. Colby was handling things well, but he was less experienced than Zac and needed his input from time to time. And he'd been agreeable to Zac's new idea, one he'd had churning around in his mind for some time.

It wasn't such a farfetched plan as to be easily dismissed—the opening of a branch of Midwest Construction somewhere in the St. Clair area. From the city all the way to Port Huron, acres of land that had been held for years by old-timers were being made available for sale by their heirs as the owners were dying off. Subdividing and rezoning were already under way. A reputable, experienced construction firm could get in on the ground floor.

Zac had in mind lakeside homes and inland wooded lots of no less than one acre apiece, to be offered to people who wanted privacy and could afford the price tag of custom construction. His company had built everything from tract housing to commercial buildings, but Zac had always had a desire to get involved in custom homes, for the change and the challenge. He and Colby had contacted a young architect, innovative and hungry, and had formulated tentative plans. Zac's task now was to find a site for their branch office and to get some preliminary feasibility studies going. His larger task was to convince Lainey to be a part of his future.

Turning onto the road that led past both their ranches, Zac glanced over at the package on the seat next to him. He'd brought her a present, one that meant something to him. His mother had died only last year, and he'd wound up with her cameo, very delicate and very old. It had been handed down from his grand-mother, and his mother had worn it on a fragile gold chain for as long as Zac could remember. He'd noticed that Lainey rarely wore jewelry, but hoped the cameo would be something she would treasure.

He'd missed her. God, how he'd missed her. He'd left, worried and wondering if she were making plans to exit from his life. He'd spent a lot of time thinking, and had come to the conclusion that he hadn't gotten where he was today by letting life just happen to him. He needed to talk with Lainey, to tell her how deep his feelings for her were, to convince her that they could have a future together. Her life in New York had un-doubtedly been exciting. It was up to him to persuade her that a quiet life could be exciting, as well. Turning into her drive, he felt confident that he could.

The lights were ablaze in both house and barn. Climbing out of the car, he checked his watch and saw that it was already ten. Then he noticed Charley's truck and realized that Juno must have gone into labor. As he approached, the door swung open and Lainey stepped out. In the half circle of light, she looked exhausted but pleased.

Blinking to adjust her eyes to the darkness, Lainey saw Zac walking toward her and stopped. His name came out on a sigh as he rushed to scoop her into his strong arms. His mouth claimed hers, and the weari-ness fled from her as she put her arms around his neck and let him sweep her away. At last he set her back on her feet. "I'm sweaty and I smell like a horse's mid-wife, I'm afraid."

Another kiss, another touch. Would there ever be enough? "You're beautiful and you smell wonderful." He kissed the top of her head before straightening. "I gather we have a new foal?"

"Yes, a colt." She took his hand. "Come see. Oh, Zac, he's beautiful."

Her eyes were shining as she led him to the stall. Juno was lying down and swung her huge eyes up to his for a moment, then resumed licking her newborn son. The colt was curled up near her head, his coat more red than brown, though Zac knew it would likely deepen to a darker chestnut later. His eyes were closed, but he wiggled a bit, leaning into the tongue that was bathing him, loving him. Zac slid his arm around Lainey as she hung over the stall door. "It's exciting, isn't it? A new life being born. I imagine you watched?"

"Watched?" questioned a low voice behind them. "She assisted," said Charley as he came alongside. "Good to have you home, Zac."

Home. Yes, it was beginning to feel like home. Zac grinned at his ranch foreman. "Thanks. It's great being back." He tightened his arm at Lainey's waist. "I appreciate your helping out."

Charley set aside the bucket he'd used to dispose of the afterbirth and nodded. "Lainey here's already thanked me a dozen times. I told her I could assist in a birthing in my sleep after helping nearly two hundred foals into this world." He nodded toward the newcomer. "He's a fine healthy one, looks like."

Lainey was still in awe of the spindly-legged colt. "Now we have to think of a name for him."

Charley picked up his battered hat and stuck it on his balding head. "You'll think of one. I'll be leaving now, but I'll come back in the morning, if you like, just to check him out."

Lainey gave him a grateful smile. "That would be great, Charley. Thank you."

"Good night." With that, Charley walked out.

"How about Domino?" Lainey suggested, her eyes back on the colt. "He's got two white dots on one front paw and one on the second."

"Whatever you say." Turning her from the stall, Zac guided her toward the door and closed it behind them. "Let's let mother and son get acquainted, shall we? I could use a cup of coffee, if you're not too tired."

She was exhausted; emotionally and physically drained. But she wanted him, needed him with her. For the first time, she noticed he was wearing suit pants and a white shirt, the sleeves rolled up. "Looks like you just stepped out of a board meeting."

Zac reached into the Mercedes and grabbed the package. "Actually, I did. I drove right through." He took her hand as she started to the house. "I couldn't wait to see you again."

Lainey stopped. No one had ever been dying to see her again, leaving an appointment and driving several hours nonstop to be with her. Her heart fluttered in her chest as she looked into his eyes, silvery in the moonlight. With a shaky hand she traced the day's growth of beard on his square jaw. He was watching her expectantly. It was time for a little straight talk.

"I was afraid you weren't coming back," she whispered.

Her simple admission touched him. "You needn't have been. Don't you know how much I care about you?" He saw the doubt in her eyes and wondered what he'd have to do to remove it. "Will you ever believe me?"

Her mother had professed to care, too. Lainey felt a shudder whip through her. She looked down the length of her damp shirt and soiled jeans. "I need a shower. Let me get you something to eat and then get cleaned up."

The shadows were back in her eyes, and he wanted to know why. "All right."

In the kitchen, she opened the refrigerator. "Not a lot here," she said apologetically. Without him there to nag her, she hadn't been shopping. "How about scrambled eggs?"

He took the carton from her. "I'll fix them. You go shower. Did you have dinner?"

Lainey rubbed her forehead. The throbbing was gone, replaced by a dull ache that even the joy of witnessing the colt's birth hadn't been able to prevent. "I don't think so," she said absently. She left him there and made her way to the bath.

Frowning, Zac set the table and broke eggs into a dish, wishing he knew what had happened while he'd been away. Something had, he was certain. Lainey's moods were changing and shifting faster than the night breezes at the screen door.

He had just put the toast on the table when she joined him, her hair still damp. She had wrapped herself in a comfortably worn chenille robe of pale blue, and somehow he found it sexier than the finest satin. She tightened the belt and touched the draped collar, as if needing the consolation of something familiar.

"Mmm, that does smell good." Surprised to find herself hungry, Lainey took a bite. She swallowed and heard her stomach gurgle, then looked up. "I guess I haven't eaten in a while."

"It looks like I can't leave you alone because you don't take care of yourself."

The past five days without him had been so lonely. She grew solemn. "I think that's a very good plan."

Did she mean it? Zac set down his fork, no longer hungry, suddenly eager. He held out the package to her.

"I brought you something." He saw genuine surprise on her face. Was she so unused to receiving gifts?

"Why?"

"Because I wanted to. Open it."

She fumbled with the lid, then sat staring at the delicate cameo resting on a pad of white cotton. Reaching in, she removed the dainty chain and held the necklace in her hand. The ivory oval was of a woman's head, a woman with long hair and a sweet face. "This is beautiful."

"It was my mother's. As far back as I can remember, she always wore it. It originally belonged to her mother."

She touched the raised work. "I can't accept this, Zac. Surely your wife must have..."

"My mother died last year, after Nancy. I want you to have it."

Tears sprang to her eyes, but she fought them back. At least Zac had had a mother who was warm and traditional and loving. Perhaps that was why he was. "No one has ever given me anything like this, a family heirloom. You need to keep this, to give it to...to..."

He took her free hand. "To the woman I love. I have." He watched her struggle with her emotions and with the tears that suddenly spiked her lashes. Her eyes were huge and haunted as she looked at him. She was like a dam ready to burst. He realized he'd never seen her cry, not really cry—not even when she'd poured out the story of the rape. "What is it, Lainey?"

She shook her head helplessly, the words refusing to form. Carefully, she replaced the necklace in the box and rose to stand with her back to him.

He went to her, touched her shoulder. She whirled around and moved into his arms, clutching him fiercely to her. "Zac, I need you."

"I'm right here," he murmured, holding her tightly. Her declaration of need was more moving than the words of love he'd been hoping to hear. It had been so long since someone had needed him. His face in her hair, he held on.

She was crying now, sobbing into his shirt, trying to get closer still, burrowing into him. "I don't *want* to need you," she said with a catch in her voice. "But I do. Oh, God, I do."

He rubbed her back gently. "It's all right to need, Lainey. I need you, too." She made no sound, but her silent weeping was worse than open sobbing might have been. He could think of nothing to say, so he let the cleansing tears flow. She clung to him, accepting comfort as she so rarely allowed herself to do.

It took a while, but gradually, she relaxed, and the wrenching sobs ended. She reached into her pocket for a tissue to blow her nose.

"What happened, Lainey? Did someone come here, someone who hurt you?"

She shook her head violently, as if shaking off a memory. "I don't want to talk about it." Raising her damp face to his, she clutched at his sleeves. "Make love to me, Zac. Make me forget everything else."

Making love answered many needs, he knew, not the least of which was comfort, the obliteration of some of life's harsher realities. As he led her to her bedroom, he hoped he could find the gentleness that would erase all her pain.

There was a candle in a brass holder on her nightstand. He lit it as she pulled back the crocheted spread. He watched her lie down on the bed, her face pale in the flickering candlelight framed by the black cloud of her hair fanned out on the pillow. Leaning down, he kissed away the tracks of her tears, then kissed closed her eyes.

As his mouth touched hers, Lainey felt herself relax, trusting him to soothe, to heal. The kiss went slowly, seducing, enticing, as if he were memorizing the shape of her lips. She let herself drift with it. His hands glided into her hair, his long fingers massaging her scalp, then sliding to the base of her neck, removing all traces of lingering tension. How could he know just what she needed? she wondered on a sigh as she felt him shift his weight.

Lazily she opened her eyes and saw him removing his clothes unhurriedly. As the first time, when she'd seen him naked in the stream, she lay admiring his body, the strength behind the hard, rippling muscles, the taut skin turning golden in the light of the candle.

Finished undressing, he sat down and untied her robe, spreading the fabric to reveal her slight frame. She wore a short satin gown underneath. Her pointed breasts beckoned, and he could no longer resist pressing his lips to one swollen peak.

Lainey arched at the first contact of his wet mouth, finding his kiss doubly arousing through the soft fabric. He took his time, giving equal attention to her other side. Her flesh swelled to his touch, fueling him further. So lost in feeling was she that she was scarcely aware when he slipped the robe and gown from her and angled her onto her side.

Now his big hands were kneading her back, moving to her waist, then stroking the bunched muscles of her calves. She'd never been touched like this, revered like this. Like a cat, she stretched, seeking the gentle warmth of his hands.

Her total trust in him moved Zac. She'd never been loved as she deserved to be, but now he would show her. The first man had used her and the second had abused her. He would do anything to erase those memories from her and replace them with his loving touch. He would treasure her as he'd longed to do.

Lainey felt a prickle of desire as his mouth replaced his hands and journeyed along her shoulders and down her back, coaxing a response, relaxed and unrushed. There were so many secret, untouched places to pleasure, and he knew them all.

Through the open window, Zac heard a night bird twitter fretfully in a nearby tree and felt a rush of sympathy that he didn't have a mate beside him, too. Lainey's eyes were darkening now, her breathing becoming more labored as her passion mounted. Watching her face take on a rosy hue, he ran his fingers over her, his touch light and undemanding. Her skin was dewy, damp with the beginnings of arousal, and it excited him more. Her body was long, yet almost too slender, her feet small, and her wrists fragile as he held one to his mouth. Turning over her hand, he kissed her palm and felt her fingers curl and cup his face as she made a soft sound.

"Zac," she murmured, then raised her hands to trace the width of his shoulders and trail down his arms to thread her fingers with his. Hands locked together, she waited for his mouth to come to hers, then drank in the pleasure of his kiss. She felt like a desert walker opening herself to rain. If she lived to be a thousand, she'd never forget this moment.

She felt his leg brush hers and ran her bare foot up the length to his knee, shivering at the contact. He was rock solid in a way that delighted her, making her feel small and fragile. With increased anticipation, she tasted his desire.

Now she learned that a kiss could be so tender, so sensitive as to bring tears to her eyes. There was no demand and no hurry; there were only gentle explorations and sweet searchings and a quiet awakening. And his hands never stopped touching, until her skin was humming and her blood rushing. Still he lingered, to brush his lips across her cheek, along the line of her throat and between the fullness of her breasts.

This, then, was love. Lainey let the thought take root. Passion driven by love, need answered with understanding, comfort given unselfishly—love as she'd once dreamed it would be, but never believed it could be. Fearful that what he felt couldn't even come close to what she now knew, she could only cling to him. If he rejected her now, she would never survive it.

He felt the change in her and shifted to look into her eyes, saw her lips trembling. Braced on his elbows, he framed her face. "Tell me what you're feeling, Lainey."

She swallowed past a dry throat. "I can't."

"Then I'll tell you. I love you."

She felt a surge of hope, but fought it down, afraid to trust. "Don't tell me things you don't mean. Too many—"

"Too many others have? I won't. Not ever. I love you, the woman you are. And I want you with me always. Always, Lainey."

She sucked in a deep breath as she tried to think back. No, her memory was not faulty. No one had ever spoken those words aloud to her. No one. God, how she wanted to believe him, to give to him all the love she'd stored away for so long. And yet . . .

He watched the emotions flicker across her face. "It's all right," he told her, smiling down into her troubled eyes. "When you're ready, you'll be able to say what you feel."

He kissed her, and Lainey wrapped herself around him, trying to show him with her body what she couldn't put into words. When his tongue slipped into her mouth, she welcomed its honeyed taste. When he slipped inside her, she welcomed him home.

He took her then; took her to a place vaguely familiar, yet always brand-new. A place only two lovers could share.

He was a light sleeper, having been conditioned by months of lying alongside his dying wife, attuned to her every need. Zac opened his eyes and saw Lainey's head shift restlessly on the pillow. He'd blown out the candle, but moonlight drifted in and played across her damp face. He rose on an elbow and saw she was clutching the sheet in tight fists.

"No," she whispered aloud. "Please, no." Her body seemed to sink into the mattress as she struggled with her unseen demons, her head thrashing now. "No!" she called out again.

Zac touched her arm. "Lainey, it's all right."

But she didn't hear, lost in a world he couldn't see. It was dark, so dark, and she was cold. She fought the hysteria building in her throat, pulling back from the dreadful stench of cigars and sweat. She had to get free, to get away. "Let me go," she screamed, and sat upright in bed.

Her eyes flew open as she gulped in fresh air, listening to the pounding of her heart. Disoriented, she turned to see a man beside her, and for a moment the fear returned. Focusing at last and recognizing him, she sagged limply forward. "Zac. Oh, God."

Sitting up, he pulled her to him, soothing her as he would a small child. She was warm and damp and trembling. "It's all right. It's over, and I'm here."

Drained, she let him hold her, let the fear dissipate and his strength flow into her. For a moment longer, she allowed him to smooth back her hair, to whisper words of comfort. Then she eased away, feeling the aftermath of the nightmare mingled with the embarrassment of being observed.

"I once told you I was a mess. Now you know."

"No one can control their dreams, Lainey." He stroked her bare back. "Were you back in that alley?"

She nodded, then took a deep breath as she pushed her hair back. "I thought they would stop after... after I got over being afraid of a man's touch." Weary, deeply disappointed, she dropped her head to rest on her raised knees. "But it's not over." She closed her eyes. This wasn't fair to Zac, to burden him with her unending problems.

He shifted to face her. "Maybe there's something else bothering you deep inside." He didn't want to upset her further, but he needed to know. "Lainey, what happened while I was gone?"

She was quiet so long he thought she might not answer. Finally, she raised her head. "My mother was here this afternoon."

He cursed himself inwardly for not having talked with that newspaperman and warned him. "And you quarreled?"

Lainey gave a bitter laugh. "You don't quarrel with my mother. You have *discussions*. And she always has the last word. Always. The last word this time is that I'll be hearing from her attorney."

"Over what?"

"Money, of course. Money rules my mother or, I should say, the lack of it." Her sigh was ragged. "I didn't make very much until I moved to New York, and even then not during the first year. But once I became the Temptation girl, things changed. Irene quit work, and we lived off my income, but when I turned twenty-one, Anne Blackburn had a long talk with me. She was shocked to learn that Irene was spending every dime I was earning. My mother likes nice clothes, a chic apartment, the good life. I was too busy to pay much attention.'' Lainey shivered, remembering, and drew the sheet around her.

Banking his rising anger, Zac waited for her to go on.

"Anne taught me how to manage my money, where to invest, guiding me every step of the way. Well, Irene didn't like that; the two of them had never gotten along. I thought it was because Irene was jealous of my affection for Anne. Now I realize that Anne was on to her and Irene knew it and resented her interference.''

"So she did something about it?''

"Oh, yes. Several of us younger models lived with Anne, and that arrangement didn't suit Irene. She coaxed me away, telling me she missed me, that I was all she had. I can't believe I fell for all those lies.''

He took both her hands in his. ''Don't blame yourself. Most of us are raised to trust our parents, and you were young.''

"Young and gullible. She had no trouble manipulating me. An apartment with a *good* address, new furniture, trips to the Bahamas in the winter because she caught cold so easily. I worked and she played. I'd been conditioned to please her, to try to make her happy. My father hadn't been able to do it, so I took on the task. Why did it take me so long to see?''

"Wanting to please people we care about is part of living.''

The eyes she raised to his were filled with anguish. ''She never loved me. She used me. She chose a career for me—one she'd wanted as a girl—then pushed me into it. Now, she tells me I owe her half of everything I have for all the sacrifices she's made for me, so I could become this big-time model.'' She squeezed his hands hard. "She asked me to go back, she lied to me about everyone missing me, and when I still refused, she told me I'd be sorry, that she'd get a court order and force me to pay her. Zac, I was only a meal ticket to her. My own mother."

Zac struggled to control his rage. Yes, someone would be sorry, all right. But it wouldn't be Lainey. He'd make sure of that. "Giving birth is a biological act, Lainey, like what Juno did tonight. It doesn't mean love automatically follows." He thought of Colby, whose father had disappointed him deeply. "I could tell you stories about parents that would rival Irene. Forget her. Don't let her upset you. I know a lawyer who will take care of her."

"She may not do anything. She often threatened me. It was a way to keep me in line."

From what he'd heard, Zac doubted Irene wouldn't try. "If she does, we'll be ready for her."

"She's still my mother, and she did support me all those years before I started making money."

"Didn't your father pay child support?"

"Well, yes, but . . . Listen, I don't give a damn about the money. She can have it, all of it. I just want her out of my life, and I feel guilty even thinking that."

He pulled her to him, cradling her head on his shoulder. "I told you once that guilt and I are not strangers. But in this, I see nothing for you to feel guilty over."

"I don't love her. I don't even *like* her. But I can't help wondering what will happen to her."

Zac smoothed her hair, awed by her enormous capacity to care. "She'll have to try something called *getting a job*. Her future's not your concern." He shifted so he could look into her face. "Your future's with me." He kissed her, long and tenderly.

But Lainey sat up, shaking her head. "How could you want a future with someone whose past is a nightmare? Someone who has more problems to overcome than . . . than all those children she's trying to help?"

"Maybe because of those very things. It isn't what happens to us that counts; it's how we handle it. Despite the pain, you're overcoming your past, slowly but surely. And look at you. You've been used, hurt and emotionally battered. And yet you rush to your father's side when he needs you, you worry about what will happen to your mother even when she wants to drag you into court, and you work daily to help those children put their hurtful pasts behind them. How could I *not* love you and want to be a part of your future?"

Lainey swallowed. "You make me sound far better than I am."

"We've got years ahead of us for me to convince you that I'm right."

"Zac." She watched her hand play with a tuft of hair on his chest. "I'm uncomfortable making plans for a future that seems very uncertain at the moment. I have too much unfinished business to clear up. The nightmares, the problem in New York with my mother, whether or not I can make a go of this ranch. I've been pressured all my life. Please, can we just take this one day at a time?"

He wanted to tell her about his plans to open a branch nearby, to assure her that he'd be there for her as she worked out her problems. But she wasn't ready to hear that right now. If he pushed, she'd back away even more. He'd have to be content to wait her out. He kissed her nose lightly. "Sure. Just as long as there's room for me in your life."

How could there not be, when she loved him? But the words wouldn't come, not yet. When she could go to him a whole woman, free of the past and certain of a future she could share with him, then she would tell him everything that was in her heart. Before then, it would be unfair of her to expect anything from him.

She stroked his roughened cheek. "I very much want you in my life, though it seems like all the risks are yours. I've been used, and it's not a good feeling. I want to be sure I'm not using you to get well."

"You're not. Trust me."

But her trust had been trampled on by nearly everyone she'd known since she was a child. It would take time. "I'm learning to."

Slowly he slid the sheet from her and cupped one lovely breast. Her response was instantaneous, and he smiled. "You've come a long way."

"Yes," she said, feeling the heat. She lay back and pulled him down to her. "This time, don't hold back. I know you do, thinking you'll frighten me. I'm not frightened anymore—not of you. I want to feel everything, all your passion."

It was all he needed to hear, Zac thought as he reached for her.

Chapter Twelve

Domino was a week old and about to have his coming-out party. Lainey smiled as four of her students, all holding hands, walked into the corral where he stood near his mother on legs that were still a little wobbly. Zac was at Juno's head, holding her reins and talking softly to her. A very protective mother, Juno had to be watched carefully whenever anyone came near her baby.

"He's so skinny," Danny commented.

"He's got red hair like me," Melissa said proudly. She touched the white yarn tied around her ponytail. "We should give him a ribbon, too."

"Nah," Bobby asserted disgustedly. "He's a boy, and boys don't wear ribbons." He held out a tentative hand. "Will he come to me?"

"He will if you offer him this sugar," Lainey said, placing the cube in his hand. "Just hold steady."

Domino's nose caught the scent, and he pranced over, his gait hesitant. Venturing closer, he lowered his head and scooped the treat from Bobby's outthrust hand.

Making a face, Bobby wiped his hand on his jeans. "He sure is wet."

Finishing, the colt sniffed at the other children, looking for more. Juno, uneasy, snuffled and bobbed her big head. Zac patted her sleek neck.

"His mommy's getting mad," Danny said, taking a step back.

Lainey felt Shelly grip her hand tighter. "She's just looking out for him," she told the children. "Zac's holding her, so don't worry."

"Yeah, that's what mommies do," interjected Melissa, who'd recently been adopted by a family where there were two other little girls, lots of toys and an abundance of love. "Mommies take care of you, and they make sure you grow up healthy and strong."

Bobby dared to stroke Domino's neck, but his small face was sad. "Some mommies do. Other mommies don't like kids."

Wishing Dionne was here to listen to their comments and perhaps interpret them, Lainey stooped down to their level and guided small hands that itched to touch the friendly colt. Unsure what to say, she changed the subject. "Isn't he soft?"

"Did he get a bath?" asked Bobby.

"No," Danny answered before Lainey could. "His mommy washes him with her tongue."

"Oh, yuk," Melissa said, obviously disenchanted. "My new mommy washes me in a big blue bathtub, and then she brushes my hair. She reads me bedtime stories, too."

Pleased for her, Lainey smiled. "I'm glad you're happy in your new home, Melissa." A sudden sound to her left had her turning as she felt a hand slip out of her own. Looking up, she saw Shelly running toward the gate. "What on earth!"

Shelly squeezed herself between the wide boards of the gate, then continued running, heading toward the woods. Lainey shot a frantic look toward Zac who was already tying Juno's reins to the tree limb.

"Go after her," he yelled. "I'll take care of the others."

Lainey set out, hurrying through the gate, then following the path the child had taken, keeping Shelly's bright yellow shirt in her line of vision. Shelly was fast, driven by some new fear or ghosts from her past. Lainey lost sight of her around a curve, then saw her again, moving deeper into the trees. "Shelly! Stop! Wait for me!"

But the child ran on, forcing Lainey to increase the length of her strides. Finally, at the base of a gnarled tree, she caught up with her and stopped. Shelly was bent over and beating the trunk with a stick she'd found, beating and sobbing. For a long moment, Lainey just watched while she caught her breath, wondering at the fury being vented, the frustrated rage she was witnessing. Then she touched the child's arm. "It's okay, Shelly. Please stop."

The girl dropped the stick, then pounded on the tree bark with small fists. "She's gone, she's really gone," she sobbed.

At last, she understood. Firmly, Lainey pulled Shelly to her and hugged her small frame. "Yes, she's gone."

Her breath catching, Shelly drew in puffs of air, her cheek against Lainey's blouse. "My mommy's never going to give me a bath again or brush my hair." She raised huge blue eyes filled with pain to Lainey. "She used to sit on my bed and make up stories that made me laugh."

Lainey touched the ends of her hair. "What kind of stories?"

"My favorite was about a rabbit named Rebecca. That's my middle name." Shelly dragged a smudged hand down one cheek.

Lainey dried the child's cheeks as she talked. "You have wonderful, warm memories of her then, don't you?" Shelly nodded. "That's more than Bobby has, more than a lot of people have." Myself included, she thought, hoping she was saying the right thing. "You know your mommy loved you, and that's very important to remember."

Shelly dabbed at her streaked cheeks. "She's never coming back, is she?"

Lainey fought a few tears back herself. That had to be the saddest question she'd ever had to answer. "No, she's not. But there's still your daddy and your aunt and uncle and your cousins. Lots of people who love you."

The child nodded glumly and took the tissue Shelly handed her. She blew her nose loudly. "Aunt Joan's nice, but . . ."

When she didn't go on, Lainey finished for her. "But she's not your mommy. Aren't you lucky to have had two such nice ladies love you? Some kids don't even have one."

The nod came more easily this time. Lainey tipped the small, trembling chin up so Shelly would look at her. "And Dionne cares about you, too. Very much. And so do I."

She actually managed a small smile at that. Lainey pulled her into another hug, then stood. "Are you ready to go back now?"

"Yes."

They retraced their steps slowly, Shelly's hand in hers. "Do you like Domino?" she asked, hoping to keep the child talking.

"He's pretty."

"Next time you come, maybe we'll take him into the back pasture, the small one, and watch him romp around. Would you like that?"

Her eyes were shiny with anticipation as they looked up at Lainey. "No one else, just you and me?"

Hungry for individual attention. She should have guessed. Poor Joan Morgan was too busy to spare much time for a lonely child. "Yes, the two of us."

"I'd like that."

She'd have to take Joan aside when she came for Shelly, Lainey thought as they left the woods. And she'd have to call Dionne.

"Yes, that was a tremendous breakthrough," Dionne said into the phone after hearing the whole story. "Shelly's finally accepting that her mother's gone and not returning. Now she can heal and start to build a new life."

"Do you think she'll keep on talking now?"

"I believe so. Lainey, you've damn near worked a miracle. Thank you."

Taken aback, Lainey shook her head. "Not me. I didn't do anything. The other children's conversation triggered a reaction in Shelly."

"And you followed, and came up with the right things to say to her. Instinct, lady. I knew you'd be good with these children."

That's what Anne had told her. Lainey hoped they were right. She'd like to think she'd played a small part in helping Shelly. "Thanks, Dionne. It's so much easier to work on someone else's problem than my own."

"Another nightmare?"

"Yes. That's two within a week." Zac hadn't been with her this time so she'd toughed it out alone. She'd been torn between needing his comfort and not wanting him to witness her failure to conquer whatever it was that was eating at her. "I wish I knew what was causing them."

"How are things between you and Zac?"

"Good, I think. He's so patient." She gave a short laugh as she lay back on her bed, twirling the telephone cord around her index finger. "I'd have walked away from me ages ago."

"He loves you."

Lainey sighed. "So he says."

"And you don't believe him."

"Sometimes I do. I've known him less than two months." She heard the screen door slam and booted footsteps coming toward her. "Speaking of Zac, he's just walked in. Can we continue this another time?"

"Sure. And thanks for calling about Shelly. It's the best news I've had all week."

"Bye." She hung up the phone as Zac walked toward the bed. His face was unsmiling. "What is it?" she asked, sitting up.

He'd driven two of the children home and picked up the mail on the way back. The moment he'd seen the envelope, he'd debated about giving it to her. But he knew it was selfish to want to keep bad news from her. He placed the pale gray envelope in her hand.

Lainey looked down. The postmark was New York, the return address that of a law firm she didn't recognize. Heart hammering, she ripped open the envelope.

* * *

It was growing dark by the time Zac finished painting the new addition to the porch. He'd cleaned the brushes and his hands in the barn before walking back to the house. Odd that there were no lights on, he thought as he knocked once on the back door, then walked in. "Lainey?"

Hearing no response, he went through the living room toward her bedroom, again calling her name.

"Mmm? In here, Zac." She reached to switch on the bedside lamp as he walked in.

She was sitting on her bed, back against the headboard, legs drawn up, hugging a pillow to her. "What are you doing here in the dark?"

"Thinking. I guess I lost track of time."

He sat down beside her, reaching a hand to touch her, because the need was always within him. "What are you thinking about so hard?" As if he didn't know. She'd read the letter from her mother's attorney, mumbled something about how she should have known Irene wouldn't give up without a fight, and gone out to work in the garden. She'd accepted the inevitability of a court battle easily, he'd thought. Too easily.

She raised dark, determined eyes to his. "I'm going to New York."

Zac felt his stomach muscles tighten, but didn't let it show. "To do what?" he asked quietly.

"I need to check on my investments. And I need to have it out with my mother."

"You can check on your investments by phone or mail, and I told you that I have an attorney who will make mincemeat of Irene. Why put yourself through all that?"

Lainey turned to gaze out the window. Leaves from the maple tree brushed against the screen, shifting with the evening breeze. The air drifting in smelled so good, clean and fresh. She loved it here. But she had unfinished business. She looked back at Zac, who was waiting for her explanation.

"It's time I went back. There are things I need to do that I can't do from here. I want to see Anne and a couple of other people." She set the pillow aside and laced her fingers with his. "Dionne is always telling me that I won't be able to face the future until I resolve my past. I need to do this, Zac."

Unreasonable fear raced along his nerve endings, but he forced himself to nod. "All right. I'll go with you."

"It's not necessary. Because of you, I'm stronger than I was before. I'm not afraid."

But *he* was—suddenly and terrifyingly—of losing her to a past that still held her in its grip. Perhaps if he went with her, she would not so easily walk away from what he had to offer her. "It's necessary. For me. Unless you don't want me along."

She squeezed his hand. "I always want you."

Zac reached for the phone to make plane reservations.

He hated New York. Zac stood at the hotel window, looking down at the snarl of traffic ten floors below, and frowned. He could never understand why people wanted to live in large cities. Even Detroit was too big, too crowded for his taste, which was why he'd moved his company some time ago to the suburbs and now planned a rural branch. He felt stifled in an urban atmosphere, needing the serenity of wide-open spaces and quiet wooded areas. He wished he felt secure enough about Lainey to ask how she honestly viewed the Big Apple.

The truth was, after spending the day here with her, he was afraid of her answer. They'd arrived late last evening, taxied directly to their hotel and shared a late dinner before turning in early. Had it been jet lag or nerves that had kept him awake half the night? he wondered. Lainey, too, had been restless, and he'd held her to him, reluctant to give voice to his feeling of unease.

Zac turned from the window and strolled into the sitting room of their suite, his hands thrust into his pants pockets, reliving the morning. Another Lainey had emerged before his very eyes, the one he knew she'd been but that he'd never seen. He'd looked up as she'd stepped out of their bedroom, and he'd all but spilled his coffee.

She was every inch the stunning model, wearing an expensive ivory suit, beautifully cut as if made for her, and it likely had been. The silk blouse had a high neck, and she'd fixed her hair into an intricate twist that added a look of sophistication. He'd never seen her in heels, noting that the top of her head now came just to his eye level. He hadn't smiled until he'd noticed that she was wearing his mother's cameo. She'd touched it lightly and told him she'd put it on for luck.

Only in this town, Lainey didn't need to rely on luck, Zac thought as he crossed to the bar and poured himself a generous splash of Scotch. She'd strolled these streets as one who belonged. He saw none of the hesitancy he'd seen in her when first they'd met in St. Clair. Had he really been responsible for the return of her confidence? he asked himself as he took a sip and felt the trailing heat. Perhaps a little.

She'd taken him to meet Anne Blackburn in her lovely apartment overlooking Central Park, and he'd been impressed by the woman and her warmth. Tall, somewhat regal, Anne had eyes that missed nothing and yet were tinged with kindness. She'd listened to Lainey, then asked some hardball questions with the genuine concern of a caring friend. As they'd left, she'd shaken Zac's hand and told him that she hoped they'd meet again, and sounded as if she meant it.

They'd walked along Fifth Avenue, had lunch at Trump Tower and then Lainey had called her mother. Anne had told them that Irene had had to move after losing Lainey's income, subletting a small apartment in the Village on 13th near Washington Square, in an area that had known better times. Irene, also, had known better times and was anxious to recapture them. Surprised at Lainey's call, she'd refused her daughter's request to meet at her place and had instead agreed to come to the suite at four this afternoon.

Lainey hadn't told him what she was planning to say or do, and Zac's curiosity was as aroused as Irene's. Taking another swallow of his drink, he sat down in a wing chair. Over an hour ago, she'd left him, saying she had some banking business to take care of, and he'd returned to the suite—to pace and to worry.

He'd debated about grabbing a cab and paying an unexpected and most likely unwelcome visit to Irene Roberts and letting her in on some hard facts of life. He wanted her to know that no one—absolutely no one— was ever going to take advantage of, use, or hurt Lainey again; and that if someone tried, they'd have him to answer to. But after thinking it through, he'd decided that Lainey wouldn't thank him for his interference, and he'd have had to tell her. Instead, he'd made a couple of phone calls and knew his opportunity would come. Lainey wanted, *needed,* to do this herself—to exorcise the ghosts of her past, to be free. Perhaps then, her nightmares would stop.

And his would begin. Zac drained the glass and grimaced. It had been a revelation, seeing her here, looking different, fitting in. In Anne's apartment, he'd stared at a large, framed photograph of Lainey taken about two years ago, and seen what she had been, what she could be again. Confident again, coming to grips with her past, she could reach out for that dazzling future. Or a future with him, peaceful and quiet, raising horses and, hopefully, children. Growing old together. Her choice.

Loving someone enough to let them go was the hardest kind of loving. He'd done it once before, without having had a say in the matter. This time he had a choice: to walk away or fight for her. He chose to fight. And he'd lost very few fights in his lifetime. Zac got up and made himself another drink.

As he dropped ice cubes into his glass, he heard a knock at the door. Pleased that Lainey had returned a good twenty minutes before Irene was due, he swung open the door.

The woman wore a silk dress, designer shoes and a surprised look on her face. He saw the resemblance and thought she'd once been almost beautiful; but there was a discontented look about the too-red mouth. He saw frank admiration in her eyes as they swept over him, and undisguised curiosity.

"You've got the right room, Mrs. Roberts. I'm Zac Sinclair, a friend of Lainey's." He held out his hand.

Irene shook it briefly, her gaze narrowing as she tried to place the name. "Is Lainey here?"

"She will be soon. Come in, please." He ushered her inside and watched her glance around. Fate, it would seem, had taken a hand in things, and Zac was not one to turn away from an opportunity. He walked to the bar. "Would you like a drink?"

"No, thank you." She took the wing chair by the window and openly studied him—the pale blue shirt, loosened tie and Italian leather loafers. "Do you live in New York, Mr. Sinclair?" she asked.

Turning with his drink in hand, Zac leaned against the bar. "No. I met Lainey in St. Clair, Michigan. I believe you've been there?"

She didn't bother to hide a look of distaste. "Yes. It's very... provincial."

"Isn't it? That's one of the things Lainey and I like about living there."

Irene raised an eyebrow. "You live with Lainey?"

"Mrs. Roberts, I intend to marry your daughter."

Irene leaned forward for a closer look, then sat up straighter and sent him a frosty look. "I think you should know I won't have you taking advantage of my daughter's generous nature."

Zac crossed one ankle over the other. "Like you did?"

She rose to her feet. "I don't have to listen to this."

"I believe you do. Sit down." His voice was low, authoritative, the one even burly construction men listened to. He took quiet satisfaction in seeing her ease back into the chair, her pale eyes widening. "I know all about what you've done to Lainey. Everything."

"I'm not taking this from some drifter who... who..."

"I thought that's what you were thinking." He smiled, but there was no warmth. "Ever hear of Midwest Construction, Mrs. Roberts? You're from Detroit, you should have." He paused a moment while she made the connection, saw her reassess the situation.

"Yes, that's right," he went on. "An old firm, well established. It's mine, as well as a highly successful thoroughbred breeding ranch and various other financial holdings. Not quite a drifter, Mrs. Roberts.''

Zac watched her face as his words sank in and saw that she believed him. "Lainey will be here soon, probably to offer you a check. You're going to take it and never contact her again. You're going to call your attorney and drop the lawsuit. And you're going to thank your lucky stars that we don't take you to court for extortion."

Ignoring the blaze of fury in her eyes, he removed a slip of paper from his shirt pocket and handed it to her. "This is the name and number of a friend of mine who owns a public-relations firm here in Manhattan. I've arranged for an interview for you with him."

She frowned, puzzled. "What for?"

"A job. After you run through Lainey's money, you'll need one."

Irene's face reddened. "I don't need a job. I have a protégée, a beautiful young model. Much more grateful than my own daughter, I might add. She's got a great future ahead of her."

He nodded. "That would be Dominique. Yes, we spent the morning with Anne Blackburn and we're well aware of Dominique's future—and yours." He saw her shoulders sag a fraction and almost pitied her. "I was against Lainey giving you any of the money she's worked so hard to earn, but she wants it that way. You can keep the money on one condition, that you never contact Lainey again."

She was livid and struggled not to show it. "This won't work, you know. Lainey will come back to me. She cares about me."

"Not anymore. Violating trust does that to people. Lainey's cut the umbilical cord this time, Mrs. Roberts, and you handed her the scissors." He heard the key moving into the lock and leaned back against the bar. "I trust this conversation will be our little secret?"

Irene's eyes flashed fire at him as he turned to the door.

Lainey rushed in, wishing the bank manager hadn't taken forever to honor her requests. Seeing her mother sitting stiffly across the room, pinpoints of anger on her cheeks, and Zac casually leaning against the bar, made her doubly upset that she hadn't arrived sooner.

Zac walked to her, slipped an arm about her waist and bent to kiss her lips, finding them cool and dry. She was nervous, and he intended to lend her every ounce of support he could muster. "I'm glad you're back."

Lainey took courage from the warmth of his smile, then turned to look at her mother, feeling the familiar flutter of unease. If only she could get over feeling twelve years old in front of that icy gaze. She took a breath, needing to get this over with, yet wanting to keep it civilized. "I see you two have met."

"Yes," Zac commented with a smile. "We've had a nice chat." He saw Irene purse her thin lips together as he moved back to the bar, drawing Lainey along with him. "Would you like a drink, Lainey?"

Her eyes went from one to the other, wondering just what they'd chatted about. She stared at the glass he held out, but shook her head.

"You're looking lovely, Lainey," Irene stated a little too loudly. "Quite like your old self again. I knew you'd come to your senses. Why, a beautiful woman like you doesn't want to spend her life with smelly horses, wet-nursing children who are disturbed or from broken homes."

"I'm from a broken home, if you'll recall. And you're the one who broke it."

Irene waved a dismissing hand. "Be that as it may, you're back now, back where you belong. I hated having to hire an attorney to frighten you into returning, but I had to wake you up. You see that, don't you?"

For a long moment, Lainey just stared at the woman who'd given birth to her, seeing a stranger—one she didn't like very much. Then she reached into her purse and took out a folded check. "Yes, you did wake me up, and I'm grateful to you for that. Otherwise I might not have figured out quite so quickly where I do belong."

Turning to Zac, she took his hand. "With Zac, in Michigan, or wherever he wants to be. If he'll have me." She watched his frown disappear and the worry leave his dark eyes.

"Are you sure?" he whispered.

"Very sure." She held out the check to her mother. "This should compensate you for all your sacrifices."

Irene unfolded the check and glanced at the amount. "This is, this isn't—"

"That is exactly half of everything I've put aside. Take it or leave it."

Irene's blood was boiling and her temper mounting. "I can't believe..." Her eyes flew to Zac as he straightened, his dark eyes issuing an unmistakable warning.

Clearing her throat, she tucked the check into her purse and stood. One last time, she narrowed her eyes at her daughter.

"I hate to see you waste your life like this, but then you've never been good at making decisions on your own, have you?" Ignoring Zac completely, she swiveled toward the door. "Goodbye, Lainey."

Only when she heard the door close firmly behind Irene did Lainey let out a trembling sigh. All she felt was relief and a rush of sadness.

Turning back toward Zac, she stepped out of her heels. "Oh, am I glad to get those off." Angling her head, she looked up at him. "Would you like to tell me what you and Irene chatted about before I got here?"

He shrugged and took a swallow of his drink, then put down the glass. "You told me you were worried about what would happen to her. I called an old friend who owns a PR firm not far from here. He agreed to give her a job. When she goes through your money, she'll probably call him."

There was more, she was certain. "And that's all?"

He slipped his arms about her loosely. The rest he would take to the grave. "Would I lie to you?"

"Not exactly lie. Alter the facts a little, maybe."

"Never." He kissed the end of her nose. "Let's get on to more important topics. Did I hear you propose to me a few minutes ago?"

"Propose? You mean as in marriage?"

Slowly, he nodded.

She considered that a moment, then smiled. "I guess you did."

But Zac wasn't totally convinced. "Lainey, I've watched you yesterday and today. You fit in here. You were a very successful model. Are you sure you won't miss this life, get bored with country living and . . . and maybe me?"

"Yes, I'm sure." She stepped closer, placing her hands on his chest. "I never liked modeling, never enjoyed myself, never had fun like some of the girls did."

"But it's such a glamorous life."

She shook her head. "It's a superficial world. There's no creativity to it. The makeup artist changes your face into artificial perfection. The fashion designer delivers a certain message. The photographer with his selective eye sets the scene, the lighting, the angles, even the wind. The model is just shoved about, molded, twisted into their vision, their combined creation. She has no say in any of it."

"Then why'd you do it for so long?"

"You know why. The reason just left here. I hated that life. The hours are endless, tiring, hot and boring. You can't ever eat when you want because the camera picks up an extra quarter of an ounce. You can't drink or it shows on your face. Lose sleep and a close-up reveals it. You're a thing, a commodity, a pliable creature who takes directions all day and lessons all evening." She raised her hands to touch his face, willing him to believe. "I hated being a thing."

He kissed her finally, no holds barred, deeply, then pulled her into a rough embrace. "I was so afraid to come here with you, afraid I'd lose you."

"No, never." Reaching for her purse, she pulled out the newspaper article on her ranch. "Look at this picture, the one taken alongside Trixie, and tell me what you see."

Zac studied the photo, wondering what she was getting at. "I see a beautiful woman—"

"Stop right there. People have been telling me that I'm beautiful for as long as I can remember. But I never once *felt* beautiful, not until you came into my life. Now, what else do you see?"

"Well, I see this beautiful woman looking at this lucky guy who's crazy in love with her and scared to tell her so."

"And I see a woman who *feels* beautiful because she's looking at the man she loves. I didn't see it at first, but it's all right there. Even my mother spotted it." She moved closer, her arms tightening around him. "Love was only a word, a feeling I'd imagined, till I loved you. No one ever was able to break through to me, until you tried."

He felt her heart beating against his and thought his own would burst. "Tell me again."

"I love you, Zac." She waited for his mouth to claim hers, scarcely able to contain her happiness. She who had had no one suddenly had everything. When the kiss ended, she smiled up at him. "I feel like celebrating. Where would you like to go tonight?"

"Home. I want to take you home."

"There's a man after my own heart."

"I went after it, all right."

"And you won it, for all time." Smiling, she went up on tiptoe for his kiss.

* * * * *

It was no secret that tension ran high between Dr. Dionne Keller and Zac Sinclair's partner. But can it translate into love? Find out who is able to make the good doctor happy in Pat Warren's next novel, AN UNCOMMON LOVE, a June 1991 Special Edition.

SILHOUETTE·INTIMATE·MOMENTS®

NORA ROBERTS
Night Shadow

People all over the city of Urbana were asking, Who was that masked man?

Assistant district attorney Deborah O'Roarke was the first to learn his secret identity . . . and her life would never be the same.

The stories of the lives and loves of the O'Roarke sisters began in January 1991 with NIGHT SHIFT, Silhouette Intimate Moments #365. And if you want to know more about Deborah and the man behind the mask, look for NIGHT SHADOW, Silhouette Intimate Moments #373.

SILHOUETTE'S "BIG WIN"
SWEEPSTAKES RULES & REGULATIONS

NO PURCHASE NECESSARY TO ENTER OR RECEIVE A PRIZE

1. To enter the Sweepstakes and join the Reader Service, scratch off the metallic strips on all your BIG WIN tickets #1-#6. This will reveal the potential values for each Sweepstakes entry number, the number of free book(s) you will receive and your free bonus gift as part of our Reader Service. If you do not wish to take advantage of our Reader Service but wish to enter the Sweepstakes only, scratch off the metallic strips on your BIG WIN tickets #1-#4. Return your entire sheet of tickets intact. Incomplete and/or inaccurate entries are ineligible for that section or sections of prizes. Torstar Corp. and its affiliates are not responsible for mutilated or unreadable entries or inadvertent printing errors. Mechanically reproduced entries are null and void.

2. Whether you take advantage of this offer or not, on or about April 30, 1992, at the offices of Marden-Kane Inc., Lake Success, NY, your Sweepstakes numbers will be compared against the list of winning numbers generated at random by the computer. However, prizes will only be awarded to individuals who have entered the Sweepstakes. In the event that all prizes are not claimed, a random drawing will be held from all qualified entries received from March 30, 1990 to March 31, 1992, to award all unclaimed prizes. All cash prizes (Grand to Sixth), will be mailed to the winners and are payable by check in U.S. funds. Seventh prize will be shipped to winners via third-class mail. These prizes are in addition to any free, surprise or mystery gifts that might be offered. Versions of this Sweepstakes with different prizes of approximate equal value may appear at retail outlets or in other mailings by Torstar Corp. and its affiliates.

3. The following prizes are awarded in this sweepstakes: ★ Grand Prize (1) $1,000,000; First Prize (1) $25,000; Second Prize (1) $10,000; Third Prize (5) $5,000; Fourth Prize (10) $1,000; Fifth Prize (100) $250; Sixth Prize (2,500) $10; ★ ★ Seventh Prize (6,000) $12.95 ARV.

   ★ This presentation offers a Grand Prize of a $1,000,000 annuity. Winner will receive $33,333.33 a year for 30 years without interest totalling $1,000,000.

   ★ ★ Seventh Prize: A fully illustrated hardcover book published by Torstar Corp. Approximate Retail Value of the book is $12.95.

   Entrants may cancel the Reader Service at anytime without cost or obligation to buy (see details in center insert card).

4. This Sweepstakes is being conducted under the supervision of an independent judging organization. By entering this Sweepstakes, each entrant accepts and agrees to be bound by these rules and the decisions of the judges, which shall be final and binding. Odds of winning in the random drawing are dependent upon the total number of entries received. Taxes, if any, are the sole responsibility of the winners. Prizes are nontransferable. All entries must be received at the address printed on the reply card and must be postmarked no later than 12:00 MIDNIGHT on March 31, 1992. The drawing for all unclaimed Sweepstakes prizes will take place on May 30, 1992, at 12:00 NOON, at the offices of Marden-Kane, Inc., Lake Success, New York.

5. This offer is open to residents of the U.S., the United Kingdom, France and Canada, 18 years or older, except employees and their immediate family members of Torstar Corp., its affiliates, subsidiaries, and all the other agencies, entities and persons connected with the use, marketing or conduct of this Sweepstakes. All Federal, State, Provincial and local laws apply. Void wherever prohibited or restricted by law. Any litigation within the Province of Quebec respecting the conduct and awarding of a prize in this publicity contest must be submitted to the Régie des Loteries et Courses du Québec.

6. Winners will be notified by mail and may be required to execute an affidavit of eligibility and release, which must be returned within 14 days after notification or an alternate winner will be selected. Canadian winners will be required to correctly answer an arithmetical skill-testing question administered by mail, which must be returned within a limited time. Winners consent to the use of their names, photographs and/or likenesses for advertising and publicity in conjunction with this and similar promotions without additional compensation. For a list of our major prize winners, send a stamped, self-addressed ENVELOPE to: WINNERS LIST, c/o Marden-Kane Inc., P.O. Box 701, SAYREVILLE, NJ 08871 Requests for Winners Lists will be fulfilled after the May 30, 1992 drawing date.

If Sweepstakes entry form is missing, please print your name and address on a 3″ ×5″ piece of plain paper and send to:

In the U.S.	In Canada
Silhouette's "BIG WIN" Sweepstakes	Silhouette's "BIG WIN" Sweepstakes
3010 Walden Ave.	P.O. Box 609
P.O. Box 1867	Fort Erie, Ontario
Buffalo, NY 14269-1867	L2A 5X3

Offer limited to one per household.

LTY-S391D

This April,
Silhouette *Special Edition* is pleased to present

ONCE IN A LIFETIME
by Ginna Gray

the long-awaited companion volume to her bestselling duo

Fools Rush In (#416)
Where Angels Fear (#468)

Ever since spitfire Erin Blaine and her angelic twin sister Elise stirred up double trouble and entangled their long-suffering brother David in some sticky hide-and-seek scenarios, readers clamored to hear more about dashing, debonair David himself.

Now that time has come, as straitlaced Abigail Stewart manages to invade the secrecy shrouding sardonic David Blaine's bachelor boat—and creates the kind of salty, saucy, swashbuckling romantic adventure that comes along only once in a lifetime!

Even if you missed the earlier novels,
you won't want to miss

ONCE IN A LIFETIME #661

Available this April, only in Silhouette *Special Edition*.   OL-1